Praise for Rich Zał

LIGHTS OUT SUMMER

2018 Shamus Award
for Best Paperback Private Eye Novel

"Zahradnik nails the period, with its pack journalism, racism overt and subtle, and the excesses of the wealthy at places like Studio 54, as he shows how one dogged reporter can make a difference."

—*Publishers Weekly*

"[A] descriptive, fast-paced story that is very well researched. Readers will fly through the pages in order to reach the climactic conclusion."

—*RT Book Reviews*

A BLACK SAIL

Best Mystery,
2017 Next Generation Indie Book Awards

"Starred Review: Offers a blast from the time machine back to New York City's bad old days in the 1970s. Taylor, while out to get the story and get back to the crime beat, is complex and has a good heart. Verdict: Fans of the late Barbara D'Amato and Bruce DeSilva will relish this gritty and powerful crime novel."

—*Library Journal*

"Zahradnik ratchets up the action in this novel, which quickens the pace and keeps readers engaged ... a truly enjoyable read."

—*RT Book Reviews*

"If you love a good murder mystery, check out this series—I promise you'll be hooked in no time flat."

—*Feathered Quill Book Reviews*

DROP DEAD PUNK

Gold Medal Winner, mystery/thriller e-book,
2016 IPPY Awards

"The New York City financial crisis of 1975 provides the dramatic backdrop for Zahradnik's frenetic sequel to 2014's *Last Words* ... Taylor, who lives for the big story, makes an appealingly single-minded hero."

—*Publishers Weekly*

"*Drop Dead Punk* provides hours of engrossing entertainment ... Book two of the Coleridge Taylor series is a thoroughly satisfying read that will keep readers guessing until the end."

—*RT Reviews*

THE BONE
RECORDS

ALSO BY RICH ZAHRADNIK

Last Words

Drop Dead Punk

A Black Sail

Lights Out Summer

THE BONE RECORDS

Rich Zahradnik

1000 WORDS A DAY PRESS

1000 Words a Day Press
36 Clifford Avenue
Pelham, N.Y. 10803

For more information go to www.richzahradnik.com

All rights reserved. No part of this book may be reproduced or transmitted in any form or by any means, mechanical or electronic, including photocopying, recording, or any information storage and retrieval system, without the written permission of the publisher.

This is a work of fiction. Names, places, characters, media, brands, and incidents are either the product of the author's imagination or are used fictitiously.

Cover and interior design by Rafael Andres

The Bone Records
Copyright © 2022 by Rich Zahradnik

ISBN: 979-8-9859056-4-9 (trade paper)
ISBN: 979-8-9859056-1-8 (mobi e-book)
ISBN: 979-8-9859056-2-5 (epub e-book)
ISBN: 979-8-9859056-3-2 (pdf e-book)

Library of Congress Control Number: 2022905835

Printed in the United States of America

This one's for *all* the Examiners

CHAPTER 1

Friday, August 19, 2016

Grigg's reunion with his father was brief—eight minutes to be exact—and ended when a man with a nickel-plated revolver shot Dad twice.

Three hours before the violence began, Grigg struggled through the crowd on the Coney Island subway platform. He was the last to reach the stairway to the station's exit. Again. Even the old folks were gone. His wrecked knee held him back.

Outside the station, Deno's Wonder Wheel turned slowly, towering over the amusement park that took its name from the ancient fifteen-story ride. The wheel's spokes glowed a hot neon white. Hazy coronas surrounded all the lights.

Tick-tick-tick-tick.

Grigg had started wearing his father's Timex soon after he had gone missing. He put the watch up to his ear, as he'd done too many times before. It wasn't loud enough to be heard. The clockwork noise was in his head. Maybe a reminder to keep looking. Maybe a reminder that six months was already too long in missing persons cases.

His father's watch read 8:18 p.m.

He limped away from Coney Island's amusement parks toward his house on West 28th off Mermaid Avenue. As he did, the street darkened. He checked behind him more than once. The neighborhood became far less amusing as night came on—and the farther you went from the fun parks. Mugging wasn't the thrill ride Grigg needed. He didn't want any more trouble. He had a lifetime's supply. His long days pinballed him between two jobs and the search for his father.

But despite Grigg's best efforts, the minutes and hours and days kept spinning off the Timex, found by the police in a Howard Beach motel room, the last place his father was seen before he vanished into the thin March air. Their empty house waited to reflect Grigg's loneliness back at him. His mother had died when he was eighteen months old. His boss at the city's claims adjustment office rarely talked to him outside of giving orders. All of his connections—he couldn't really call them friends—in the neighborhood he owed to his father. Dad, like the rest of them, had immigrated from Russia. Unlike the rest of them, he'd married a woman from Jamaica, a union that guaranteed Grigg would always be on the outside in Little Odessa.

The rubber soles of his cheap dress shoes slapped the wet pavement. A thunderstorm had blown through while he was on the subway, leaving behind the sticky-thick humidity. His messenger bag tugged on his shoulder.

He went over the lead he'd uncovered tonight. Going door-to-door in a Midwood apartment building full of Russians, he'd talked briefly to a tenant named Freddy Popov, who recognized Grigg's father when shown a photo. Popov said a man—maybe a cop—had been canvassing the building with a picture of Grigg's dad four weeks earlier. Inside the man's apartment and shielded by Popov, someone said something in Russian. Popov got hinky, then said he didn't know anything more and slammed the door. Grigg banged on it until a woman across the hall threatened to call the cops. He left with only the knowledge that someone else—maybe a cop?—was also searching for Dad. Still, that bit of info was his biggest lead to date.

Grigg limped up to the small, two-story brick house—kitchen, living room, two bedrooms over a garage—a duplicate of the other attached homes on the street. He unlocked the steel gate, then the front door, and stepped inside.

The thunk of the door closing echoed through the house. Two days ago, Grigg had moved everything out except for the sleeping bag in his bedroom of twenty-seven years and a blue duffel, readying the old house for its new owners. He turned the deadbolt.

He shouldn't be staying here tonight. He'd spent all his free time on the search for Dad, right up until the closing on the sale of the house. Even at the end, he'd hoped for a breakthrough that would save him from selling. He'd signed the papers yesterday, writing a check for $1,650—most of his savings—because the house was underwater on a second mortgage his father had taken out. Grigg knew the out-of-state buyers wouldn't be moving in for three weeks, so he'd kept a copy of the key.

Trespassing in my own house. Inviting trouble when I already have too much.

The plan was to use the next three weeks to find an apartment share, but the lead from Popov tugged at his thoughts. Would it pull so hard that he'd spend his free time searching for Dad and end up homeless? He ducked his own question and instead pictured going back to demand Popov tell him more. He shook his head. He could barely keep his mind on his housing problem for the space of a single thought. He took a beer out of the refrigerator, went up to his room, and rolled his sleeping bag into a fat pillow to lean against.

Grigg popped open the 90 Years Young Double IPA. Nine percent alcohol. The strong stuff he'd dubbed "floor softener." He downed two sixteen-ounce cans, and the ache faded from the muscles in his damaged leg.

He took out his phone. He'd run through his data allowance last week. Three days until the new billing cycle. At least he had his music. He played the Decembrists, their songs about revenge and ships at sea set to jangly indie rock. He followed with the Killers, then Vampire Weekend.

Tick-tick-tick-tick.

His father's watch read 11:20 p.m.

He opened his notebook and wrote down "Day 191" along with what he'd learned. It was longer than any previous entry—yet not long at all. So many days. The silence in the house chilled him, sending goosebumps in waves over his arms and thighs. He got up and turned down the air conditioner. It wouldn't help. He missed his father's voice, the way it had warmed their home. They could talk about everything and anything, a lot of anything, but such interesting anything. Dad was always there with his questions, his curiosity, and his deep interest in whatever Grigg was up to. There were days his father was more intrigued by Grigg's job than Grigg was. Even that helped.

A fourth beer. He floated on the wood floor of his empty bedroom. Slept.

A thump. The floor hardened underneath him. Another thump. Half buzzed, halfway to a headache, Grigg opened his eyes. He heard it again. Not a dream. On the roof. He followed the steps above him to his father's empty bedroom. He was about to switch on his phone's flashlight when legs—silhouetted by the glow from the street across the way—dangled over the room's tiny balcony. They descended slowly, inching, hesitating, as if the intruder were no expert at this sort of move. The toes stretched to touch, and finally, the person dropped, stumbled, and landed on their knees.

Grigg didn't know whether to laugh or arm himself. If this was a robbery, then the joke was going to be on a thief who'd picked a house with nothing in it. Grigg decided discretion was the better part of whatever, returned to his bedroom, and pulled the stun gun from his messenger bag. Ever since he'd been attacked when he was in the police academy—suffering the knee injury that forced him to drop out—he hadn't felt safe unless he carried the weapon.

He placed the messenger bag next to his duffel in the hallway in case he needed to get out fast. In the kitchen, he grabbed his second six pack as a backup weapon.

Of course, he could escape by the front and leave the intruder for the police to deal with. But if he did, then the buyers would be notified, and he'd lose the three weeks of temporary housing he'd been counting on.

He crept through the doorway into the main bedroom.

The figure, whose face remained in deep shadow because of the streetlight glow from behind, rattled the handle to the single balcony door, used his elbow to smash in the square pane nearest the knob, reached in, and turned the simple metal lock. As he pushed the door open, Grigg stepped forward, hit his phone's light, and thrust forward the stun gun.

"Get the fuck out of my house!"

The figure froze. "I'm not going to hurt you, Grigg."

Grigg moved closer.

"Dad? Dad!"

Full beard and longer hair, but it was him.

Grigg didn't know whether to hug his father or scream at him.

"I came to say goodbye," Dad said.

"Goodbye?"

"I'm leaving. For Russia. I don't know when I'll be able to return. It's the only way."

"I don't understand." *Any of it.* "You said you'd never go back."

"It's the only way to fix things."

"Things? What things?" *Popov's suggestion about a cop.* "Are the police after you?"

A click came from the front door, and Grigg spun. Seeing his father and not an intruder had put the brakes on his fear. Now, his heart raced. He squeezed the handle of the stun gun with a sweaty hand. *Keep it together.*

The knob turned.

The front door flew open.

CHAPTER 2

Friday, August 19, 2016

The man was tall and red haired with a short beard and a flattened nose. He held a long-barreled, nickel-plated revolver. Looked like a .357 magnum.

"Shit." Grigg grabbed his bags—there wasn't time to recover the sleeping roll from his room and stuff it in the duffel—dropped back into the bedroom with his father, and shut and locked the door, though it wouldn't hold for long. "Guy's armed. Is someone after you?"

"Yes. But no, not *now*. That's why I came across the roof."

Grigg's thoughts spun like he'd boarded the Tilt-A-Whirl at Deno's Wonder Wheel. This was fucking nuts. His dad came back and moments later they were under attack. His stomach flipped as if he were actually on the ride.

A hundred questions.

A thousand.

Something hit the bedroom door hard.

No time for any.

"We'll go out the way you came in."

"I can't make it back on the roof. I barely made it down."

"I'll boost you."

They were on the balcony in seconds. Grigg grabbed his father's thighs and lifted upward, bearing as much of the weight as he could on his good right leg. It wasn't enough. He nearly fell over; instead, he leaned against the iron railing to regain his balance and shoved until Dad was able to drag himself onto the roof.

Another crash from the bedroom door.

Grigg tossed his duffel down into the backyard for later retrieval.

The bedroom door gave way after the third blow.

Grigg ripped free a can of 90 Years Young and hurled it hard into the shadowed darkness of the room. The man yelped in pain.

Grigg didn't wait to learn more. He moved to the side and climbed onto the balcony railing. Two loud gunshots, the weapon aimed at the space he'd vacated. He dropped the remaining beers and started pulling himself onto the roof. His arms were strong, but the left leg slowed him. Scrambling with all his strength, he made it up.

Below the asphalt roofing, in the attic, was the weapon he really needed, a registered .32 in a gun safe. No way to get it now.

Should've been better prepared.

"Run!" Dad whispered.

Run was right. There'd be time for should-haves later. Right now, Grigg had pissed off the gun-wielding asshole who was after his father for reasons unknown.

He went as fast as his left leg would allow, which meant he and his sixty-eight-year-old dad kept about even. They dodged around the boiler chimney and an AC unit. Neither structure looked tall enough to block a clear shot. They needed something bigger between them and that nickel-plated revolver. Like *now*.

They crossed to the roof of the next attached house and the next.

"How'd you get up here?" Grigg gasped, trying to picture a way down to street level and coming up empty.

"The Kiev Bakery at the corner has a fire escape."

That meant winning a block-long race over rooftops. Against bullets and a faster runner.

"Stop!" came a deep voice from behind them.

"Why's he after you?"

Instead of an answer, the report of the gun, then another.

Dad grabbed his side, groaned, and slowed but kept running, slewing off to the left. Grigg stayed with him.

"Get to Katia. Katia Sokolov—"

"Katia?"

Dad jerked and spun nearly in sync with the sound of the third shot. Hot blood sprayed Grigg's face.

His father listed hard to the left, veering toward the edge of the roof and the backyard two stories below.

Grigg grabbed for his dad's arm, but his hand slipped on blood.

He reached again to get a hold, but his father, as if

driven by the red jet from his neck, took two more steps.

And disappeared off the roof.

Grigg stopped.

Stared at the twisted body below.

The next gunshot lifted the messenger bag hanging from his shoulder.

Shock made way for raw panic. Flee or die. The fire escape. Too far. He had to get down the way he came up. He dropped to the balcony of the house beneath him, then repeated the maneuver to reach the ground, bad knee screaming from the punishment of the twin blows, shirt drenched in sweat and blood.

His father's body lay face up with an arm under his back and the right leg bent at an unnatural angle. A two-story drop wouldn't necessarily kill you. But the neck wound …

"Stay there or I will shoot you." The killer began taking Grigg's route to the ground.

The man had one shot left before he needed to reload. Or had he reloaded already?

Grigg knelt. Pressed his hand to his father's neck where the blood pulsed.

His father's eyes were open. With the slightest of movements, he patted at his blazer pocket. The jacket was no surprise. Dad always wore blazers. Weekdays and weekends. All seasons. *Why the hell does that matter now? Tilt-A-Whirl thinking.* A black tube protruded from the pocket. Grigg pulled it out.

Another shot.

Dirt leapt inches from Grigg's foot.

The gunman stood on the second-floor balcony and looked to be reloading.

Warning bells almost drowned out the unending ticking in Grigg's head as he held the tube up for Dad to see. "Is this what he's after?"

Dad's eyes didn't move. Stared upward. Locked in on something. Or nothing. His mouth was a black hole ringed with blood and spittle on thin lips. Grigg checked for a pulse. Neck first, then ear to chest. Nothing.

The gunman hung from the balcony, preparing to make the drop to the ground.

Fighting the nausea creeping up from his gut, Grigg ran as darts of pain shot from his left knee into his thigh. He climbed over the fence into the opposite yard, then into another next door, and found a shed to crouch behind.

From two backyards away, the gun went off.

A kill shot when Dad was already dead.

Grigg heaved up what was left of his dinner and the beers. Heaved again. Too much noise. Ground down his teeth to stop. He spat quietly to clear the taste of puke. Failed.

He couldn't see or hear the shooter, but he didn't dare move. Grief, anger, and fear threatened to swamp anything like clear thinking. A tidal wave against a rowboat. He needed to save himself. He needed to be a coward. Five minutes, then ten ticked off on his father's watch as he looked at the fence. Shadowed darkness. A deep purple oozed across his vision from staring too hard at the wooden slats.

Finally, he ordered himself to leave.

Be practical: the duffel bag.

He crossed two more backyards until he could approach his house—what used to be his house—from the other side. He saw no one in the yard where the body lay, looking from this distance like a dark mound. But the killer could be waiting somewhere to take him out. He inched with his back up against the wall (it was darkest near the houses), grabbed the bag, and slipped out to the avenue without incident.

His destination: the Conquistador Arcade in the Coney Island amusement area. He worked there most evenings. He had a key.

Cleaning the blood from his face and arms and out of his hair took an hour. Might have taken less time, but he kept scrubbing long after his skin was clean. If only he could scrub tonight away. After searching for six months, he'd had mere minutes with his dad before the attack. Grigg was too exhausted to cry. He knew the shirt was a write-off but left it soaking in the sink anyway, now the least of his lost causes.

He needed to go to the police. He knew that. But they hadn't given a shit when Dad disappeared. Grigg had been the only one looking. Murder was different than missing, right? Then again, he knew of too many unsolved killings in Coney Island.

He found it hard to think. Ideas, memories, discrete facts were fireflies inside his head. They whirled, collided, and spun off into the darkness. The lights led nowhere. Connected nothing. Would it help if he could catch them all in a jar like he had on an upstate trip with Dad? Or would that only mean the same confusion jammed in a smaller space?

He exited the bathroom of the arcade, which had closed hours ago, and moved to the Skee-Ball machines against the back wall. Rows of blinking arcade games shielded him from the front windows. He sat down. It was ironic. No, just sad. Grigg had dreamed of becoming a cop since he was a kid. The police academy hadn't worked out. Worse than that, it'd cost him his knee. Failed. Failed to find his father. Then Dad found him too late. Another failure. Exhaustion pressed down on him like the air had thickened, had weight. Maybe he'd lie down in the lane of this machine. He absently pulled out the black tube he'd taken from his dad's pocket. The shock again. He'd forgotten all about it. He took off a blue rubber band. The flimsy, plastic-like material unrolled: a super-thin black disc with a hole in the middle, like an old record. One of the arcade games flashed, and Grigg caught sight of something in the translucent black material. Film? He played his phone's light through it from behind, and the image of a skull materialized. He held the light closer. An X-ray of a skull, though like no X-ray he'd ever seen. For one obvious reason, it was circular; on closer inspection, the edge was uneven, like it had been cut by hand. The disc bore handwritten Cyrillic lettering. Grigg couldn't read or speak the Russian language, but smaller English script had also been written on the film: "Not Fade Away," right above the skull's eye sockets. He tipped the disc sidelong and scanned the surface. *Wait … are those grooves?* Grooves, three inches' worth, cut into the X-ray disc, but only on one side.

Grigg would have sworn he was holding an old-fashioned record album—if an album were thin, translucent, and had a skull X-ray on it but no proper label.

He turned it over again. Connections came together in his head. The sting of memory going back six months, the night before his father disappeared, the second to last time Grigg had set eyes on the man.

Dad had stood in the living room, whistling and sorting through the mail: a couple fliers, a bill, and a manila envelope. He had opened the envelope, and Grigg had glimpsed a black thing—maybe disc shaped—slipping from it.

Was it a disc? Maybe he only wanted it to be. It seemed so long ago.

The way he remembered it, Dad froze, stopped whistling, then turned away from Grigg to hold the object over a table lamp before hurrying to his bedroom. His father hadn't come out again—no goodnight, no nothing—and was gone when Grigg awoke the next morning.

In the aftermath of his father's disappearance, he'd forgotten about the envelope and the black thing.

Grigg reached further into his memories but could find nothing else. That period had become a blur. He'd been overwhelmed by the search—plus two jobs and money running out fast. Finding his father had seemed more important than figuring out why he'd left. Maybe he had gotten it backward. Maybe the why came first.

He looked at his phone, useless as a tool to identify the object for certain. That would have to happen in the morning. And on the chance it played like a vinyl record, he needed to listen to it before he turned it over to the cops.

The strange disc generated enough adrenaline to further clear the fog in his brain. His father's last words: get to Katia Sokolov. If his thoughts hadn't been scrambled by the murder, he'd have wondered at that name sooner. First, probably. He couldn't talk to the cops until after he spoke with Katia, something he hadn't done in more than a year. Still, there was no way he'd sic a pack of homicide detectives on her. He owed her that much. More.

Thinking of how he'd lost Katia took him to losing Dad for good and wrenched sobs from him for twenty minutes, a half hour. He wasn't sure.

God, I so need sleep.

Grigg risked the chance of being seen, snuck out, and bought a four-pack of strong ale at a bodega on Surf Avenue.

He was asleep midway through the second can.

CHAPTER 3

Saturday, August 20, 2016

Grigg sipped a mug of tepid coffee in a diner next to a check-cashing place on Mermaid Avenue. He'd cleared out of the arcade before it opened—in spite of soreness, a thumping headache, and the inability to put one good thought after another. He didn't want to be there when his boss, the ancient Mr. Petrushkin, showed. He liked Grigg but wouldn't want to find him sleeping at his business.

Grigg was new to grief. Ideas ran away, dropped into a nothingness beyond his reach. At eighteen months old, he'd suffered no grief when his mother had died. Only an absence, a hole that had always existed and was a part of him. Not now. Stop-motion thoughts were interrupted by intruding images of his father's murder.

As a result, he'd been circling the same questions through breakfast. Why had Dad left? Why did he come back to … to say goodbye before leaving for Russia? He'd always said he never wanted to return to the motherland. He'd sounded desperate in the few moments they'd had together. Had he been running the whole time he'd been gone? Grigg had learned so little in six months of investigating. He'd thought for a while his father had already left the city because Grigg came up with no sightings, no clues. That whole time, he never once imagined his father was dead. He couldn't. He was finding it almost impossible now. The images intruded again. His father on the bloody grass, two limbs bent in the wrong directions. Grigg rubbed his eyes hard to erase the picture. They had been close as father and son, partnered as neighborhood oddities, each in his own way. Dad was a playmate when Grigg was little and a ready ear once he got into his teens and twenties. His gentleness was so different from the autocratic, vodka-fueled Russian fathers Grigg met growing up. His laugh was a low chuckle, almost a whisper, though one Grigg could pick out in a crowded room. A generous teacher loved by his seventh-grade students. Free English tutor to anyone. A hobbyist of a writer on Coney Island's history (books typed but never published). Dad was the only person among the Russians in the neighborhood who seemed to take no notice of Grigg's skin color. If Grigg struggled with how he was treated, his father made things easier by speaking little of his own Russian roots, his life before America. *Was that a choice he made for me—or just the way he was?* He had been Grigg's island in Little Odessa's sea of judgment and prejudice. Now, six months of Dad's life were unaccounted for. What secrets had he kept from Grigg? What did he do that got him hunted down and shot?

Grigg cried.

After a while, he blew his nose with several napkins from the dispenser and wiped his eyes and face with another.

He stared at his phone and forced himself to focus on Katia Sokolov. He dragged one memory, then another, from the black molasses gumming his thoughts. Mr. Sokolov and Grigg's dad had come over from the Soviet Union in 1987. In fact, they had grown up together in St. Petersburg, then called Leningrad. Grigg and Katia, in turn, were raised as friends and playmates until middle school yanked them apart. That should have been the end of the story, but they found each other again late in high school, started dating, and kept dating until Grigg fucked the whole thing up because of his insecurities over money—the money the Sokolovs had and he didn't.

Dad was right. I was an idiot for breaking it off.

He pictured the Sokolovs' six-room apartment in a Brighton Beach tower. Beautiful, expensive furniture everywhere. Dark wood bookshelves covered an entire living room wall. Her father's high-end stereo system … *a stereo system. Shit, with a turntable.*

Katia's father had died in 2011. She lived alone. He picked up the phone.

"Little early in the day to be drunk dialing." If Katia didn't sound angry, she didn't sound happy either.

"No, I'm not … I never—"

"Right, you never."

He had.

"What do you want, Grigoriy?"

She knew he hated that name. Looking for an argument. He wasn't going to fight with her—or tell the full story over the phone. Could not drop the bomb about Dad that way. Had to be in person.

"I found this disc. It looks like a record. It's probably from Russia, but it's weird." He was talking too fast. "It's hard to explain. You need to see it, if you're up for it. I'd like to play it on your turntable—"

"You ... you want to use my record player?"

"Uh-huh."

"Are you okay?"

"Yeah, fine."

"You sound odd."

"I'm intrigued by this disc."

She'd know he was holding back the real news. This was the only way he could play it.

A dead silence followed. He thought she'd hung up.

"I guess you better come over. Say twelve-thirty."

Tick-tick-tick-tick.

His father's watch read 11:05 a.m.

Katia opened the door. "Grigg?" Unspoken: *Why do you look like shit?* Her thick raven hair was braided in a single plait. Her large, dark brown eyes gave him the once-over. "What's going on?"

"I ... It's my dad." To say the words for the first time was to make the terrible thing real. "He's dead."

She tilted her head, confused, and motioned him inside.

He started telling her the story standing next to the couch. By the time he got to the part with him and Dad in the backyard, he was choking up. He'd become an adult who cried without warning. Would it ever stop?

"You'd better sit." She pulled on his arm, staring up at him, tears running down her cheeks.

He took a step, halted.

He had to tell her right now.

"Listen. I left something out. The last thing he said to me was your name."

"My name?"

"'*Get to Katia. Katia Sokolov.*' Those were his exact words. Then the second bullet hit him in the neck."

"I don't understand."

"Neither do I."

Quiet sobs joined her tears. "I hadn't seen him in so long, even before …"

She pointed to the couch, which was so white it glowed.

Despite trying to clean up at the arcade, he still felt filthy; he sat on the floor.

"I'm really, really sorry, Grigg." She wiped her eyes, blinked, and gave her head a little shake. He'd seen her cry. Held her some of those times. "I liked your dad so very much."

"He liked you. One of the few times he got seriously angry with me was when I … I was stupid."

Katia ignored the comment. "Did you really want to play a record?"

The implication was he'd lied to get in the door with the bad news. At least, that's how Grigg heard it. Everything, everybody had become dark to him. Dark designs. Dark motives.

He nodded. He pulled the messenger bag onto his thighs, opened it, pulled out the file folder he'd taken from the arcade, slid out the disc, and handed it to her. "Hold it up to the light."

"A skull? A skull record? I've never seen anything like it."

"You studied a lot more about Russia than I did …"

Katia held the disc at arm's length, then brought it closer. "The English and Russian say the same thing. 'Not Fade Away.' It's scary—beautiful too."

She took it to the stereo, a Bang & Olufsen component system as shiny as everything else in the living room. She flipped the disc over once, then twice. "Looks like only one side has grooves."

The needle dropped. The sound was deep and stretched out, unrecognizable as any song. "Wrong speed. Forty-five." Katia lifted the stylus and moved a switch. Now, words could be made out, but the singer still sang too slowly and too low, like he was performing underwater. Was it a *he*?

"Does it play 78s?"

Katia looked at him like he'd forgotten something important. "This turntable does everything." A shrug. "That was Dad."

She went through the steps again.

Now they heard "Not Fade Away." Old time rock and

roll. Grigg knew the song but sung by someone else, probably from the jukebox at Ruby's Bar & Grill on the boardwalk, his favorite place. Beer, sea breeze, the ocean. There was nothing better. After last night would he feel that way again?

"Originally recorded by Buddy Holly," she read from her phone and looked at him. "Died in a plane crash in '59. 'The day the music died.'"

"The what?"

"'American Pie'—that long song all the old-timers sing along with at Ruby's. Nikki the bartender told me it was about the day this guy died," Katia pointed at the stereo, "Buddy Holly. I'm guessing this is him. Sounds like it's from way back. Says here the Grateful Dead, the Rolling Stones, and Florence and the Machine covered it."

"The Stones. That's the version of this on the jukebox."

Katia typed on her phone again. "Lemme look up 'X-rays and recordings.'" A pause while she tapped, tapped again. "There're a handful of links. If yours is one of these … how could it not be?" It was like she was arguing with herself. She read more. "There's Russian slang for them. Several different words and phrases. Bone music or—just—bones. Ribs, music on the ribs, and rib rock."

"So, it's a bone record?"

"Not the exact translation."

"Guess it's good I never learned the language. Looks like a record to me."

"In the Soviet Union, from the forties to the early sixties, the only way to listen to Western music was to buy bootlegs printed on used X-rays." Her eyes came up again. "They were sold when our dads were growing up."

"If that's what this thing is, what was my dad doing with one now?"

"Here's something from another site. Bones let people listen to banned jazz, rock and roll, and Russian singers who had immigrated or been denounced. Black marketeers cut the discs one at a time on a turntable that served as a lathe. Customers bought them from dealers on the street in places like flea markets."

"Why X-rays?"

She moved her thumb up on her screen and paused to read, did that again. "This is it. The inventors figured out that one side of a used X-ray was soft enough to take a groove. The film could be bought with bribes to hospital workers. Each only holds one song. They're singles, not albums."

As if on cue, the song ended, and the needle slid across the smooth surface. Katia stepped over, lifted the stylus, and played the record again, speaking over it. "One song per disc, each disc a picture of one person's bones. Each an original. And all illegal for those who made them, sold them, played them."

"Dad was a big fan of American oldies. Fifties oldies, not eighties oldies. Maybe it began with bone records?"

"Still doesn't answer your questions. Why did he have it, and why did he want you to take it?"

Grigg shook his head. The clue left him clueless.

"And the biggest question of all." Katia picked up the

folder, waiting for the song to end again. "Why did your dad send you to me?"

CHAPTER 4

Saturday, August 20, 2016

Katia invited Grigg to stay for lunch. Liverwurst sandwiches on rye with mustard. Never mind the food. They had so much to talk about, not least what Grigg was going to tell the cops. The dam holding back all the words felt like it would break, but he wanted to take it slow to keep his thoughts from jumping all over the place. He was pretty sure she'd let him.

"Still working as a paralegal?"

"For my sins."

"Thought you liked it."

"I don't like doing it for a lawyer who's defending the big banks that fucked people over during the crash. Maybe if the firm and the cases were different ... but it's more than just that. I've learned that I don't want to work my ass off with no way to move up. Lawyers climb. Paralegals don't. I want to go to law school and then help people."

"When would that happen?"

She laughed a little, a stranger sound, given his state, than Buddy Holly at 33 rpm. "When I save a lot of money.

I could sell the apartment. Dad left it to me paid off."

He sensed his old insecurities about money trying to circle up past the grief.

Katia shrugged. "I'm not ready to do that."

"Still training?"

"Made black belt end of last year."

"As I recall, you were already kicking ass with the lesser belts in Shotokan."

"Stand up."

He did as he was ordered. She rose and moved to the other side of him, where there was more floor space in the kitchen. She pointed to her foot. "I'm going to put the outside of my left foot on the right side of your head."

She moved as promised—without connecting—and held the position for several seconds with a statue-like stillness that had to take focus and strength. Then the foot went down and the other came around in a blur.

"Double roundhouse kick. Black means I do things faster and know a few extras."

"I'm impressed."

They sat.

She nibbled at her sandwich. She wasn't eating much. "You're still working for the city?"

"One of my jobs. Assistant claims adjuster."

"What's New York doing in the insurance business?"

"That's the point. The city is self-insured. It pays out all the claims itself, so it investigates them too. You fall and break your arm on the steps of Brooklyn Borough Hall, I go out with my boss to figure out what happened."

She nodded like it made sense, though her eyes took on the same bored look he got whenever he talked about his job. "They make any headway finding the guys who jumped you when you were in the academy?"

"Two years gone. Zero. They're sworn officers by now and riding patrol in our great city."

"They were really academy classmates. I saw the news stories."

"They had on jumpsuits and masks, but at least one of the idiots left on his spit-and-polish uniform boots. Another was theatrical about it. He had a swastika armband. Clocked those from the sidewalk while they stomped on me. They were quite specific about their objections. 'We don't need your kind on the job, nigger. This is a white man's position.' Afterwards, I had my eye on four cadets from Staten Island. Racists can come from anywhere, I guess, but I picked that backwater first. Loaded with cops and mobsters. Italian on both sides. The four I knew were tight—and a match to the size and shape of my attackers. The investigator said she'd look into it. Didn't sound motivated, though." He put the last bite of the sandwich in his mouth. He felt guilty for being hungry, but his stomach wanted food and the grief stayed busy slithering around his brain. He reached for a change of subject. "I've missed talking."

She looked away.

Mistake.

"I'm sorry. I shouldn't have said that. I'm an idiot. I was a complete idiot back then."

"You never gave me a reason. You left me hanging."

"I didn't have a good one."

"Was it someone else?"

"No. And there was nobody for a long while after. I tried a couple of apps. That's a special sort of torture, like dogs sniffing each other's asses. Sit down and wait to see if you'll need to sneak past the bathrooms for the back door. Or if your date'll do the same. Had one bail on me like she was in a plane that caught fire."

That little laugh. "Then why?"

"We were scraping by. You had everything—"

"That's ridiculous. Ridiculous you should care. We were together. We were good. Your dad was the best. Even my dad got over us."

"*Even.* Anyway, like I said, I was an idiot."

"You hurt—then you hurt me."

"That's fair. Now, everything hurts. Thank you again for seeing me. You had every right to say no."

"Of course I'd see you. We were family before we were dating, before we were exes. The trips with our dads. The beach. They talked. We played. You're still *that* friend."

"I don't know. Could be one-sided. I'm trailing trouble like Jonah with an albatross around his neck."

"You need to go to the cops. They're probably already looking for you."

"I'm going to find his killer."

A that's-a-terrible-idea frown. "Let them handle it. Be a witness. Mourn."

The flood of thoughts he'd had during breakfast at the

diner coursed again through his head. The dam almost burst. He took a breath and reset. "I … can't get the shooting out of my head. The whole scene. I should have found Dad and helped him before last night ever happened. Given how the cops ignored the case when he was missing, I don't trust them. I owe my father this. The cops can do what they want."

He sipped lemonade, trying to calm down so he could focus on what was important. "It's Dad's last words … If I tell the police, they'll be all over you."

"Go ahead. I'll say I don't know anything—I have no idea why he said my name."

Her eyes were unblinking. No side glances, no other tells. If she ever guessed he'd tested her … Now, he needed her to understand the consequences.

"That won't be the end of it. The cops will have a bone record—a thing they've never seen—that points who knows where. And the last words of a dead man. They'll barge into your life. You don't know where they'll take the investigation. Your job. Finances."

"My asshole boss?" Her brow furrowed, wrinkling her smooth forehead. "They're not going to find anything."

"I know. But *they* don't."

Katia's eyes flashed. "I'm not afraid of the police."

"See, I'm making you angry." He sighed. "Settles it. I'm not telling them about you when they interview me. We'll figure it out ourselves."

Katia looked ready to argue the point, but at that moment, the front door opened.

"I'm home." A loud female voice.

"My roommate Irina."

A buxom, sandy-haired woman wearing a gaudy cover over a bikini came into the kitchen. She stared at Grigg.

"This is my friend, Grigg Orlov. We grew up together."

"You're Russian?" A bit of a boozy slur, but Grigg recognized the tone of disbelief his skin color produced.

"On my father's side." He got up. "I better get moving."

Katia walked him to the door. Irina trailed.

"Call soon."

"I will. Thanks. For everything."

The door shut.

He stood out in the hall for a moment, sad their time together ended so fast, though he had plenty to be a great deal sadder about.

Irina's piercing voice came through the door. "I didn't know you like them in chocolate."

"Shut up."

"He's really Russian? Can't be all *that* Russian."

"Shut the fuck up."

The anger in Katia's voice lit a fire in Grigg's chest. He'd learned to tolerate most of the daily attacks that came from being a color that didn't match his name. Or just from being brown. But not when they hit Katia first and rebounded. He'd never handled those well.

A door in the apartment slammed. His finger shaking, Grigg pushed the button to call the elevator.

CHAPTER 5

Tuesday, September 6, 2016

Tick-tick-tick-tick.

Coming from a giant clock tower. Like Big Ben, but all black.

Boxes packed for moving were stacked everywhere in the house. Grigg slalomed through the maze to a wooden crate in his father's room. He strained with a crowbar to pull out dozens of nails. New nails appeared in place of the old ones. The lid finally off, he found a smaller box inside. It went on like that, like the Russian *matryoshka* dolls, a box nested inside a box nested inside a box. He woke as he pulled open the lid on the smallest to find a bone record glowing with the ghost image of his father's face.

He'd had the same nightmare the last two and a half weeks.

A spider crawled across the ceiling of his empty bedroom in the empty house. The buyers would move in on Friday. Last night, he'd promised himself—*really* promised himself this time—he'd spend all his free time apartment-hunting, starting today. He'd even scheduled three interviews this evening for flat shares. *Oh joy.*

Grigg had returned to his job in the city adjuster's office six days after the murder, using the department's resources to research the bone record and look for other leads. There wasn't much helpful information online about the strange Russian discs. He'd learned their history, listened to songs recorded on them, and viewed pictures of surviving discs displaying a femur, broken forearms, a rib cage, and a cracked skull. He'd twice visited Freddy Popov's apartment in Midwood to try to get a description of the man who had gone door-to-door with Dad's picture. Nobody had been home. He'd left a note both times with his number. No call back.

The big problem—massive, really—was he didn't have clues, only hints pointing in too many directions. He gave himself headaches hoping Katia would suddenly remember the reason Grigg's dying father had said he should go to her. Every time her name appeared on his phone, hope launched like a rocket—and exploded as it left the pad when her call was about something else. He kept that to himself. He didn't dare ask her again. The trust between them was fragile, a thin thread.

Grigg stretched. He'd gone to bed on four cans of floor softener and woken up with the usual hollowed-out sensation, a feeling worse than a hangover.

He rose from the sleeping bag, walked to the kitchen, and poured Sugar Pops straight into his mouth from a box that came in a Kellogg's Variety Pack. A sadness like something suddenly remembered, something repressed, crept from the corners of thought and mutated into the black molasses that mucked up his brain. There were beers in the fridge. The desire to open one, to wallow, to do nothing, almost got him. But the daily cycle—would it ever end?—spun past that urge as he remembered the night of the murder. The red-haired gunman pursuing them across the roof. Anger at the killer sparked into a hot glow, then a fire burning, driving back the black gunk. It helped him focus, which was good. No one else cared about the murder, not like Grigg.

Detectives Ho and Wilson at the 60th Precinct, who'd been assigned the case, cared about all the wrong things. He'd met with them following lunch with Katia on the day after the murder. *The day after.* Yeah, that didn't play well with the cops. They'd interviewed him for three hours and spent a lot of time on why he took almost a day to come in. He'd said he didn't feel safe at the scene and then the shock hit him, which maybe they bought in the end because they already had a theory—pulled out of their asses—that his dad, a man in a financial hole, had gotten involved in something illegal. He'd kept Katia out of his statement, as he'd promised, and with great reluctance turned over the bone record to the detectives. That had won him another lecture, this one on forensics and fingerprints. At that point, he'd snapped and stepped in it at the same time: "I didn't have time to get rubber gloves with a killer chasing me."

"Another reason you should have come in here right away," Ho had said.

This morning's anger burned hotter at the thought of a police report reading *Borrowed from a loan shark,* or *Drug deal gone bad.*

With grief transformed into anger, he'd nearly completed the cycle's first spin of the day. Wrapped inside his fury over the murder was anger at his father for leaving him once—and returning only to be taken for good minutes later. He'd come just to say goodbye? "I'm going to Russia." What the fuck? Why not stay safe? The anger didn't last long; instead, it mutated into gray-toned guilt over getting mad at his father—and at his father for being murdered. The cycle halted after one spin, a relief in a way, at least for the moment. Guilt didn't slow him down like inky, gummy grief. Guilt made him work almost as hard as anger did, driven to pay a debt. Running on emotional spin-dry every day wasn't healthy, probably was some sort of psychological problem. He couldn't go through those feelings over and over without doing damage. But he didn't know how to do anything else.

He showered and dressed, and as he came into the kitchen, his phone rattled on the counter: Vasiliev, the mortician.

"We're getting the body from the medical examiner Monday, and we can have the cremated remains ready by Wednesday. Nothing religious at the memorial, as you asked."

"Thank you again. I'll get the rest to you."

"I know you will. Your father was a good man."

Dad had taught Vasiliev English, like anyone in the

neighborhood who wanted to learn. Never charged a cent, and he could have made lots.

Grigg had decided not to hold the service at the funeral home. There was a charge for that. Several. Vasiliev didn't mind. He'd even helped Grigg book a room at the Coney Island Community Center.

A non-religious service would be what his father wanted, but it wasn't his actual last wish.

Get to Katia.

The spin cycle started again. Grigg moved for the door. He was already running late for work.

CHAPTER 6

Tuesday, September 6, 2016

The morning cool was leaving the air like it was sneaking out of town. Grigg walked along West 28th Street to Mermaid Avenue and rounded Romanov's at the corner. At night, when multicolored bulbs splashed light across it, the local Russian cabaret took on some of its grand old style. Now dowdy in the daylight with its plaster cracking, it looked like the faded wedding hall it was.

He passed stores with signs in Russian. Furniture warehouses, restaurants, tea shops, clothing stores, discounters stuffed with a mix of everything. He didn't know the language; he didn't look the part. Maybe once he'd solved his father's murder—that didn't sound crazy at all—he'd move away from Little Odessa. Disappear to a neighborhood where people looked like him. He'd be invisible there, at least. What did that say about him? He answered his question with a question. How *could* he leave? Coney Island's beaches and rides and freak shows anchored him; they were his midtown, his Times Square. His best memories were of the hours spent in those places with Dad. He supposed some people would want to flee from such reminders. He didn't. Anyway, where else would a true freak live? Back when Grigg started at the police academy, he'd thought the force might give him a way to become an insider in a neighborhood where he was perpetually on the outside. A mistake. He'd learned the NYPD was still much whiter than the city it policed. Even a home to neo-Nazis.

After twenty-five minutes, the subway reached the stop Grigg wanted. He walked to the NYC Sanitation garage in Flatbush and found his way to the office area at the back.

Tick-tick-tick-tick.

His father's watch read 9:25 a.m.

Grigg pulled out his clipboard and took up his customary position. His boss—tall, bulky, gray-haired Jamie Carmichael—started questioning a claimant. This was the routine of his job, and Grigg found concentrating on filling in the form as he listened to the answers stopped the sickening whirl of emotions for a few minutes.

"Start from the beginning, Mr. Holcomb," Carmichael said.

"I was halfway onto the crosswalk—"

"Halfway?"

The man, short with stringy brown hair, crutches, and a cast on his right leg, startled at Carmichael's question. "A third of the way?" Holcomb said it like he was seeking the right answer.

No surprise. Grigg had seen the guy twice before, most recently four months ago, with a cast on the other leg. Grigg was sure his boss had some kind of racket going, giving out settlements to a roster of five repeating characters, presumably for part of the take.

"Go on."

"The garbage truck jumped the light. I moved fast but not fast enough." Holcomb flashed a smile that didn't seem appropriate. "Knocked me down." He rapped a crutch on the cast.

Grigg didn't have rock-solid proof his boss was dirty. He'd never witnessed cash changing hands with the Jamie Carmichael Players, Grigg's private name for the three men and two women who'd made repeat appearances making claims on the city in the last year and a half.

As assistant adjuster, he filled out the form, then transferred the information to an ancient PC at the office. The position had come along a few months after he'd had to drop out of the police academy, some kind of bureaucratic make-good—probably a hedge against Grigg suing the city over his injury and lost opportunity.

Carmichael asked another half-hour's worth of checkbox questions. Finally finished, Holcomb crutched his way past a clot of burly sanitation workers outside the office and left the garage fast for a guy with sticks and a cast. Hard stares from the blue-collar crowd followed him to the door.

Carmichael spent another twenty minutes going through the garage's paperwork on the truck that was supposed to be involved. "We're outta here," he said, already through the office door.

Tick-tick-tick-tick.

His father's watch read 11:10 a.m.

A shop worker stepped in front of Carmichael. "Why you gotta fuck us over?"

Three more came up behind.

"Doing a tough job, sport. Just like you."

"Nothing tough about the shit you're pulling."

A wrench in the man's left hand came from behind his back. His bald head gleamed with sweat.

Carmichael was fast. He pulled a revolver from a shoulder holster and stepped toward the worker. The barrel made a deep impression in the skin of the man's damp dome. The other men fell away, and the wrench clanked to the oil-stained concrete.

"What would be *tough* is the mess your buddies would have to clean up."

As fast as it appeared, the gun was gone. Carmichael strolled out of the garage like he was the Commissioner of Sanitation. Grigg hustled behind him at a quick limp.

The bald man yelled, "You can't do that. We're calling the cops."

"Say hey to my friends at the Six-Seven. Great bunch of guys."

Carmichael slid into the city-issue Dodge and turned the key. "Got any questions?"

Innocuous enough. But Carmichael only asked that question after one of his bogus cases. It was a challenge. It was a there-are-no-questions question.

"Nope." Grigg waited, spoke at the next light. "You

were a detective with the NYPD?" Grigg knew, but he'd never asked Carmichael directly.

"What's that have to do with anything?" Carmichael's red-cheeked face had a smile on it, but the grin was pure threat.

"My father was murdered." It was stating the obvious, but Carmichael hadn't mentioned it since Grigg came back to work.

"I know. And?"

That's pretty cold.

"I'm trying to figure out what happened."

"Not your job."

Grigg had known it was a bad idea to bring it up, but he was down to bad ideas. Since he'd started the job in February of 2015, Carmichael hadn't shown much interest in any sort of conversation with Grigg. He mainly talked on the phone. To old police pals, from what Grigg could tell. That or criminals.

After forty minutes in stop-and-go traffic, Carmichael pulled the car over less than halfway to their office near Borough Hall. "Lunch."

Tommy, ex-detective and bartender at Kennedy's, gave Grigg the usual cold stare like he'd never seen Grigg or anyone else black or brown in the place before. Today, Grigg was over it.

"What?" he asked.

Tommy didn't answer and turned to Carmichael, his best lunchtime customer, and poured the first course: Jameson.

Carmichael failed to notice the brief exchange; as always, his focus was on the whisky. He sipped off liquor poured right to the top of the glass. A double and a half.

Aside from Tommy's chilly welcome, this was the one part of the job Grigg liked. Couple or three beers made keying in the interview sheets less boring. No one ever complained about errors—there must have been errors. He doubted anyone checked.

The steamy weather called for Mermaid Pilsner, but they were too far north for that brewer, so Grigg settled for Sixpoint's Alpenflo lager.

"Yeah, I was a homicide cop." Forty-five minutes after they'd arrived, Carmichael was halfway finished with his third Jameson. He spoke to the mirror, which advertised the brand he was having for lunch. "If you're thinking about solving your dad's murder, I'd think again."

Grigg nodded but didn't respond.

"What? You think you're a detective after a few weeks' training at the academy?"

"I was halfway through."

Carmichael laughed. "You're running your own investigation, aren't you?"

Grigg nodded. He would stand his ground without getting in an argument with his boss, if possible.

Carmichael finished the drink and waved for another, one more than usual. Probably celebrating this morning's score. He looked at Grigg through the deep-brown Irish whisky in the glass, almost like he was about to toast. Grigg knew that wasn't happening.

"I'm telling you this because I know from personal experience the department can make mistakes. The Six-Oh. Not the best detective squad in Brooklyn. So lemme give the amateur a couple tips." He threw back half of the Jameson and clacked the glass on the bar. "There's only three things in an investigation that matter. Witnesses, witnesses, witnesses. I don't give a shit about forensics. Closed-circuit cameras. Facial recog-whatever. Ballistics, yeah, you want a match. But it starts and ends with witnesses, witnesses, witnesses. Interview people. Ask them for other people to talk to. Listen to what they're saying. Sometimes they'll tell you something, and you won't realize it's *something* till later. Go back and talk to them again. You get any of that in the academy?"

Grigg shook his head.

"Never give an informant money unless you've got something on him. Unless you can charge him. Which you can't. So, don't give fucking anyone any money."

Like I have it.

"Families looking for help in a case get ripped off fucking left, right, and center by scam artists. Talk to everybody in your dad's life. Because somebody close to him knows something."

Grigg gulped half the can of beer because he wanted another for his own small celebration at this break in the gloom. It felt like he was getting an assignment. For the first time, someone else was telling him how to find his father's killer. He lifted a hand to order.

"Forget it." Carmichael slid off the stool. "You're driving back."

Another first. Grigg never drove the city-issue car.

He slung his messenger bag across his back and walked toward the door while Carmichael paid his tab.

"Yo, Yeltsin."

Grigg turned to find Carmichael a step behind him.

"I don't care what you think you saw at the garage today. When I was a murder cop, I nailed every doer I could. No deals. No special favors. Highest clearance rate in the Six-Seven."

Grigg nodded and stepped out into the rotting garbage, puke, and dog shit stink of a Brooklyn sidewalk in summer.

CHAPTER 7

Wednesday, September 7, 2016

Grigg turned onto West 15th Street and headed for The Bowery. A squealing noise. His stomach clenched. He turned. A homeless woman—young, old, who knew?—pushed a grocery cart with one bad wheel. Grigg's heart rattled in its bone cage. He reached back and touched the stun gun in its holster. He didn't need to check for the sap he'd bought. The weapon weighed down a cargo pocket of his shorts.

He was headed for job number two, counterman and mechanic at the Conquistador Arcade. He was going to ask for more hours. Rent would soon become a major expense, plus the student loans … fuck, why even bother adding it up? The Great Recession was supposedly long over, yet Grigg was working harder to dig out of the crater it had left behind. If you kept digging, didn't you end up down deeper in the hole?

All the interviews last night for rooms in shared apartments had been short, which wasn't a good sign. Two people at each of the three flats, all around his age with

Russian last names. All had some version of a suppressed surprise reaction when they got a look at him. Eyes went briefly wide. A slipped look at the other roommate. They weren't much interested in his answers.

At least tonight held the promise of new information in the case. Mr. Petrushkin, the 74-year-old owner of the arcade, was full of stories about the old Soviet Union. He was better with events than names and tended to tell his tales out of order. That didn't matter. Grigg's hope was Mr. P would know something about bone records that the Internet didn't. Carmichael's words had become Grigg's guide: Witnesses, witnesses, witnesses. Mr. P had been a good friend of his father's. Grigg could envision Dad and Mr. P sitting at the kitchen table with little glasses of iced vodka, pickles, and brown bread.

"You need to let go of your nostalgia for a failed system," said Dad.

"You don't respect what we had that worked for us," Mr. P said. *"Putin does."*

"Putin's a thug."

"Maybe Russians need thugs."

"He peddles memories of things that never happened."

Whenever Mr. P threatened to return to Russia, Grigg's father would shoot back: *"You go to Putin's Paradise. It's just another name for the Gulag."*

Most of their get-togethers didn't turn into arguments. Mr. P would talk about his arcade and the other Coney Island businesses that manufactured fun. Dad took it all in and asked questions, interested in anything about the neighborhood. He'd lived in Coney Island a long time by then, yet he could never learn enough. He'd passed that curiosity on to his son.

Grigg had been so lonely the six months Dad was missing. But all that time, there had been hope. He would come back. To turn around in the house and not see him. To know he'd never see him. It was tearing him up.

Tick-tick-tick-tick.

His father's watch said 6:55 p.m.

Half a block from the arcade, The Bowery, which ran parallel to Surf Avenue for the two and a half blocks of its length, was dead quiet. Three businesses were closed, shutters down. After that stretch, things picked up a little with two food stands bracketing a nondescript building for rent across from the arcade. He let one of Dad's mini-history lessons fire up his imagination to push the sadness off for a little while. This little alley, Dad had said, was once famous citywide as an entertainment center. The short stub of a street was crammed with buildings on both sides, some leaning over the sidewalks—music halls, restaurants, whorehouses, freakshows, penny arcades, gambling dens, carousels—all hoping to pick up customers who came for the beach and the three massive Disney-scale-and-beyond parks at Coney Island. Then it was two parks after a huge fire; then one after another couple of fires; then the great parks were gone, dreamlands that few remembered.

As a teen, with some idea of the oddity of a Russian man's interest in a seedy collection of Brooklyn tourist attractions, he'd asked his father why he loved the place.

"Because Coney Island is not a lie," he'd said. "It's called The People's Playground. Which it is. The boardwalk, the beach, all of it is open to anyone. They called everything the *people's* this, the *people's* that, in the Soviet Union. Yet none of it was ever ours. Until finally it was, and then it was stolen."

Grigg let the memory go as he entered the arcade. Mr. P gave him a project right away. The place was crowded. Kids yelled; machines rang and buzzed. Half the children were there for a birthday party, careening from game to game. The single arcade on what was now a backwater of modern Coney Island could still do business on a September night.

After thirty minutes unjamming a Skee-Ball machine, Grigg manned the prize counter. Hours passed. Much of the crowd disappeared for snacks or to go on rides at Luna or Deno's Wonder Wheel, the two small fun parks that now operated.

Grigg went over to Mr. P at the register. "What do you know about bone records? Or bone music?"

One bristly gray eyebrow went up. "It's been a long time since anyone said those words, or the Russian ones, at least. Why on earth do you ask?"

Grigg told him about the record his father was carrying when he died. He pulled out his phone so Mr. P could look at the pictures Grigg had taken before he gave the disc to the cops. There was wonder in the old man's watery, pale blue eyes.

"I wish I could have held the thing. It's been so long. A different life." He started speaking in Russian, then switched back to English. "Bones, X-ray music. We had many names for them. I haven't seen one in more than fifty years. For a time, this was the one way we could hear …"

Mr. P looked over Grigg's head as his words trailed off. He handed back the phone.

Grigg turned.

A fat man stood two feet inside the arcade's entrance. Grigg knew who he was. Joe the Borscht—Borscht because his blood was as cold as the traditional soup. Head of the Coney Island Neighborhood Benevolence Association, aka The Mob. Question was, why was he here? Mr. P had somehow avoided making protection payments. One of Joe's black-clad goons blocked the glass front door.

"I want to talk to him," said Joe the Borscht. He pointed at Grigg.

Grigg didn't think it was ever just talk with Joe.

Tick-tick-tick-tick.

His father's watch said 10:38 p.m.

CHAPTER 8

Wednesday, September 7, 2016

Joe the Borscht stepped closer to the counter. A frown laced deep canyons in his rectangular forehead. Out from behind his girth appeared a third man—thin and short, looking miniature next to Joe. A face that would probably be called handsome, medium-length blond hair, dressed in a dark gray pinstriped suit and a light blue floral tie. He looked like a bookkeeper who'd wandered into the wrong place in the wrong neighborhood.

Grigg ran the scenarios as an unwelcome, squirmy warmth spread through his gut. This was connected to his father, right? But how? Run. He wanted to run. The stun gun and the sap wouldn't get him past three men, two of whom were certainly strapped. His revolver was in his locker in the back of the arcade, where he'd stowed it before the police searched his house—actually former house, now his squat with the clock ticking on when the locks would be changed. *Why don't I have it with me? Screw the carry permit. They could be the murderers.*

Mr. P smiled.

Like he didn't care they were here? That it was okay they wanted Grigg? His stomach, hot, squeezed as hard as a Skee-Ball. His mouth filled with saliva. Nowhere to spit. He swallowed.

Skee-Ball. He glanced at the one he'd pulled from the jammed machine. Throw it at them? Right … one more reason for them to beat the crap out of him. Or shoot him. Sweat soaked the collar of his red Conquistador Arcade polo shirt.

Mr. P picked up the ball as Grigg was discarding the idea of using it. He tossed it once. "Your man at the door I know from the streets going back to when he was knee high. Likes to call himself Frank. Bullied younger kids before he graduated to your school." He pointed with the index finger of the hand holding the ball. "Who is your new friend, Josef Viktorovich? He's not from the neighborhood."

Grigg noted that Mr. P had used the respectful form of Russian address.

"I know many people from outside your small world, Petrushkin," Joe shot back, not interested in returning the compliment.

"Grigg's on the clock, and he's got work to do. To what do we owe a visit from the Coney Island Neighborhood Benevolence Association?"

"I want to know if there's anything I can do for our poor Grigg."

Mr. P turned to him. "Grigg, is there anything you need?"

"Work. It takes my mind off things."

"I'm afraid I've also got questions," said Joe. "I want to make sure there are no misunderstandings between Grigg and myself."

"Is that so?" Mr. P leaned on the counter. "Since when do you bother a family member in mourning? These are old rules you're breaking, Josef Viktorovich."

Joe the Borscht tipped his head to the side like he didn't get why the conversation was going the way it was. Grigg didn't either. How could a 74-year-old arcade owner stand up to Joe the Borscht?

The Bookkeeper took a step closer. His light blue eyes watched the players in the scene like there was something here for him to learn.

One of the regular beat cops, Lanzonni, passed the window spinning his billy club in intricate circles and figure eights. Even a cop on the Island had to put on his own sideshow. On busy weekend afternoons, Lanzonni'd come inside and entertain the kids with his stick tricks.

The place was too damned empty for that now.

Lanzonni waved at Mr. P and Grigg, then gave Joe the Borscht and the other two men a long stare through the plate glass window.

Joe the Borscht turned slowly, stopped at the door held open by Frank, and spoke without looking back. "I have accounts I need to settle with Grigg."

"Whatever you're going to settle, it can wait until after the service," Mr. P said.

Joe the Borscht left, walking down The Bowery away

from Lanzonni, the Bookkeeper and Frank in tow.

Grigg was safe for now. Good. He'd learned nothing. Bad. Had Dad borrowed money from Joe? Anything was possible, given the financial hole his father had put himself in. Put Grigg in. Russian rules meant Grigg inherited the debt. Why not say so? Joe the Borscht wasn't shy about collecting. About anything.

Almost as important, what made the gangster leave? The cop's look-in? Mr. P's bold refusal to let him talk to Grigg? It didn't add up. Grigg opened his mouth to speak. Petrushkin raised his finger, then said, "Your father never mentioned anything about Joe to me. Why is he interested in you?"

"No clue. Maybe Dad borrowed money. He needed it."

"Your father wasn't stupid like that. He hated the mob. I will see what I can do about our friend. There are other *associations*. I am owed a favor or two. Much better than owing favors to *those* people."

Mr. P has dealings with the mob? Grigg wanted specifics. "You can—"

"My business is my business." A favorite line. "Let me do it and say thank you after. For now, watch how you go."

Grigg nodded.

"May I see the pictures of the bone again?"

Grigg handed over the phone.

"It is a fascinating story of innovation and bravery, completely forgotten in this world of music on computers." Mr. P picked up from where he'd been interrupted.

"For twenty years or so, this was the only way to play music banned by the authorities."

Grigg knew this from the web, but he listened, hoping the old man would offer something he didn't.

Mr. P dipped his head to stare at the skull record intensely, as if he could make it play using his eyes.

"Your father and Sokolov bought many of them, you know."

Here was something: His dad and Katia's father? "No, I didn't."

"Those two were real *stilyagi*—or more like you would say, wannabes. *Stilyagi* mostly came from families with power and influence. The teen rebels of the Soviet Union during that period. Back then it meant something like beatniks or hipsters. The kids dressed in what they thought—imagined, really—was the cool, colorful clothing of the West, rather than the drab garb of the Soviet worker's paradise. Their presence in society mirrored the appearance and disappearance of the bone music. The *stilyagi* were the ones who most desperately wanted to hear it. There were other boys your father and Sokolov ran with. Two brothers."

"Who? Are they here?"

"Not that I know of. The oldest one was a rough customer—and got rougher. He went from buying X-ray records to selling them and then was sucked deeper into the world of the black market, into a gang. Was sent to a work camp, in the end. My old head can't recall his name. Before he went bad, all four boys would go searching for the elusive *Amerikanski* rock and roll at the flea markets. Ended up owning a lot of blues and tangos because many discs weren't labeled, or the labels were a lie." He shook with quiet laughter. "Even that was considered good. *Cool.* Because it was forbidden."

"Weren't you in their group?"

"I was older. Already in university. That was a ticket to a better life. Party membership and a good job. I couldn't jeopardize it. They told their stories when they got back. Our families' flats were in the same building. Some of them connected."

"Did Dad ever talk about the records as an adult? When you met again here?"

"Never. You know your father wasn't much for nostalgia about those days." He stared off over the pinball machines, a look that meant he was digging deeper. "Eventually, the KGB had a special unit working to shut down the bootleg music business. It got bad. The suck-ups in the Communist youth league—kids their age—reported those buying bone music. You'd get time in a work camp for making them—even owning them. As I said, some like that older boy—what *was* his name?—got started with the Russian mob by dealing in the bones." He handed back the phone. "How is the sound on this recording?"

"Not great."

"Yes, yes. You might get crackling and popping so loud you could hardly hear the music. Some were nothing more than three minutes of noise. In Russian, we called that *buying sand*. If the police ever give it back, may I see it?"

The *if* was like a slap. "Sure."

"Old songs recorded on the bones of dead people. Few would know what they are. Fewer still would have any interest in them. Enough of the memories." Mr. P put his hand on Grigg's shoulder. "How are you getting through all this?"

His response was flat and pat: "As best I can."

Mr. P's shoulders dropped into their usual slouch, the excitement of the bone record passing. "I need to do some paperwork in the back. You take care of things here. Watch those girls." He pointed to three that looked around twelve years old, short shorts, halter tops. "They've been hip-checking the crane machine."

After work, Grigg stopped at Nathan's for a late dinner: two dogs with cheese sauce and chili, small order of frog's legs, and a draft Mermaid Pilsner. He stood eating at an inside table.

Mr. P had connected his father to the bone records. Back when Dad was a teenage … what? Russian greaser? Hippie? Punk? Grigg could hardly picture it.

The discs were black market and linked to the mob. Or rather, mobsters operating five decades ago. He'd take it: a lead was a lead, and one he hadn't had four hours ago. And another surprise: Mr. P somehow had the pull to keep Joe the Borscht off Grigg's back. Or so Grigg hoped.

A number he didn't know set off his phone, and he answered.

"We met at door to my apartment." Heavy Russian accent. "When your father was alive."

"Freddy Popov? I've been trying to talk with you. You said the guy who had my father's picture might be a cop. How sure are you of that?"

"My neighbor talked with guy. Now we think maybe government agent."

"What agency? I want a description of him. Everything you know."

"Even better. Man gave her his phone number in case there was another sighting of your father."

"My dad was seen there?"

"She said that to him. Think she was hitting on the fed."

"Okay, so what agency *is* he with?"

"Just have number written on a card."

"What is it?"

"Will cost you."

"Cost? My dad was murdered."

"Then you need lead. Two hundred bucks."

"Are you shitting me?"

"If you have better …"

"Okay, fine. I'll be right over."

"No. Busy. Friday night. Be here at seven."

Two straws to grasp at in one night. Grigg was a phone number away from someone who had been searching for his father. Maybe he was a fed, maybe he wasn't. He could be the guy who'd trailed Dad to their house. Shot him on the roof. Grigg had to be prepared for that. Right, with half a cop's training and a bad knee.

If Grigg ate only bologna sandwiches and skipped his

floor softeners for two days, he might have the money to pay Popov.

He started the walk home, planning a zigzag, backstreet route rather than straight west on Surf Avenue. To be extra careful, he started out going the wrong way on Surf in the direction of Brighton Beach. As he came to Eldorado Bumper Cars, he stopped as if to watch the crashing and slamming, skids and sparks. A male in a navy hoodie not far behind halted in front of a closed store and made like he cared about the merchandise. Blue, red, and green cars raced around the oval track, sparks spraying from the paddles topping the poles that drew the juice from the wire-net ceiling. Heavy metal music blared. An adjacent arcade added bells, beeps, gunfire, and explosions. Both places blasted all that noise from outdoor loudspeakers to attract customers, modern sound systems replacing the old-school Coney Island barkers.

Grigg moved ahead to the arcade. The guy in the hoodie moved the same distance. The Skee-Ball dropped back into Grigg's stomach. His breathing came fast; electricity ran up his spine. Fear and focus combined. *Stay calm. Might not be one of Joe the Borscht's men.* Tourists, drunks—drunk tourists—were often followed out of the amusement district before being mugged. Coney Island might be the fun capital of New York City, but real-life thrills of a deadly sort lurked on the streets around it in Gravesend and Sheepshead Bay. Mr. P couldn't have had time to call off Joe the Borscht, so it could be a mob tail. Either way, embarrassing to get jumped in his own neighborhood.

Grigg crossed the street to the Coney Island-Stillwell Avenue station, where the subway platform had a good crowd to get lost in. He didn't see Hoodie come up. He rode one stop to Bay 50th Street. Still no shadow. He got on again going back to Coney Island, left the station, and followed Mermaid Avenue two blocks. He turned into a twenty-four-hour Russian supermarket, roaming the aisles, checking out foods, though he couldn't read the labels. A fat, ponytailed man at the register stopped reading one of the local Russian papers and tracked Grigg around the store. The reaction was familiar. Happened whenever Grigg shopped. Didn't care. At this point, he was worried about the tail.

After five minutes, the man said, "Is there something you're looking for? You don't look like our sort of customer."

"They have a special look?"

"We may sell food for the soul, but it ain't fucking soul food." His shoulders bounced as he laughed at the stupid joke. "Not for your kind."

Grigg wanted to lecture the man about his name, his dead father's name, the food his father had taught him to love.

What good will it do? What good will it ever do?

Instead, he bought a pack of Dentyne and hustled along Mermaid.

Sadness settled over him because of the one problem he could never solve: the way the world—his Little Odessa world, at least—reacted to the color of his skin. Many here would never accept him.

As he turned at Romanoff's, he checked behind. Hoodie? Might be. Still, there were a lot of hoodies in the neighborhood. Street uniform. His heart wasn't convinced. It thundered in his chest. Rule of the street said don't be the first to run. He limped at a regular pace, head tilted to pick up footsteps behind. As he closed in on his house, he broke the rule and went as fast as his knee would allow. It hardly counted as running. The pursuer stopped three houses down and crossed to the other side of the street. A match bloomed flame to light a cigarette. The man's face stayed in darkness under the hood with the glowing ash pointed at Grigg. A tail rather than a mugging? Joe the Borscht keeping track?

Inside, he took out a can of beer.

May as well enjoy one I already bought.

Grigg sipped half of it. Carefully, he peered out a front window. Hoodie, still across the street, lit another cigarette.

Grigg stopped at one beer. Researching the Russian mob in early sixties St. Petersburg was too daunting for tonight. He watched *Deadpool* on Netflix, checking the window every fifteen minutes. Halfway through the movie, Hoodie got on his cell phone, turned, and walked back to the avenue. Grigg went out on the stoop and watched for two hours. The street stayed quiet. He went to bed.

CHAPTER 9

Thursday, September 8, 2016

Pounding. Let it be a dream. He opened his eyes. He didn't want anyone banging on his door. He didn't want anyone knowing it was *his* door. Again, real pounding: *Bam. Bam. Bam.*

Grigg got up from the sleeping bag. The guy who followed him last night? Why wait so long? Couldn't be the new owners. They moved in tomorrow and had keys. He edged into the hallway and looked at the escape route he and Dad had used that awful night: the balcony in the master bedroom.

His gut tightened. He was fully awake, though weary from the fight-or-flight spikes that'd been roiling his system since last night.

I can't go through it again.
"Open up. NYPD."
Ah, shit.
"Coming."
He pulled on jeans and a shirt.
Ho and Wilson grabbed Grigg by the arms as soon

as he opened the door. They hustled him down the stairs. Old lady Belochkin stood on her porch next door, arms crossed over her bulldozer of a chest. She shook her head at Grigg. She'd never liked him. Hadn't liked Mom either; his father had told him that once with a couple swear words mixed in. Dad never swore.

The cops put him in an unmarked car and drove to the precinct house. The concrete building was stained like some kind of rot had set in, and it had tiny windows—perfect for not seeing inside. It resembled a massive bomb shelter accidentally left aboveground.

Wilson moved ahead down the corridor, took out a key, and unlocked a door. Ho pulled Grigg in by his hair.

"Goddammit, that hurts!"

"Shut the fuck up." Ho slammed him hard into a chair. The room was almost as narrow as the hall they'd left. Grigg only rated an interview closet.

Acoustic tiling covered the walls and ceiling. Ho unclicked the cuffs off one wrist and onto the chair bolted to the floor. He sat opposite without a table in between, while Wilson stood behind him. No window, no one-way mirror, no sign of any cameras.

The black hole of interview rooms.

His stomach burned. The acid leapt up his throat. He'd had bad encounters with cops. Too-rough stop and frisks. If he came out of this box busted up—or didn't get out at all—who would do anything about it? The sour taste wouldn't go away.

"We don't want to have to work hard today," said Ho.

He had close-cropped black hair, narrow-set eyes, and a small mouth. His face was impassive, bored, even. He'd already used that line too many times in his career. "What were you doing in the house?"

"How'd you know I was there?"

"We know everything you're up to."

"The guy following me last night?"

Ho leaned in close. His breath was awful, starting at cigarettes and going downhill through his last three meals. He yanked Grigg off the chair by his hair and let go.

"Fuck. Ouch."

Wilson checked his fingernails.

Excellent. Bad cop and who-gives-a-shit cop.

"You don't own the house anymore."

"Why are you looking into my real estate dealings? The buyers don't move in until tomorrow. We have an arrangement."

"We're looking into every fucking thing about you. Be careful. The more lies, the worse it gets. You like living so close to where your father was murdered?"

"Nowhere else to go."

"You had nowhere else to go the night of the murder?"

"What are you talking about?"

"You were on the roof when your father was shot."

"Yeah. I told you I was."

"We have a witness who says it was just you and your father."

Grigg looked in disbelief from one detective up to the other.

"That's bullshit. Who's your witness? They'd have seen the shooter."

"If you don't start telling us what really happened, you'll get to view *all* the witnesses at your murder trial. Back up. Go over it again. You're in the house. Your father shows up. Was this meeting planned?"

"No, of course not. Or I would have let him in the front door. He completely surprised me, like I told you. He was only with me a couple minutes or so before the guy with the gun came in the front door. Had a key or picked it. We got the hell out the same way Dad came in."

"It's a nice story. Why should we believe you? You tampered with evidence at the scene. Tell us why you murdered your father."

"Is that what your witness claims? I did it? Really? Because if you had it solid, we wouldn't be talking. What was my motive? I was the *only* one looking for Dad when he went missing. You guys sure as shit weren't."

Ho shook his head. "Flunked out of the academy. Otherwise, you'd know all the terms—*motive, alibi,* and *opportunity.* You don't have an alibi. You certainly had fucking opportunity."

"I didn't flunk out. Everyone seems to keep forgetting. I was attacked by four racists who work for your department now."

"Keep taking us through your story—once the shooter got in," said Wilson, whose brown hair was parted down the middle and matched dull brown eyes. A picture of him would appear next to *nondescript* in the dictionary.

"Fuck. How many times? I only saw him in the light briefly when he came through the door. Six-foot-one or two. Short red hair. Beard cut close. Flattened nose. Dressed in a dark suit. *Again*, the revolver was nickel-plated. Looked big to me. But I bet they all look big when someone's coming after you." Grigg retold the escape out the balcony, climbing, running, running, shooting, shooting. Sprayed with Dad's blood … He broke down, the bottom dropping out of his thoughts, falling away—and he was going to fall after them, become a complete blubbering idiot.

Get yourself under control. Can't do this here.

Wilson left, came back in, and dropped a roll of toilet paper on the floor in a way that didn't say, *Take your time*. More like, *Get on with it*. That actually helped. Grigg wiped away the tears and blew his nose hard, filling the tissue with snot, and left it on the floor.

"Dad fell off the roof. I went down after him."

"Then you ran?"

"Y-yeah—"

"After taking the record?"

Frustration boiled up like steam, filling his head, pressing to get out. "I told you all this before too. Dad showed me the bone record in his pocket. Then he was dead. The gunman was climbing down, told me to stay where I was. He'd already shot at me. I didn't think me staying would end so well."

"What reason did the mystery man have to come after your father?"

"That's what I've been trying to figure out! That's what *you* should be working on. Not coming up with fake witnesses to squeeze a confession out of me."

Ho was out of his seat. "Listen you fucking nig—"

Wilson interrupted: "Let's get this on the record."

Ho remained standing, looking down at Grigg. "Your father said *nothing* the night of his death? Nothing to explain what was going on?"

"No." A lie. He'd never tell them his father had named Katia. "Like I said, when Dad came inside, he told me he'd come to say goodbye because he was going to Russia and might not return. You tell me what that means. Then the gunman showed up. Maybe the guy had the house staked out, hoping Dad would return. More likely, he was following him. Let's be honest. You thought he came back for something. So did I. You've tossed the house. I searched the whole place before you did. I didn't find anything. Did you?"

"First time we interviewed you, I told you taking the record was stupid. Now we have a witness. You're hiding something. Maybe you were angry he disappeared and left you with two mortgages on the house. Maybe it was something else."

"There's no witness. You're lying. Or … or being manipulated." Grigg's voice rose. "Everyone will tell you I was the one trying to find Dad. Then he was taken minutes after he returned." Desperation. "Joe the Borscht came looking for me last night. Pull *him* in."

"What did he want?"

"We didn't get that far. Really good news for me, I'm thinking."

"We'll check with organized crime if we think it merits our time," said Ho like it didn't. "For now, you're our suspect. We're going to give you some more rope. Don't think it'll take much. We'll talk to everybody you know. Everybody they know. Everybody with a view of that roof. We'll find out what you're hiding."

Grigg's stomach gurgled, making the burning worse. The cops wanted an easy case—or wanted him for how he looked. Joe the Borscht plain wanted Grigg.

"Don't go far," said Wilson. "We'll know if you do, and it'll only make things easier for us."

Wilson opened the door and pointed the way. No escort on the long walk toward sunlight. As soon as he exited the precinct, Grigg rushed home to pack up. He couldn't come back to the house tonight. Or ever again. He saw that the stuff in his bedroom had been rifled through, what little there was, by other detectives while he was being interviewed. He threw his gear back into the blue duffel, rolled up the sleeping bag and stuffed it in too, and threw his messenger bag over his shoulder. He briefly fingered the bullet hole high on the outside flap of the bag. Like he needed one more reminder of that night.

He'd caught one break. His gun safe was in his locker at the arcade.

The way these cops are working the case, they'd find a way to make the ballistics match.

He thought of Carmichael's advice: *Witnesses, witness-*

es, witnesses.

Wilson and Ho said they had one. The statement was either a bullshit ploy to rattle him into doing something stupid or the witness didn't give them enough to arrest Grigg. If the witness was real, it had to be someone connected to the murder trying to frame him. Bad to worse didn't begin to cover it.

He limped fast back to Mermaid Avenue because he needed to get to the day job. One quick call before the subway. He leaned against the wall of Romanoff's, a stitch sowing pain in his side. His knee throbbed.

He touched Katia's number as soon as he caught his breath.

"Just finished getting roasted by the cops. I'm a suspect. *The* suspect, they say."

"Did you find a place? Today's the last day, right?"

"No takers for me as a roomie. Hate to do it, but I'm going to have to sneak in and out of the arcade. Will mean some early mornings."

"Come over tonight. We'll figure it out."

"I can't put you in jeopardy."

"Are you being followed?"

"Was last night. Think it might have been a cop. Detectives were at the house this morning."

"My building has a back door into the basement. I'll unlock it just before six. Come along behind the buildings. You'll have a clear view if anyone's behind you."

"I really appreciate this. Everything."

He hung up.

His dad had taught him a Russian proverb: *Who feels worse in the trap, the cheese or the mouse?*

He turned for the subway.

CHAPTER 10

Thursday, September 8, 2016

"Not Fade Away" played from Katia's Bluetooth speakers for the third time.

Grigg shook his head. "I got nothing."

"How could there even be some kind of code on the record if it was made more than fifty years before the crime?" Katia touched her phone to stop the playback of the bone record recording.

"I know. After what Mr. P said, I hoped I'd hear a clue. Anything."

"Maybe it's something in the lyrics themselves?" she asked.

"Fodder for late-night web searches."

She looked at him, a beautiful stillness in the way she sat on the couch, except her eyes, which were the blue of a quick-running stream.

Tick-tick-tick-tick.

His father's watch read 6:15 p.m.

"You need to lie low." Her dark eyebrows rose slowly like she knew a secret. "And I have an idea."

"I can't hide under your bed." It was a joke. And wishful thinking. "I don't think your roommate likes me."

"You heard her?"

"She's kinda loud."

"I ripped her a new asshole for that. No, you can't stay here." She laughed. "I have a friend. You went to high school with her too. She's got an interesting sort of squat. You might be able to crash."

Might.

"She might also be able to help with the case. She digs into all sorts of weird stuff. She said to stop by."

Since no one had followed Grigg in, they left the apartment building by the front door, heading south on Brighton 4th Street toward the ocean. They crossed Bridgewater Court and passed Café Restaurant Volna, which had some of the best *pelmeni* in the neighborhood. They weren't on the boardwalk long before Katia jumped down to the sand. Grigg followed. The honey glow of the late summer sun warmed the beach. Native Americans called Coney the Island without Shadows—something like that—because it ran east-west and the beach faced south, so the sun beamed down on the sand throughout the entire day as it arced across the sky. Grigg wanted his life back without shadows.

"I don't even know why they went crazy over Hurricane Hermine." Katia waved at the pristine, sparsely populated beach, a few folks getting sun on the Thursday after Labor Day. "Sunday was a perfect beach day. Everyone laid out. But we couldn't go in the water because of riptides. Ropes and cops. Same on Monday."

"Because of Superstorm Sandy. Nobody wants to make that mistake again."

They walked west toward Coney Island's entertainment district. Katia's sandals were off, and she dodged the water, laughing as waves reached up toward her. She loved the sand, the ocean, everything about the beach. Always had. Grigg wasn't pushing it. He figured she'd tell him who they were meeting when she was ready. No amount of time had changed how much he trusted her. Seeing Katia again was the only good thing that had happened to him in the last six months. He thought back to the break-up scene, his twitchy insecurities.

Stupid with bells on.

Grigg's calves burned from limping across the sand, but it was for the best. The less he was seen on the streets, the better. Cops, Joe the Borscht, and an unknown killer could all be after him. They passed the New York Aquarium, which had been designed to present its back to the sea. All steel and cement. Inside was better. His dad had loved visiting the exhibits.

After the aquarium came the heart of the amusement area, primarily made up of the two parks, Deno's Wonder Wheel and Luna. Some of the Wonder Wheel's cars slid back and forth like the contraption was broken. Screams came from the ride. It had been designed that way, a so-called eccentric Ferris wheel. *Thank you, Dad's history lessons.* Other rides flashed, and metal screeched on metal.

Music drifted out of Ruby's Bar & Grill up on the

boardwalk. In his memory, the perfume of fried clams, corn on the cob, and good beer. The massive skeleton of the Parachute Drop—long out of use but still a symbol of Coney Island, its Eiffel Tower—stood where Steeplechase Park had been, with the Brooklyn Cyclones ballfield behind it. Quickly enough, they passed the existing amusement parks, which weren't that large and struggled to survive from season to season. Next, giant public housing projects huddled up to the boardwalk, offering poor tenants some of the best ocean views in the city. *The real estate boys must drool over those.*

Katia took the next set of steps up to the boardwalk, pulled her sandals back on, and picked up the pace. "Charlotte texted me. She just got home."

His curiosity was piqued now. "Who's Charlotte?"

"You'll see."

So much for curiosity.

They walked to the end of the boardwalk and turned inland on West 37th Street. A fence crowned with barbed wire ran along the other side of the street. Beyond was Sea Gate, emphasis on *gate*, the private community that occupied the western point of Coney Island. They passed one of the gates that gave the neighborhood its name—a roof-like structure spanning two buildings with a booth for the Sea Gate Police, the private force that operated independently from the NYPD.

Sea Gate was full of Russians—Jews from the earliest migrations, plus White Russian Orthodox, atheists, mobsters, and everything in between.

"We're friends, aren't we?" Katia's voice dropped.

He turned, startled. "Of course. I could never repay you for everything you're doing for me."

"It's just … after everything, I want our friendship to be real. Not about owing me."

"It's real. We. Are. Friends." *Though if I could go back in time and do it differently, we'd be more than that.*

She reached out and touched his elbow with two fingers. Electricity coursed through him so powerfully that she may as well have hugged him close and fierce.

She pulled her hand back.

They walked by the Mermaid Spa, on the other side of the Sea Gate fence. Many called it the best Russian bath in New York.

Katia turned right onto Neptune Avenue and stopped in front of two buildings, one complete, one still under construction, the latter a girder frame behind a fence. There was no equipment on the site. Pieces of plastic on the unfinished tower snapped in the light ocean breeze rising in the cooler evening air.

Katia walked up to the completed apartment tower. A brass sign read Neptune's Manor. She pushed the button to ring apartment 4D.

"Nice digs."

"Charlotte may be a squatter, but she knows how to do it right. No one will ever find her. She's invisible." Katia pulled the door when it buzzed and walked to the elevator. "This place opened in 2006. In two years, condos on every floor were empty. Foreclosures. The Great Recession. Then the developer went bust. That's why the other building was never finished. Charlotte moved in and made her apartment disappear from the bank's records."

"Nice skill to have."

"Olympic-class hacker. But she's picky."

"How so?"

"Doesn't like Russians, from our school days. I'm the only one she's friends with. So far."

"You tell me that now?"

CHAPTER 11

Thursday, September 8, 2016

The doors closed, Katia pushed four, and the elevator rose.

"We bumped into each other a few years ago on the avenue. Hadn't seen her since high school. Got coffee. I volunteered to look up the bankruptcy filing on this building. With what I found and her skills … Like I said, no one will ever know she's here."

She led him down the hall and knocked on the door to 4D.

"It's Katia."

Fiddling with the chain, and the snap of one lock, then another. The door opened to reveal a woman taller than Grigg or Katia with sun-streaked brown hair in a ponytail. She had full lips, brown eyes, and a stare so intense Grigg thought he was in trouble before she spoke. She wore dark blue sweats and a white T-shirt that read *urFucked now*. He didn't remember her from Lincoln High. No surprise. The place had 2,500 students.

"Charlotte, this is Grigg."

"Come in." She closed the door and locked all the

locks. "I'm not a fucking Russian," she told him by way of introduction.

"That's not a concern for me," Grigg said.

"It was for most. Still is. Course you don't look the part." She saw his face change from confusion to anger, and she laughed, a bold sound that matched her intensity. "Don't get yourself bent out of shape. I don't care about color, shape, sex, or anything else. Well, except for most Russians. Not a fan of fucking Russians. Their tight little circles in school. Acting like they own the whole neighborhood."

"Believe me, I wasn't on the inside in high school. Or anywhere."

"Yeah, guess that makes sense. Anyway, Katia's done me some favors. I owe her."

This rankled him. "Don't put yourself out. I don't want to be payback on a debt."

"So, I'm not good enough for *you* either?"

Katia stepped between the two of them. "Aren't my two good friends getting along so well. You'll be in the bedroom in the back, Grigg. Why don't you set your stuff down?"

He carried his duffel and the messenger bag over his shoulder past a full-sized inflated mattress made up with sheets and blankets and positioned in the middle of the living room. A large laptop lay open on it. Cardboard boxes set on their sides and stacked along the other wall held neatly folded clothing.

Before he got to the doorway to the back bedroom,

a glinting flash blinded him for an instant. He put up his hand and followed the light to the balcony, which had a sliding glass door that was closed but for two inches. A thick black cable snaked from the balcony through the opening to a metal box on the floor, along with a narrow blue wire that went to what looked like a router; it had a row of flashing lights that meant computers were talking to each other. The metal thing reflecting the last of the sunlight stood on three legs.

No way.

He couldn't help himself. He turned around.

"Solar panels?"

"Pretty cool, huh?" Katia said, obviously trying to encourage a conversation. "Electricity. Charlotte stores it in the battery. The building provides water."

"They can't help it," Charlotte said with a shrug. "The Great Recession produced some excellent squatting opportunities."

"How long have you been here?" Grigg said.

"Since 2011."

"Katia's right about you." Charlotte dropped her head a little but kept her eyes on him. "You are invisible."

"I'm motivated. Left high school in junior year. Bounced around. Shelters. Awful. Scary." She shuddered.

If they were scary for her …

"Found this place. Katia keeps me up on the bankruptcy of the building's owner. She told me a little about your father's murder. Awful. Sorry." She sat down cross-legged on the bed. "What have you got on the case?"

"Bits and pieces." He started with what was top of mind. "When Dad was missing, a guy named Freddy Popov told me he'd been shown a picture of my father by a guy—maybe a fed—who was on the hunt. Freddy's offered to sell me the guy's phone number tomorrow night. Two hundred bucks."

"A fed, huh?"

Uh-oh. "Wanna throw me out now?"

"No, I love feds. I love *fucking* with feds." She briefly tapped the keyboard. "That's an expensive phone number. This guy legit?"

"No idea. He is a *fucking* Russian. As in, from there very recently."

"I'll check him out."

He gave her the address and apartment number in Midwood.

"That all you got?"

Grigg nodded. He told her about Joe the Borscht.

"Whatever you do," Katia said to both of them, "stay away from him."

Grigg shook his head. "Not sure I can. Joe knows something. Somehow, I have to find out what. Be nice if I had a plan for that."

He started describing the bone record, but Charlotte waved him off. "Katia told me. Some dark shit there. The oldest music hack ever. I'll do a deep dive on those. There are engines that'll compare the lyrics with what's on the web. See if any part of the song has been referenced or echoed."

"Like it's code for something?"

"Like the language was used at a later date to mean something else. That might be a reason to pick that particular record. Then the big fun. Sites on the darknet where bad guys go to brag. Good place to ask around, given how rare a bone record must be these days."

Charlotte handed Grigg a deflated mattress-style pool float that would definitely be more comfortable than the floor. He went in the other room and blew it up. He and Katia sat on it. Charlotte tapped at her keyboard so fast it sounded like she was in a race.

"What else does she do on there?" he asked Katia quietly.

"She got me some information for these homeowners a bank client of ours ripped off. I passed it on. I was a whistleblower, really."

"Doesn't that violate some kind of code of ethics?"

"Laws too. That's why I used Charlotte. If it ever gets out, my career's done. Law school, over."

An hour and a half passed. Katia had to leave.

The cops, work, walking the beach. He fell asleep without going out to buy beer, though his last thought before he dropped off was that he'd have to lay in a supply tomorrow. The beer didn't only soften floors. It quieted his thoughts, which could keep him awake as easily as the hardwood underneath him.

CHAPTER 12

Friday, September 9, 2016

Grigg perched on a folding chair in Freddy Popov's apartment. The place was sparsely furnished, which made an obvious lie of Freddy's claim he'd lived in the place for three years. Freddy sat on the only chair with cushions, plastic-wrapped and new, and stared at Grigg with light green eyes. His hair was blond and slicked back with so much styling gel that it looked like he had a product addiction; his suit was cheap and neat. A crate served as the coffee table. Nothing about him looked legit.

"When did you come over from Russia?" Grigg asked, testing.

"2009." Another lie. His accent was thick as a tourist's.

Grigg fingered six twenties and eight tens. Katia had lent him sixty of the two hundred bucks, which he had taken because he needed it so bad—and wished he didn't. Whatever ridiculous long shot hope he had of getting back together with her, he didn't want money to get in the way again. His overactive imagination had already dreamed up a theory that she'd offered the loan because she knew nothing was going to happen between them.

"I have the money. Can I get that phone number?"

"Things have changed small bit. Maybe more than—"

"Don't dick around with me."

"Calm, my friend. You'll get what you want. More than. I have an errand I need you to do."

"I run this errand to get the phone number?"

"No, you run errand, I tell you everything you want to know about murder of your papa."

"Do you have the phone number?"

"No."

"You lie too fucking much." Grigg stood up.

"Sit down, friend. There *are* feds in this game. Plans must change. Put your money away. Take this." He handed over a piece of paper with two long decimals on it: 40.676841 and -74.148313. "At that location is shipping container. Very specific container. Yellow. Trans-Global Logistics. At a certain time, I will want you to retrieve items from that container. I let you know when."

"Where is it?"

"Those are the coordinates."

"Why not just give me the goddamn address?"

"Is more precise."

"Or really difficult to get to. You're nuts. I came here for that number. I'm not—"

Loud, hard thumps on the apartment door.

Am I safe behind any *door in this town?*

"You were followed?" The cushion squeaked as Popov got off the chair.

"No. I'm careful these days. You don't know how careful."

"I hope. Or you've killed us both." Popov went to the window and opened it.

"Uh … we're three stories up."

The pounding on the door sounded like the kind meant to unhinge it, not convince someone to open up. Whoever was on the other side didn't speak, didn't yell. They knew who was inside. They weren't cops. Popov opened a big cardboard box under the window and pulled out a rolled-up rope ladder.

Like he knew someone might come after him. Like Dad did.

Popov hooked the ladder on the sill and let it go.

"I'll go north around building." Popov put his leg over the windowsill. "You go south. At least we split them."

Wood cracked.

Freddy Popov disappeared down into the dark.

A gunshot sounded and the faceplate of a deadbolt that had been holding out buried itself in the coffee table. Whoever wanted in had run out of whatever patience they had.

Grigg went for the ladder.

A second shot.

He swung his strong leg over, secured a foothold, brought over the bad leg, and took the descent one rung at a time, the smashing noise above making him wish he could trust his left knee. He jumped from the third rung and landed on his right foot, shoulder-rolled to standing, and sped along the building's wall.

That's when the shooting from Popov's window started.

Out in front of the building, Grigg slowed to a walk among the folks on the sidewalk. He couldn't afford to stand out. Wouldn't achieve much by trying to run anyway.

A man flew out the front door of Popov's building, semi-automatic drawn, yelling at Grigg.

He dodged into the street as a bullet blew off a car's rearview mirror. Bent low, he moved across the thoroughfare, throwing himself out of the way of a cab, the driver leaning hard on her horn.

A second gunshot.

Grigg plunged into a darkened space across the street from the building. A sign read KOLBERT PLAYGROUND.

Moving was going to get him killed. This wasn't his neighborhood. He didn't know which streets were escape routes. He wasn't fast enough. He had to hide somewhere and stay still.

From behind him, the shooter yelled in Russian—probably calling others to follow.

Grigg slalomed around trees, his knee sending a jolt of pain every time he leaned left, and turned to where swings, a jungle gym, and other playground equipment loomed out of the dark. He crept beneath the slide, which he judged to be the darkest spot in the play area, and hunched underneath where the metal sloped to the ground.

Good thing I'm short.

He heard steps from the direction he'd come.

A flashlight.

Tick-tick-tick-tick.

No fucking way he was looking at his father's watch.

The flashlight searched in a methodical pattern—tight circles drawn by a beam of light—leading two men across the park toward the playground. Muffled crunching on wood chips. They'd crossed from the grass into the play area.

Grigg tried to squeeze farther underneath the slide, sitting on the ground with his back against metal, bad knee lancing pain that flashed blue lightning at the back of his eyes.

The only good news: Dusk had turned to dark.

The beam flashed along the swings. Angled steel bars and chains loomed like a threat with the gunmen approaching.

He measured the distance to the fence on his left, which was lit by the stale yellow of a streetlight. A dash of twenty or thirty feet. Meant to keep little kids in, so it wasn't too high. But his left leg made Grigg kid-equivalent. He saw himself hanging upside down from the fence as three spots of red spread across his yellow dress shirt until they merged into one large blotch. The empty eyes of his imagined self stared at him.

His gut burned like the acid was sizzling through his stomach's lining. His back ached from bending. His knee demanded that he ignore the rest of it.

Air hissed over his teeth in panicked breaths. He tried to slow it. He couldn't afford to make any noise.

Inhale slow through the nose, exhale slow from the mouth.

Clear your head. Make a plan.

Nothing came to him. He didn't know what to do. He'd trapped himself.

The circle of light slid past the jungle gym toward the slide, stopped, came nearer, went back, and rose up and around the jungle gym. Back down, it edged so close it passed inches from Grigg's work shoe.

Halted.

He took in a deep breath and prepared for the deadly run to the fence.

The light flicked away out of sight. He dared to peek from under the slide. The beam was pointed the other way and moving out of the playground into the park proper. He exhaled. Wanted to collapse onto his side but didn't dare.

A hand grabbed his shoulder. He fought as he was yanked to his feet. One of the goons had snuck around the other side of the slide. The man ran him at the slide's ladder and slammed him against it. Just in time, Grigg got his arms in front to protect his face. White flashed across his vision, followed by sharp pain when his arms struck the steel.

"Ow! Fuck, dammit!"

"Shut up or I do again." The man raised his voice. "You were right! Slide! Got him."

Grigg bit his lip against the stinging ache in his forearms. The flashlight bounced as the other man ran back. Grigg was turned around and found a narrow-headed man with a ponytail and something wrong with the left side of his face. Or that was a trick of the shadows.

White light in his eyes. Blinded in a halogen tunnel surrounded by black.

"Where's Popov?"

"I have no idea."

"You're Orlov's son." The one with the flashlight spoke. It wasn't a question. "You were searching for him."

"Who are you?"

The goon holding him pulled him away from the metal and prepared to throw him at the ladder again. Grigg had no way to protect the back of his head.

Before the thug could, he said, "Yeah, I'm Grigg Orlov. Andrei was my dad. I was looking for him."

He was set back against steel.

"Why do you meet Popov?" The Russian accent was thick as Freddy's. He liked his questions short and simple.

"He said he wanted to talk."

"He met with your father. When Papa was running. Several times. Did he tell you?"

"Yeah, sure."

It took control to get that out and not act surprised. If Grigg finished the night intact, he'd learned something new, but not from that liar Freddy.

"You're no good at lying."

"I'm not lying."

"Maybe not yet. What did Popov say?"

"Nothing before you interrupted our conversation."

I'm screwed if they search me and those container coordinates mean anything to them.

"See, now you lie. Where did he go?"

"Your sudden entrance made him want to leave just as rapidly. He went out through the same window I did. Didn't share his plans for the rest of the night."

A pause, maybe because Grigg had strained the man's English vocabulary.

"Let's go." The other one pulled him away from the ladder. "Running around out here, Grigoriy Andreiovich could get his head cracked open."

"The name's Grigg."

"No respect for the land of your fathers. Typical."

"Heard that before."

His eyes adjusted once the beam was taken away, and the playground objects began appearing out of the darkness.

"What the fuck are you doing on my real estate?"

The flashlight flew up the walkway. It lit a white man, legs apart, with a handkerchief on his head and a gun held away from the side of his body, a pose that said, *I've got one too.* The goon holding Grigg let go of one arm.

The new gunman raised his hand to block the light. "Get that fucking thing out of my eyes. These fucking corners are NBS. That means the fucking park is NBS territory. Second and last time, what the fuck are you doing on my real estate?"

"Easy." The semi-automatic came up next to the flashlight in the Russian's hand. "Just a little private business. We leave now."

"Don't fucking draw down on me."

Russian goons versus North Brooklyn Skins. My name just changed to Caught in the Crossfire.

Fight-or-flight pinned the needle at flight, but the Russian gripped Grigg's right arm even tighter with one big hand. Sweat ran down Grigg's neck and onto his chest.

"You leave park," said the Russian, "and we leave behind you. Gone for good."

"Fuck that shit. Fucking Russian mob doesn't come here ever."

A crack and the one holding Grigg crumpled with a grunt, dragging Grigg to the ground with him. Other guns—the gangbanger had friends—opened fire. A deadly snap-crackle-pop. Bullets pinged off playground equipment. Grigg flipped to the other side of the downed Russian. Not good cover. The man's partner retreated to the slide, firing as he went.

The shooting in the dark—little starbursts and big cracks—intensified.

Two more shots came from behind and left—the street side of the park—then the gunfire fell off in that direction. The gang leader retreated toward the trees, looking around, confused. Bang. His head snapped back, and he fell to the grass. A tall figure loped into the open, stopped a few feet from the chief banger, and put a bullet in his face.

Simultaneously, the flashlight came on and the goon

at the slide said, "Is that you—"

The new killer spoke in Russian, and instantly the goon behind Grigg came out.

"We didn't get Popov, but we have Orlov's son," said the goon. "He knows something. Mikhail got shot."

The tall one—bald on top and, like the other two, not a match for Dad's killer—switched to English with a foot-thick accent. "Get Orlov away."

That was it. His worst option was now his only means of escape. He took off across the open ground for the fence.

Tick-

Five steps.

"You had him. And he runs."

-Tick-

Another five.

-Tick-

"Stop!"

Grigg scrambled over the fence, letting go in his haste and falling on his back.

Ooof!

-Tick.

A snap and a *fwip* close by. They were shooting at the fence. If there was a part of him that didn't hurt, he couldn't pick it at the moment. He didn't care. He was up and running across the avenue, down unknown side street after side street until his left knee forced him to walk. He collapsed behind a dumpster in an alley. Maybe the Russians wouldn't follow. They had one wounded man. They knew the cops would be all over the park.

It was all guesses, but Grigg knew one thing for sure: no one ran slower than he did.

He waited.

CHAPTER 13

Friday, September 9, 2016

Grigg boarded Deno's Wonder Wheel. He'd dragged his sore body to the subway and then into the amusement park. The attendant shut the door, and the wheel moved and stopped to let two couples board the next car.

Nothing about tonight made sense. Freddy, his map coordinates, and the alleged meetings with Dad while he was on the run. The Russians who'd almost abducted him, but for the attack by NBS. He knew of the gang—bikers, ultra-violent and white supremacist. He hadn't heard they'd moved so far south. Midwood was white, middle-class, and known as the safest neighborhood in Brooklyn. Didn't seem like it tonight.

The Wonder Wheel, ninety-six years old, started revolving. It was one of the true survivors of the golden age of Coney Island. Grigg didn't choose it for nostalgia. He wanted somewhere he could rest, think, and see any and all possible approaches. He also needed to kill time so he wouldn't lead anyone back to Charlotte's squat. He pulled out his keychain with the Wonder Wheel souvenir fob on it, fingering two tarnished Yale keys. In high school, he'd taken a job working at Deno's that lasted five summers. The keys he held unlocked the front gates and the shed where the main power switches were, among other things. By the third summer, Grigg had been promoted to a job that included coming in and turning everything on before the general manager arrived. He'd kept the keys as a souvenir. He tried them every once in a while, just to see if they worked. They served as physical proof of his time spent working at the center of Coney Island—battered and squalid and still magical.

He and Katia had been together for all of those summers …

He tried to stretch out his back, groaned, and slumped against the seat. All the muscles from his calves to his thighs burned, double in the left leg. But he was alive and free.

Like Grigg, Freddy Popov was in the wind. Those coordinates?

He pulled out his phone, opened the map app, and plugged in the numbers. The map moved toward a spot in New Jersey … Newark airport to the left … Bayonne to the right. The satellite view closed in on the Port Elizabeth Container Terminal, a massive area of blacktop jutting into brown water. Far bigger than any pier, the terminal was covered with stacks of shipping containers. The coordinates indicated the X marking the spot was a row of containers near the water on the north side. That was as far as he could zoom in. No Street View on private property. Who knew how old the image was? There was no way to tell what was there now.

Popov had promised to tell him everything about Dad's murder if he retrieved something from a container at that location. How exactly was he supposed to do that?

If he believed the claim of the Russian thug, then Dad and Popov had been meeting in secret. Working together, then? On what? His dad was as likely to be involved in a container heist as he was to fly a fighter jet. The thug could have been trying to throw Grigg off. Disinformation. Or maybe Popov had actually been trying to help his dad escape whoever was after him? Hard to believe since everything about Popov bothered Grigg. His flat-out lying. His claim he knew everything about what happened to Dad. Who else would know everything, if not the killer? The mystery federal agent Popov said was hunting Dad hadn't been real. Bait for Grigg. Yet Popov still claimed the feds were somehow involved. He could easily have been involved in the murder, even if he wasn't the red-haired man. Especially if he did know Dad's whereabouts. Same for the Russians who came after them tonight. They killed fast and easy. Grigg had guesses, surmises, gaps, and lies. The coordinates could even be bogus. One simple fact would be nice …

Grigg had to track Popov down again before the Russian gunmen did. He only had the apartment and his cell number. Popov wouldn't go back to the flat. Charlotte had said she'd find out more about Popov. He needed her to come up with an electronic trail.

He had been so close to getting answers tonight. Instead, he'd come up with enough new questions for three investigations.

Grigg's car reached the top of the revolution. As it swung down, he scanned Surf Avenue and the crowds milling around the brightly-lit rides and game booths below. He was sure he'd spot bad guys moving in a deliberate search. Nothing so far. A few more spins on the wheel wouldn't hurt.

A block away, the Cyclone's wooden track snaked in its twisting, rising, falling path from Surf Avenue to the boardwalk and back. Its cars were cresting the top of the first steep hill for the brief panoramic view you got of the ocean before the drop—like you were going to fly off into the water. Arms flew into the air. The screams floated all the way to the Wonder Wheel as Grigg's car continued its descent.

He saw his father smiling on the bench across from his eight-year-old self. The Wonder Wheel was Grigg's first ride when he graduated from the kiddie stuff. Dad was as excited as Grigg, maybe more so, laughing when Grigg jumped as their car slid on its track toward the eccentric wheel's spoke. Grigg's squeal turned into giggles. It was one memory, but as with all his memories, it didn't jibe with Dad doing business with a crook like Freddy Popov. Running from a killer, this Grigg understood. But plotting a break-in at the container terminal? That made zero sense. It was the kind of question he would have taken to Dad, who never turned Grigg away when he wanted an answer. He missed him so. The loss made his knee, the house, the premature end of his police career, everything else trivial. The absence had become a hole in the world. His father had always, always been present in Grigg's life, while giving him room to grow, screw up, learn. When he considered everything he knew about his father, he could find nothing to explain what had happened since his disappearance.

He'd have to find the answers on his own. He wanted to protect the memory of his father. Doing both was starting to look like that freak show act: the no-armed juggler.

For the second time in almost three weeks, he'd been in the middle of a shooting. There'd be a police investigation and media coverage, either of which might yield clues he could use to learn about the men who'd come after Popov.

Grigg stepped off the Wonder Wheel dizzy. He'd knocked his head dropping from the playground fence. The rocking of the car made it worse. Nausea crept up from his stomach. He dragged his left leg against its aches and complaints to the bathroom, where he puked.

A guy pissing shook his head as Grigg washed his face. "Fucking lightweight. Don't come in here if you can't hold your beer. There's kids." The man burped.

Grigg walked to the boardwalk to take the long way around to Charlotte's place.

Charlotte's laptop was a pro model with a seventeen-inch screen, big as you'd get on a nice desktop model. She sat on the edge of her inflatable bed with the machine across her bare thighs while Grigg watched the screen from behind her.

She clicked and the monitor filled with something similar to the satellite view Grigg had seen on his phone: Newark Airport, the Jersey turnpike, water, and Bayonne. Similar, but way more detail.

"The ship channel," she said. She zoomed in; they were dropping out of the sky. Branching train tracks running parallel and crisscrossing covered the container terminal like the web of an OCD spider. Little stripes of color came closer and closer until they resolved into distinct shipping containers. Hundreds and hundreds of containers stacked in rows. Surrounded by the brown water on three sides. Big cranes at one side of the terminal waited to lift containers off ships onto train cars and trucks, or the reverse.

Charlotte slid the view toward one group of metal boxes.

"How are you doing this? I've never seen close-ups like this."

"There are *other* services besides Google Maps. You have to know how to get in and borrow a bit of time." She stopped. "That one, at the end of row twelve." Numbers were painted on the pavement. She zoomed in so the image of one yellow container filled the screen. Trans-Global Logistics was painted in black on the roof. "It's sitting right on the coordinates you gave me."

"Now I know where Freddy Popov wants me to go. But not why."

"Or how much shit you're getting into."

"How recent is that image? Is that container still there?"

Tick-tick-tick-tick.

His father's watch read 10:50 p.m.

The ticking rose in volume. The feeling of a deadline looming—or missed—rippled a charge down his spine. He was close to the thing, visually—and not far away physically, not a long drive. What was the *thing*? Ball bearings filled his stomach, rolled over each other, making him nauseous again.

"This sat-nav database updates more often than Google. Still, that shot's a week old. I need to do some digging. Get closer in time. Maybe use another database."

"Can you find out where it came from? What's in it?"

"Now you're talking needle in a needle stack. They're barcoded with all that, but I won't be able to read the code. Maybe I get crazy-lucky and find an image of the ship it came off of."

"How would I get to the container?"

"Unless you plan to swim from Bayonne, I don't know. This is a tall fence with razor wire at the top," she used the mouse to point, "and that's the security gate where this road," she pointed again, "comes in from the turnpike interchange. Lots of security. There's all sorts of shit worth stealing in those metal cans. They're guarded good."

"How does Popov expect me to get inside?"

He wasn't asking her, and she shrugged, intent on the screen. "Give me some time. I want to research the images."

"I appreciate the help. You'll keep trying to track down something on Popov?"

She nodded. "You're lucky. Katia's a good friend. Not like all the other fucking Russians. Maybe you aren't either." This time he was too tired to react. "Anyway, this is more interesting than my freelance work. Websites for co-op towers and Georgian restaurants."

"How'd you get into the work?"

"My dad's a hacker, almost first-gen. OG, right? A total thief. From people, of course. Easier marks than corporations. He forced me to do some of the work. When I wanted to stop, he hit me. I left that night. Someday, I'll be good enough to dragon-tattoo his sorry ass."

"Where's your mom?"

"Don't know. Alky. Dad slapped her around too. She left after me. That's what I heard." She pushed the same key several times. "Little bits of justice. That's what I get. Like that couple Katia was helping. None of it pays. The legit work? Some." She sighed. "I have a seasonal gig. Backup contortionist at the Coney Island Circus Sideshow. Rubber Limbed Lucinda. Also do chores. Take tickets. Help with whatever."

His eyes left the screen and took in Charlotte. A whole lot of long, slender leg ran from her skimpy running shorts to the floor. Her toenails were the colors of carnival lights. Short of her underwear, she didn't worry about what she wore around the apartment. It had nothing to do with him. She didn't care he was in the flat. Sometimes she seemed to forget he'd moved in, looking up from the screen startled when he opened the fridge. Her large brown eyes, firewalls that hid her intelligence, would clock him and drop back to the screen.

She acted freaky enough to be in the freak show.

She caught him looking. "Don't even fucking ask for a demonstration. Pervert."

"Wouldn't think of it."

"You'd be surprised. You and Katia, right?"

"No. Well, a long while back. Not now."

"Ri-ight. Be nice to her, or I'll bankrupt you."

"Nothing to bankrupt."

Charlotte laughed. The clicking resumed.

CHAPTER 14

Friday, September 9, 2016

"The container was there three days ago."

Grigg repeated what Charlotte had just told him. He looked out the balcony door. The quarter moon threw a slash of white across the ocean. The lights on Deno's Wonder Wheel went out all at once.

"How about more recently?" he asked.

"There's a lot of files to go through, and it's slow work. The closest I'll get is maybe twelve hours before."

"Then maybe we go check it out."

"First, we figure out the security at the terminal."

"Anything on the gunfight?"

Grigg had been wrong about the shooting in the park going public—wrong in the oddest way. He hadn't found a story on the *News* or the *Post's* websites. Ditto on local radio and the Brooklyn news blogs.

"Nope. Nothing at the hospitals. I even did some social engineering, called the precinct and the ER looking for my son. There's so much nothing, it's like the incident's been scrubbed. Or you imagined it."

"I didn't imagine being caught in a crossfire between Russians and neo-Nazi gangbangers. I don't have a Hollywood mind."

"Maybe someone made it go away."

"Who? How could they?"

"It would be some hack. NSA stuff. I've got another angle. It'd be a new trick for me to get the images from the cameras that cover the park. Deep and difficult. Gotta check with some other folks who know those nets better. Then see if there's video of what happened. If they're wiped, well then, you're into some deep shit."

"It's deep enough already." Grigg went into his bedroom and turned on the Bluetooth speaker and played WCBS Newsradio 880 from his phone.

Ten minutes of headlines in radio-news staccato. Fast-fast. A teenager murdered. A Bronx apartment fire. The mayor fighting with the police union. Charlotte came to the doorway. "Why keep trying? If it's been covered up, it won't be on the radio."

"We don't know for sure. Mistakes get made."

"Not with a scrub that looks this good."

The anchor slowed a little and became jocular and conversational as he introduced the political pig fight that was the presidential campaign. "Well, if you didn't think it possible, the personal attacks by Donald Trump and Hillary Clinton escalated. Trump spoke at a rally today."

Trump's voice: "Because she's being so protected, she could walk into this arena right now and shoot someone with 20,000 people watching, right smack in the middle of the heart, and she wouldn't be prosecuted. Okay? That's what's happened. That's what's happened to our country."

The anchor returned. "Meanwhile, Clinton slammed Trump's base as deplorables."

Clinton's voice: "You know, to just be grossly generalistic, you could put half of Trump's supporters into what I call the basket of deplorables. Right? The racist, sexist, homophobic, xenophobic, Islamophobic—you name it. And unfortunately, there are people like that. And he has lifted them up."

"I need to take a shower every time they talk," Charlotte told him.

WCBS cycled back around to local stories. A rape in Queens. The mayor something else. Traffic. Weather. Nothing about gangs (or anyone else) battling in a park in Midwood.

"Told you. You're onto something serious."

"It'd make me feel better if I knew what." Grigg touched the phone off. "I'm going to pick up some food at the bodega on Neptune Avenue. Can I get you anything?"

"I'm particular. *Specific* brands."

"Got a list?" Her fingernails tapped on her phone. Grigg's dinged. "What beer do you drink?" He'd seen a bottle of something on the other side of the bed.

"Belgian. I'm *very* particular about that. I'll pick some up later."

Halfway down the block, he called Katia.

"Too late?" he said apologetically.

"Almost. How's it going?"

Her voice eased his chittering anxiety from a ten to an eight. He wanted to mention that, but he didn't trust himself to do it right. There was so much grief and guilt and anger in his skull, he worried if he talked about his feelings, he'd blow up. Blow it with her.

Stay with the case.

"It's gotten really crazy."

"Charlotte?"

"No, not Charlotte." A little laugh. "I like her. She speaks her mind. She believes me. Mostly. She's helping."

"I was worried. When I've seen her with people—well, with most 'fucking Russians'—it has not gone well."

"She was a good call. Thank you. Really."

He told her about meeting Popov, their flight, and the gun battle that had left no record.

"Jesus, Grigg. Shit is getting *crazy*."

"Charlotte seems to think it's a good sign. That something big is going on."

"She would. What are you going to do?"

"Short term … my best bet is hanging out in the squat for the weekend. I know I've got to get to work on Monday—using backstreets and another subway stop. Can't afford not to. Wandering the neighborhood during a busy weekend would be bad."

"I'll come over. We'll hang. Plus, if you stare at Charlotte waiting for results while she's working, she'll flip out on you."

Which is for sure what I'd end up doing.

"I'll get extra beer. See you tomorrow."

Her visit put a lift in his crippled step.

CHAPTER 15

Monday, September 12, 2016

Grigg figured Carmichael was driving faster than usual to get to the bar because they were late for lunch. A bureaucrat up the line had assigned them two investigations for the morning. They'd just spent two and a half hours working the second one.

"Can you fucking believe it?" Carmichael said.

Grigg waited a beat. Conversations with Carmichael were still pretty one-sided. "The second call?"

"Of course, the fucking call. The department of buildings—the fucking city department of fucking buildings—has a loose handrail in one of their own stairways. They run a fire drill. Thing comes off and nine—nine!—people go tumbling. Nine interviews. Nine claims."

Grigg knew well enough how many because he'd be keying them all in.

"I'll get them loaded quickly," he said to mollify.

"What's up with your investigation?"

Grigg couldn't tell if the question was sarcastic or interested. Carmichael's smile was angry, but that could be left over from being late to his lunch date with John Jameson.

"C'mon. I knew you weren't going to listen to me. Amateurs never do. The detectives from the Six-Oh tell you anything else?"

"Oh, we talked. They say they've got a witness who saw two people on the roof. Not three. They've got me down as a suspect."

"Did you kill your father?"

Grigg turned and fixed his boss with a stare, ready to put his job in jeopardy over the remark.

Carmichael's smile broadened, like he'd told a joke, though his tone didn't change. "C'mon, asshole. That's the exact kind of question investigators ask."

"No. I did not."

"I made a call. Heard the same story about this witness. Not a big boost for you. I worked the Six-Oh before my last house. The guys on your dad's case, Ho and Wilson? Dunces. Lazy. Corrupt, I think. They don't have anyone else. You best be careful."

"Tell me about it."

"You pick up anything else?"

Grigg considered his options as a double-decker tour bus passed the car. He only had Katia and Charlotte as allies. Relying on gut and needing assurance, he told Carmichael about Freddy Popov, the attack at Freddy's apartment, the disappearing gunfight, and the shipping container.

"The Russians said Freddy met with my dad a bunch

of times when he was on the run," said Grigg. "Freddy never said a thing about that."

"Lot of loose ends there. That's okay. Loose ends lead somewhere. Ho and Wilson won't like it. They don't wanna work." Carmichael's smile shrank to a pursing of his lips as he considered the complexity of Grigg's tale. "No reports of the firefight so far? That doesn't make sense."

"None that we can find."

"Takes juice to cover up something like that. FBI juice, but not standard special agent juice. The counterintelligence guys, though, they can be innovative when it comes to breaking the rules. They have more leeway. Or it's one of the Patriot Act black-ops groups we won't learn anything about for another decade."

"A friend said the NSA."

"Them too."

"But why help the Russians?"

"If that's what they're doing. Puzzle-palace boys may want the Russians and don't want anyone to know."

"Or North Brooklyn Skins are working for the feds?"

"A stretch, but stranger things have happened. NBS would have been Hoover's kind of folks." Carmichael broke the law and dialed his phone while driving, then had to hit the horn and swerve right as a cab stopped in front of them. He spoke into the phone like nothing happened.

"Miguel, anything bad happen by Murrow High School last night? A park called …" He waved at Grigg for the name again.

"Kolbert Playground."

"Kolbert Playground? You sure? Midwood quiet all night? North Brooklyn Skins around? Don't get testy. Just heard about something." A pause. "Couldn't be better. My perps are cracked sidewalks and broken stairs. Couldn't be better." He dropped the phone into the coffee holder with a clack. "Couldn't be fucking worse." He side-eyed Grigg. "Miguel got kinda antsy. Said I sounded like I didn't believe him. Which is the first thing someone lying says. Assuming *you're* not lying, you may have some serious federal government-issue people bossing the locals."

Having already reached that conclusion, Grigg nodded.

"What about leads on Popov?"

"None yet. I have a friend researching him. She's good with data."

"Computers? Wonderful. Hate that shit. Hope you get a lead on him fast. Much more time goes by and he'll be gone—or dead."

The black molasses slipped around Grigg's brain, revealing glimpses of the Russians in the park, Popov, the detectives. His bleeding father dropping from the roof.

"This guy Popov wants to hit the container," Carmichael said. "Probably electronics, cell phones, something with a lot of value. Hard to get into those places, though—for a reason. Your father could've gotten involved in the scheme."

"Maybe." *No. Still don't believe that.*

"Men change, get changed. When they have to run.

Your dad owe money?"

Grigg's face warmed. "Yeah. Two mortgages. He could barely make the payments each month. That and keep up with the other bills. Sometimes didn't."

"That will make a good man desperate. Who else is on your radar?"

"A man named Joe the Borscht came looking for me last week."

"Know him. Coney Island Neighborhood Benevolence Association."

"Yeah. Ho and Wilson weren't interested."

"No, not those two. What'd he want? Is he a loan shark with awful timing? Or just the right timing?"

A shrug.

"Anyway, Borscht is a bad guy. Bad's a good place to look, and it's about the only thing you've got until Popov or the Russians surface. If they surface." Carmichael pulled a sharp U-turn and headed south. "Whaddaya say we find out?"

Twenty minutes later, they were parked up the street from Joe the Borscht's headquarters in Gravesend, on the other side of the Belt Parkway from Coney Island.

Carmichael sent Grigg to get coffee. Stunned, Grigg complied. He couldn't believe the man was giving up his regular lunch for a stakeout.

Maybe he misses being a cop more than he misses his Jameson.

A half hour went by. An hour. Carmichael seemed content to sip a second coffee, run for a piss break, and watch more. Grigg knew Carmichael's former job had been much like this. A detective had told his NYPD Academy class about it in what was nicknamed "The Get Over It Lecture." Real investigative work meant sitting, watching, waiting. Slow and methodical. One step at a time. None of the bang-bang TV stuff.

"He's still one fat fuck." Carmichael started the car.

Joe the Borscht left the building, followed by the little man in the suit—the Bookkeeper—who'd been with him at the arcade. They climbed into a Mercedes sedan.

"You know what I never figured out about the Russian mob?"

Grigg shook his head.

"Hitler killed twenty-five million Russians, and they still drive German cars. Must want to look like all the other drug slingers and whoremasters in Brooklyn."

"What are we gonna do?"

"Follow him. When you're on a fishing expedition, you keep casting."

Tick-tick-tick-tick.

His father's watch read 2:35 p.m.

Carmichael pulled into traffic one car behind the Merc. "Who's the guy in the suit? Bit Wall Street for the Russians."

"I don't know. He was with Joe when he came to talk with me last week. My boss didn't know him either, and Mr. P knows everyone in the neighborhood."

"Even the mobsters?"

"Seems to."

"Is he one?"

"Not that I know of."

"Arcade's a good place to launder money. Small-scale, but Russians like to run things in networks."

"I've never seen anything dirty go on in the place."

"Yet your boss was able to call off Joe the Borscht. Something to think about."

It was, but Grigg didn't know exactly what.

They cruised the Belt Parkway along the Brooklyn waterfront, cut inland after they passed Bay Ridge, and were slowed by traffic on the Gowanus Expressway. Carmichael, one hand on the wheel, stayed a car back from the Mercedes with practiced ease. This was a game he'd played many times before. The black car exited at 39th Street, but instead of driving into residential Sunset Park, took two rights and rode under the Gowanus into an area full of warehouses and other commercial buildings.

A few minutes later, Carmichael pulled over on 47th Street next to Five Boroughs Brewing.

"I could use a beer." Carmichael put the car in park. "But when I'm doing the lord's work, I don't get shitfaced."

Joe the Borscht's ride had parked on the other side of the street right across the intersection in front of a large warehouse with a yellow sign that read SUPERIOR PLUMBING SUPPLY. Underneath, Chinese characters maybe said the same thing.

Joe the Borscht and the Bookkeeper went inside.

Carmichael opened his door. "He's a long way off his patch with his new associate." He got out, closed the door, and walked away without another word, strolling toward the intersection.

Uh … how is this undercover?

Carmichael crossed and stepped into the shade of Superior Plumbing and leaned against the wall.

After a few minutes, Grigg got out, and since Carmichael was covering the front, he decided to ease around the back. Five women were standing outside smoking. As he got closer, the general babble resolved into Russian.

A skinny, dark-haired woman blew out smoke and switched to English. "If you're looking for job, you go to front office."

"They're hiring?"

"Always hiring."

"Olga, the bonus!" said a short, fat woman.

"Why should she get it?" said a third.

"She spoke to him first."

"Feh. They'll never hire *him.*"

Grigg sighed. Always the Brown Outsider.

Olga reached into her pocket and gave him a yellow Xeroxed flier. "If you give them that when you get job, I get twenty-five bucks. They prefer Russian background. That's why the bonus. With you," she waved at his face, "maybe I don't get bonus. Still, worth trying." She flipped her cigarette into a fifty-gallon drum and stepped through a door that was propped open with a red brick. Grigg leaned in and saw three, maybe four long rows of tables with computers on them. That was only one corner of the room. Women were at the workstations. Cables ran everywhere, hanging from the ceiling and bunched under the tables in colored tangles. Olga came out with a white sheet. "The application. You fill and take to front office."

"This place doesn't sell plumbing supplies."

"No, computers."

"You sell computers?"

"We type."

"Programmers?"

"No, type. That part they explain in interview. My break is over."

She went inside. He followed behind without asking and walked past one seated worker and another. That woman had Facebook on her screen. *She must be on break.* But there was another posting on Facebook, and another. Twitter. Facebook, Facebook. Instagram. Every screen displayed a social network. Eight workstations into the building, he decided he'd gone far enough. Now, he was breaking the rules of undercover work. He didn't want to run into Joe the Borscht in this strange room.

"Thank Olga for me." He said it to another woman as she came through the doorway from her smoke break. "I might apply."

"They're desperate for people." She had no accent. Probably born here.

He stepped outside the building. He met Carmichael at the car.

"Woman by herself in the front office said they're a computer services firm," Carmichael said. "Oxford Data Systems. Reception area looked like it was unchanged from when this place sold plumbing equipment."

"Why the sign?"

"Said they haven't had time to take it down. Moved in three months ago."

Grigg recounted what he'd seen and learned.

Carmichael nodded. "Gotta be some kind of scam."

"How do you know?"

"Rule in police work: bunch of computers, odd location—it's a scam. There's no high-tech companies around here. Facebook cons are big time. You're younger than me. You should know that." He started the car. "Here comes fat boy."

CHAPTER 16

Monday, September 12, 2016

They tailed Joe the Borscht back to his headquarters, then to an apartment building in Coney Island where Grigg already knew the mobster lived because most everybody in the neighborhood knew where he lived. The big goon sitting in a car parked in front of the mobster's place would probably tip some who didn't.

"All right. He's put to bed. Want me to drop you off?"

"I'm meeting someone on the boardwalk." Grigg opened the door as quickly as he told the lie. "It's an easy walk. Thanks for the help."

"It's what I do … What I *should* be doing."

Grigg moved to shut the door but pulled it back. "Are you going to do more?"

He instantly regretted asking. Today was a bonus, and if he hadn't asked, there was still the hope of more aid.

"We'll see how things go at the office. Your father was murdered, and it doesn't look like anyone's doing much about it. Maybe … if you're willing to work extra hours—extra unpaid hours—to take care of our regular paperwork."

"Yeah, definitely. Anything."

Carmichael looked through the windshield like he was searching for something. "Gotta go."

Grigg shut the door and walked. He thought about the one thing he hadn't told Carmichael. The secret he was keeping. His father's last words: *Get to Katia*. Cops hated it when you left out important facts. At his core, Carmichael was a cop; he'd be mad if he found out Grigg had held back. A chill crossed his shoulders and ran down his arms, though the evening was warm. He blamed the black brain sludge for keeping him from thinking things through. Should he tell Carmichael next time? His stomach churned.

Tick-tick-tick-tick.

His father's watch read 6:50 p.m.

He picked up the pace. He was meeting Katia across the river in the East Village. Commuting to Manhattan to hang out sucked. He missed Ruby's. But they would be safe from dangerous local eyes over there. He hopped a bus to a station outside the neighborhood, and riding the subway, his worries over Carmichael were replaced with gloom about Wednesday's memorial service. The closer the day got, the more a dread rose in him, the thought-stealing black goop squeezing between every thought. He somehow knew the service would make Dad's death real in a way he couldn't understand now. The ashes. The words. The mourners. He wanted to be on the other side of Wednesday.

When Dad was missing, Grigg could focus on the

search. He'd had hope, sometimes only the chance of hope, and that had been enough to keep going. Now, with his dad dead, the search continued—but for a murderer. Grigg feared in the end, he would find out things about his father he didn't want to know. And could never unknow. The disappearance, his murder, Freddy Popov's mystery container. They didn't add up now and weren't going to add up to anything good.

He walked to McSorley's Old Ale House on East 7th Street. Inside, a mix of NYU students, neighborhood barflies, and tourists—the perfect place to not be noticed. Katia spotted him and waved. She was at a tiny, beer-stained, initial-carved table midway back and across from the bar. Two small glass steins of beer sat in front of her. When you ordered *one* beer at McSorley's, it came as a pair. One of the idiosyncrasies of the city's oldest bar. Grigg ordered a dark and made a conscious effort to push a smile onto his face.

Didn't work.

"What's wrong?" Katia said.

Everything but seeing you.

He was trying to figure where to start when Charlotte appeared. The look on his face shifted, and she noticed. "Am I interrupting something? This a date?"

"No," he said too quickly, then checked Katia. No reaction. "I … I didn't know you were coming."

"Charlotte called me and said she had news we both should hear," said Katia. "I invited her. I called but you didn't pick up."

"We were on a stakeout."

"We?"

"Let's hear Charlotte's news first."

"Talked to a hacker who's also a serious police nerd. And a big fan of contortionists. It was fucking icky work, but I did it for you, Grigg. He listens to all the scanner traffic. There was nothing on your incident—"

"That doesn't—"

"Hold on. He flipped me to a guy who knows about the servers for the video cameras around the park. Wasn't easy, but I got in. Nothing there. Hours are missing. Brute force. Erased. Probably to make it look like a recording error."

"That won't get noticed?"

"Why would it? Officially, nothing happened. Everyone says nothing happened. No one needs to go looking for nothing. Unless you want to report it."

Grigg tilted his head like he was considering.

"You'd be some fucking dumbass to do that."

"I could report it anonymously. See what jumps."

"You can't report it until you know who to report. An anonymous source will get nowhere with that. My scanner buddy—and is he now my buddy." She shook her head. "Yuck. He walked that playground, *the whole scene*—his words. No bloodstains anywhere. Based on what you said, there should be, right?"

"Hell yeah."

"Clean as a whistle. That's my news." Charlotte downed half a stein of light.

"A stakeout?" Katia turned to Grigg.

He told the women about following Joe the Borscht to the warehouse with Carmichael.

Charlotte waved in front of a waiter's face as he passed. "You, another light!" She managed to order in a way that was ruder than a McSorley's waiter—an accomplishment in a place that prided itself on its old-school New York-style service.

"You believe you can trust this ex-cop?" Katia asked Grigg. "You already think he's dirty. You don't know much else about him outside of work."

"I'm taking what I can get. He's helping me. He's not connected to the case in any way."

"You never know."

"He thinks the warehouse is running some kind of scam. Like the calls telling you Microsoft Office has been compromised so they can get hold of your login."

"Those calls come from Bangalore," said Charlotte. "Or Serbia. Something else is going on in there. But you're right: it can't be legit. Your mobster's *not* looking to be the next Zuck."

"Zuck's more dangerous," Katia said. "Look, a rare thing. The two of you smiling at the same time."

Grigg set down his second stein. "Could you hack into the warehouse?"

"*No.*" She used the tone that was reserved for Grigg when he asked something stupid about technology. "Just because I know where the computers are doesn't mean I know what network they're on. I need to get inside."

Grigg dug in his pocket. "I picked up a job application." He handed her the sheets. "They want local Russians, though."

Charlotte shrugged. "I took four years of Russian in high school."

Katia and Grigg stared at her wide-eyed, Katia speaking before Grigg could. "You studied Russian while hating pretty much all the Russians at school?"

"I wanted to know what you fucking Russians were saying about the rest of us."

Grigg shook his head and laughed. "You're crazy. I could never speak a word of it. I never knew what they were talking about."

Katia chuckled too. "What about your freakshow gig?"

"Weekends only after Labor Day. Whatever this place is," she waved the employment flier, "it probably runs in shifts. Worth a try."

Charlotte reached in the pocket of her faded jeans for cash to pay but Katia waved her off.

"Thanks for the beers, but there's better places than this if you're going to cross the river." Heading toward the door, Charlotte disappeared into the crowd, which had thickened during their conversation.

Grigg and Katia ordered more beers and hot dogs—which had their own odd Coney Island connection, supplied by Feltman's Restaurant. They ate and drank and caught up, a mix of Grigg's investigation and their lives before his father's death brought them back together.

"I'm going to save the heavy drinking for Wednesday,"

Grigg said.

"I'll be there."

Thank god I didn't have to ask. I need someone.

After the long subway ride, he walked her to her apartment in Brighton Beach, despite her protests. She kissed him on the cheek, then shifted over to his lips. The doorman arrived to hold open the big glass and brass door, cutting the kiss off sooner than Grigg would have liked. There was no invitation upstairs.

Grigg took the boardwalk west, approached Ruby's, heard the music and the high tumult of boozy conversation—voices climbing to be heard over others. He considered sneaking in for a few more but kept moving. His buzz evaporated into the warm, starry night, letting his anxiety dream up scenes of the memorial service to come.

CHAPTER 17

Wednesday, September 14, 2016

Dad always said atheism was the only thing the Communist Party got right. The memorial service had no God in it—and not much else. Turnout was light, in spite of the friends and acquaintances Dad had made during his life in the neighborhood. Getting murdered while on the run had a way of suppressing attendance.

Tick-tick-tick-tick.

His father's watch said Grigg should have started five minutes ago.

Katia leaned over. "You can do this."

Grigg walked to the podium.

He pulled out a slip of paper. In a low drone, he listed all the good things his father had done for his students and people in the neighborhood.

A voice called out, "Speak up."

He finished: "I'll find out who killed him."

"What?"

He walked back to his seat.

The old lady who had the fourth row all to herself

shook her head at him.

Mr. P followed and was kind to Grigg—and kinder to his father's memory. He told real stories—about their St. Petersburg childhood, growing up as vast changes overtook the Soviet Union, then moving to Coney Island within a few years of each other. Grigg's mind drifted. He knew the tales, told over and over in great detail, all out of order, a patchwork, over vodka, brown bread, and pickles. They couldn't change Grigg's present or help him see a future that made any sense.

As Mr. P was finishing, Joe the Borscht walked in followed by two men carrying a huge floral Orthodox cross. There was no obvious place to put it in the community room. They propped the arrangement against the fenced-in area where toddlers spent their daycare days.

The spin dryer in Grigg's head slammed to a stop at fury. He gripped the seat of the chair in front of him like he was heading for the first drop on the Cyclone, knuckles white, and exploded: "You ass! My father wasn't part of your church. He wasn't part of any church. He wasn't part of anything to do with you."

Joe the Borscht spread his hands. His fat face attempted sadness. It looked more like indigestion. "We were only trying to honor his memory."

The other people at the service, including the man who'd opened up the room for them, stared at Grigg. Katia tugged on his hand. He shook her loose. A quick glance, and he saw the disappointment on her face. He couldn't help himself. Anger at everything that had happened up until now burned in him, all of it directed at the obscene flower cross. The sickly sweet aroma hit him, and his stomach flipped.

"You want to honor his memory, get the fuck out. Better yet, tell the cops what you know about his murder."

Mr. P loudly cleared his throat and resumed talking. Joe the Borscht walked to the back of the room. The funeral director followed with a brief speech about the English he'd learned from Anton Alexandrovich. The service ended. Mr. P joined Grigg. Over Mr. P's shoulder, Grigg saw the old lady from row four talking to Joe the Borscht. Why not? Mobsters were an ordinary part of this world. Was Grigg the problem, driven crazy by anger no one else understood? His chest felt ready to burst.

Mr. P didn't say anything to Grigg. Instead, he went over to Joe for a short conversation in low tones. Joe exited. Mr. P returned.

"Why was he here?" Grigg said. "Why is he messing with me?"

"I don't know. He should not have done that. I had things worked out. He's acting strangely. It's over now. Let us move on to lunch."

"No!" Grigg felt like he would spray his anger everywhere. "How did you get him to leave? Are you connected to the Russian mafia? Another gang?"

"Now, Grigg. You know better—"

"I don't know anything. Not until you tell me."

Mr. P shook his head wearily, sighed, and started speaking. "Chance, accident. Call it what you want. You know I'm a strong swimmer. Still am." That said with pride. "More than two decades ago, I was out swimming pretty far from the beach. My ocean laps. A kid was having trouble. Panicked. By the time I got to him, he was unconscious. I dragged him in, and a lifeguard revived him. Turned out, he was the grandson of the top man in the Russian mob that controls Sheepshead Bay. The man offered me anything I wanted. I was then paying protection to Joe the Borscht's father. I said I wanted to be left alone by all of them."

"That's it?

"I *was* left alone until Joe came calling for you. I've since made my only call to the old man … to get Joe the Borscht off of your back. Man's in his nineties now. He is far more powerful than he was when we met on the beach. For Joe, who is a minnow to this man—granted, a fat minnow—today must mean someone else powerful is pressuring him."

"And you've taken nothing else from the mobster?" Grigg's tone was belligerent. He couldn't get himself under control.

"You insult me. You insult your father's memory. He would never remain friends with anyone in the gangs. One small act bought me a lifetime of freedom. Bought you some too, until now. The grandson is a grown man. He thanked me when last he saw me. That was it." Mr. P waved his hand to dismiss the subject. "But you're upset. It's the day, the service." He leaned in close. "Something came to me the other day that I wanted to tell you. I remembered a name: Viktor Voronin. He was your father's older friend from the days of the bone records, the one who ended up in a work camp. Rumor was he died there. Voronin's younger brother was in that group of boys, too. His first name *still* escapes me. He was even closer to your father and Katia's. I'm sure I'll think of it."

They all walked outside.

The restaurant was five blocks away, his father's favorite for *pelmeni*, even though it was dark and gloomy enough that Dad said it looked like Rasputin had been the decorator. Grigg led Katia straight to the bar. The rest of the funeral party sat at three tables. Joe the Borscht and his men didn't stop in. Didn't matter. Grigg fumed about the floral cross and Joe's involvement. He ordered a vodka. The bartender poured him Stoli. Not a good antidote for anger. He knocked back the shot.

Katia asked for a chardonnay, held the glass, and looked at him. He tried to calm himself for her. He couldn't. Three quick shots hit his empty stomach. The alcohol quieted the ticking in his head but ramped up his anger and freed it from the confusion of the sticky black molasses swamping his thoughts.

That should have been the warning.

CHAPTER 18

Wednesday, September 14, 2016

Grigg sat at the bar in Ruby's, probably the worst place he could have come. He sort of knew that, sort of knew he'd had too much to drink. He'd wandered here from the restaurant, exiting the minute Katia went to the bathroom because he was unable to talk to her about his anger. About anything. He'd been thinking clearly enough to know it was better to be alone than chance saying the wrong thing to her. The bereaved son excuse would work for him later. The drunk, bereaved son. He hoped.

Ruby's was already half full. The grill was one of those special New York places where locals rubbed up against gawkers. The regulars refused to give up the place to the tourists, who wanted to see the bar built out of wood from the 1920s boardwalk. The walls were covered in pictures of the great old amusement parks and the beach crowded with millions, all real photos, unlike the fakes you found in places like fucking Applebee's with their chain-ified nostalgia. The menu included dogs, burgers, and clams, both raw on the half shell and fried. Grigg didn't want food. The bar and grill's core competency was booze. He was here for that. There were tables on the boardwalk as long as the weather was worth it, plus tables inside. But it was the long bar Grigg sought as he always did.

A fresh shot of vodka sat in front of him.

More fuel for the mental maelstrom. What of it? He'd done nothing worthwhile so far. Buried his father with poor words. Listened to Mr. P do better. Done nothing fucking real about the killing.

He slowly pushed the full glass away.

Five seats down, a muscular guy in a tight black T-shirt stared at Grigg. One of Joe the Borscht's goons? Had the right look.

Grigg didn't give a shit. Or the vodka didn't give a shit. Joe the Borscht knew something. Grigg didn't know what, but it was busy up in that villain's bowling-ball head. Bringing that cross of flowers. He was fucking with Grigg for a reason. He slid off the stool. That was where he'd take his rage. Screw Carmichael's stakeout. Screw the waiting. It was the vodka talking, but he was fine with that if it pushed him do *something, anything* on the day Dad got his pathetic goodbye.

He decided he was too buzzed to go back to Charlotte's squat for his pistol, where he'd moved it from the arcade after he'd settled in. He might lead someone there in his current state. Blowing up Charlotte's living arrangements scared him almost more than Joe the Borscht. And toting a gun in this condition rang a clanging alarm that pierced the vodka haze in his head.

Well, he had the stun gun and the sap; he'd make do with them and a little souvenir shopping. He walked two blocks and bought a Brooklyn Cyclones bat. A bat was also a stick, and his street hockey stickwork in close and up high had always been swift and dangerous. He knew where to hit people. Ten minutes later, he limped past a familiar Mercedes parked out front of the Coney Island Neighborhood Benevolence Association. Same plates as the one he and Carmichael had followed. The name of the association was engraved into a brass plaque on the building. The wood door was painted black. He pulled it open and stepped inside.

Two men played cards at a round table in the corner to his left. The sun beamed in from a front window with wooden shutters half opened. Dust motes danced in the yellow light. One guy had a half-inch Mohawk; the other had slick midnight-black hair. At a table in the middle of the room, a blond head leaned over a laptop. The bar, marble topped and painted gold in front so it looked like a church altar, ran along the right wall.

The bartender was a tall, skinny, crooked man. He looked up from fingering the screen of his phone. "Whatever you're selling, we're not buying." He gave Grigg the same stare Grigg got in Kennedy's and the Russian market, the one that said brown, black, all shades not white weren't welcome here.

"I'm looking for a little benevolence." He stepped toward the bar, weaved, caught himself. "Thought a benevolence association would be a good place to start."

"Hilarious. Members only. No weapons." His eyes flicked at the bat. "You've already had enough to drink."

"Then *they*," Grigg tilted his head, "should get rid of the guns."

Both cardplayers wore shoulder holsters. Their jackets were over their chairs.

Grigg backed up to a table near the middle of the room, stopped to steady himself, and took a seat. Placing himself between the two men and the bartender seemed a smart strategy. For once, being in the crossfire would be in his favor. If they shot at him, they'd be shooting at each other.

He moved the chair so it sat sideways to the table and let him watch the bartender and the card game. One player glanced over his cards at Grigg; the other didn't bother.

My souvenir isn't worrying them much.

The man at the computer lifted his head. Grigg recognized the blue eyes and the handsome face of the Bookkeeper. Same guy he'd seen with Joe the Borscht at Mr. P's and the Facebook Factory. Today's suit was navy blue, the tie a speckled red.

"Joe the Borscht was at my dad's memorial service." His speech was a slush of crushed consonants. "I thought I'd offer my thanks."

He leaned the bat against the table.

"I don't know anybody by that name. If you had a brain or a few less cocktails, you wouldn't be using it."

"I'll take a Stoli iced."

"I've had enough of this." The man started to come

around the bar.

"There's been a funeral," said the Bookkeeper. "Let him have a drink." No Russian accent. No Brooklyn accent either. Educated.

The bartender's eyes shifted to the Bookkeeper. Quickly, he reversed course like he'd been given a command. He pulled a frosted Stolichnaya bottle with a label in Russian out of the freezer.

The Bookkeeper closed the screen on his laptop. "My condolences."

"Yeah. Thanks."

"Strange to come looking here for a drink afterward, you must admit. Perhaps you have had a bit too much."

Deep-voiced—deeper than Grigg expected from such a small man—he spoke with confidence. Grigg thought of someone professional, someone with a real college degree. Had he been right with his guess? Did the man do Joe the Borscht's accounting? Must be harder than legit work. Two sets of books. More?

"You're rude to me, then you show up here." Joe the Borscht spoke from behind Grigg. He stood in a doorway in the back corner of the room.

"There's the man of the hour," Grigg said. "Thought you might be here. This is where all the benevolence gets doled out."

Joe the Borscht walked toward the table, legs swinging wide like a cowboy so his fat thighs wouldn't collide. He sat opposite Grigg, gave the bat the merest glance, and smiled.

The bartender put down a tall, thin shot glass frosted by the cold of the vodka. He reached for the bat, but Grigg was faster, pulling it to the other side of the chair.

"Hey. It's a rule. No weapons in the club."

Grigg picked up the glass, the cold pricking his thumb and fingertip. "That joke's getting old."

"He can have it," Joe the Borscht said. "Actually, I didn't think Andrei Alexandrovich's mutt would have the rocks to come in here. To apologize for your behavior today?"

Joe smiled but the Bookkeeper's face remained unmoved—serious and curious at the same time.

Grigg paused with the vodka. *What the fuck am I doing, drinking another one of these?* Yet the buzz had faded some from the walk.

Fuck it.

"To Andrei Alexandrovich Orlov."

He knocked it back. The iced spirit went down fast and easy. No kick at all. The voice in the back of his head telling him to worry was faint. Faded away. Gone.

Joe the Borscht ordered a vodka, and though the Bookkeeper didn't speak, he got one too. They drank the same toast. Apparently, certain rituals were observed, even here.

Grigg pointed at the door in the corner that Joe the Borscht had used. "Your command center in there? Is that where you make those special loans to street vendors and homeowners? I remember that popcorn stand that burned up last summer. Didn't pay for a note he didn't want. Some say."

"The oil must have been too hot."

Chuckling from one of the cardplayers sounded like coughing.

"What business did you have with my dad? What do you want with me?"

"Like any businessman, my interests are always in flux. Now, I want to know if you've been talking to Russians. If any have been asking questions."

Grigg laughed. He went on too long. The booze. His defenses gone. "Yeah," he gasped, "I talk to Russians all the fucking time. Must be too often for them, since they don't wanna have anything to do with me."

"Not from the neighborhood. Russians from Russia."

Popov fit that bill, and so did the three intruders at his apartment.

Change the subject. "Did my father borrow money? If you want it from me, there's none."

A smile cracked Joe's face. "If you owed, you'd already know."

"First good news today."

"We don't just take money. Your girlfriend is quite stunning."

"You keep away from her."

Joe went on like Grigg hadn't said anything. "I don't think we've heard everything you know. I'm sure of it. You've drawn too much goddamn attention to yourself—which means to us too."

The cardplayers were up and coming at Grigg. One had his gun out.

Grigg stood and swung wild. He spun. Crashed to the floor. *Lotta bravery but not enough balance.* The thug with the Mohawk wrenched away the bat. He slapped Grigg hard with his open hand. That did Grigg a favor. The pain cut through the swirling fog of his buzz, making self-preservation a higher priority than it had been a moment earlier.

"Easy, gentlemen," said the Bookkeeper. "Let's not make a mess here. They cost."

The two goons lifted Grigg and hustled him to the front door while Joe the Borscht headed for the back office. His hand on the doorknob, he said, "You should give me credit. I could have done this at your father's embarrassing little service. We do show respect for the dead."

Grigg tried to think of a response. Head not clear enough. Quick comebacks were out of reach. Joe the Borscht was gone, and Grigg stumbled outside ahead of the thugs.

One of the goons opened the door to the Mercedes, while the other guided Grigg toward the back seat.

Grigg did have one more question he wanted to ask.

Turned out Jamie Carmichael asked it for him.

"Where the fuck are you taking my friend?"

CHAPTER 19

Wednesday, September 14, 2016

Carmichael reached inside his jacket. Mohawk leveled the Glock. The shot caught Carmichael in the right shoulder. The big man staggered and pulled out his weapon.

Mohawk's face exploded.

Blood—maybe other things—splashed on Grigg as the thug went down still gripping the baseball bat.

"Move, Grigg!" Carmichael stumbled toward the parked city-owned car.

The other gunman grabbed Grigg's wrist in a crushing grip while drawing his weapon. The bartender came out the front door armed with his own revolver. They both fired at Carmichael and hit him at least once. He tumbled to the sidewalk.

Adrenaline hit Grigg's system, sobering him into action. He reached down, tore the bat out of the dead gunman's hands, cracked it on the second thug's knee—a scream—then shoulder-checked him into the Merc and rammed the end of the bat into his face, once, twice. A major penalty he'd happily take in any hockey game.

That left the armed bartender too far out of reach and already turning his gun on Grigg.

Grigg rolled over the hood of the Mercedes, scooted low with cars passing, and squeezed between two to reach Carmichael on the sidewalk. His head hung off the curb into the gutter.

He was in bad shape.

Shit.

Grigg snatched a look down the sidewalk. The bartender, who must have gone back inside, came out again with a sawed-off shotgun. He lifted the weapon and blew out the city-issue Dodge's windshield.

Sirens.

"You're coming with us *now*," the bartender called. "Or there'll be nothing left of you for the cops to save."

Shit. Shit!

He pulled at Carmichael, whose body shifted inches, if that. The man was too big. There was no way he could carry him out of here and not get shredded by buckshot. He needed Carmichael to move.

"Goddammit," he growled in the ex-cop's ear, "why were you here?"

To his surprise, Carmichael answered, his unfocused eyes looking upside down at Grigg. "Following fatso. You surprised me showing up here. The service ..." A wheeze. He coughed blood. "Couldn't work today with you off. Can't run the ... damn computer."

He shook all over, turned his head and was still.

Another blast blew out the tire inches from Grigg's

head. Definitely not a warning shot.

Grigg hunched lower, took a last look at Carmichael—*I'm so sorry*—and dashed across the street, moving as fast as he could to reach the other side.

He let the bat fall from his hand as he turned the corner.

"Jesus Christ, Grigg, what the fuck is going on?"

"Shooting. Lots of shooting."

Charlotte stood over Grigg, who sat on the floor of the squat, crashing hard as the alcohol followed the adrenaline out of his bloodstream, leaving behind exhaustion, nausea, and a banging headache.

"Why?"

"It was my fault. I went to get answers from Joe the Borscht. Bad idea. Carmichael saved me. He's dead."

He described the gunfight. Choked. Finished.

"Okay, you fucked up. But Carmichael chose to step in. You can't take that on. He was a professional, unlike you or your dad."

Every last bit of his buzz was gone. The molasses mutated into a black hole, grief and guilt sucking him down.

"I know you feel bad. You got to get past it. You're in deep. The question now is what do you do next."

Grigg's inward gaze shifted to look up at Charlotte. "Joe's really gonna want my ass. Particularly after I tell the police. Implicate him and everyone who works for him."

"The detectives don't trust you."

"They'll have to when I describe the crime scene with

complete accuracy."

"Death wish." She retreated to the other side of the room.

Grigg lay back on the floor, recounting his mistakes. Ten or thirty minutes later—he wasn't sure—Charlotte spoke up.

"Is Joe the Borscht political in any way?"

The strange question pulled him into the present. "Not that I've noticed. Enough politicians are crooks, so who knows?"

"That warehouse full of computers is political."

"Political how?"

"I started working there today."

"What? In a *day*?"

"They hire fast."

"What did they have you do?"

"Post hundreds of messages they give us. On Facebook, Twitter, Instagram. All day. They're all political in one way or the other, though I'm not sure what the endgame is. Like, they have all these Facebook groups and fake individual accounts set up so we can post memes in the forums. This one went into several groups for Texans."

She handed him her phone. The meme's headline read, "Get Ready to Secede!" and the message text said: "The establishment thinks they can treat us like stupid sheep but they are wrong. We won't put up with this anymore. The corrupt media does not talk about the crimes committed by Killary Rotten Clinton, neither does it mention the leaked emails."

"So they're anti-Clinton."

"It's more complicated than that. Confusing even. They have a Born Liberal group." She flipped to a picture of Bernie Sanders with text attacking the Clinton Foundation.

"Still anti-Clinton."

"Also, a Black Lives Matter group that talks about Ferguson." She slid her fingers across the screen. "See? 'Not my president' with an X over Trump's face. Calls on people to march."

Grigg read the rest of it out loud. "People are genuinely scared for their futures! Racism won, Ignorance won, Sexual assault won. STOP TRUMP!"

"They have us put *all* these up. Attacking this side and that, this person and that. The senior employees also turn the messages into sponsored posts, so they're advertised all over Facebook. Not just in the original groups. In people's newsfeeds. A woman who works there told me all about it ... until she said I was too curious. Good thing I like smoking. Those fucking Russians are chimneys."

Curious and bewildered, Grigg flicked through more images. "I'm a Muslim" was sponsored by United Muslims of America, with the group's name in an Arabic-style font over a montage of Middle Eastern-looking buildings. From a forum called Heart of Texas: "If Hillary becomes President of the U.S., the American army should be withdrawn from Hillary's control according to amendments to the Constitution." He looked up from the little screen. "Uh, that's not in the Constitution."

"Facts are hardly the priority at Oxford Data Systems."

"How'd you get them on your phone?"

"As soon as I posted one or saw one go up near me, I'd look it up live on my phone and grab a screenshot."

"Shit, Charlotte. You need to be careful. That's gotta be dangerous."

A shrug. "The whole operation smells like low tide after a blown sewer main."

A drawing of Satan and Jesus arm-wrestling. "Satan: If I Win Clinton Wins! Jesus: Not If I Can Help It. Press 'Like' to Help Jesus Win!"

Army of Jesus was the sponsor.

"This is comic-book, end-time stuff."

Charlotte took back her phone. "By my count, more of it's pro-Trump, but my sample size is small. The other side's represented too. Or sides, I guess. Who knows what that place puts online in a day? They've been there three months." She laid her fingers against her phone. "I kept track of some of the Facebook groups they control so I can follow them from here. Wake The Fake Up. Viral Alternative News. LaTRUTH. Area 51. Right-Win News. None of these go together at all."

He nodded. "Who's in charge?"

"Not sure, but the woman who interviewed me for the job said she was from Sheepshead Bay."

"So, locals. No real Russians?"

"Real fucking Russians? Why would you think that?"

"The email hack on the Democrats. Washington saying the Russians are trying to disrupt the election. And Joe the Borscht asked me about 'real Russians' today. He didn't say why, but it was the one thing he wanted to know about. Nothing about me or Dad. We found that warehouse because he led us there."

"I met no real Russians." She got on the bed. "I'm gonna do a deep dive on those fake accounts. Post some messages from my own bogus users. See what happens. It's all so confusing."

"Maybe that's the point. Disinformation is about confusion."

"Well, it's working. I'm confused as fuck."

He watched her open the laptop. "Any news on the container?"

"It's been there going back four weeks, at least. It was on that spot as late as twenty-four hours ago."

"Wait … so it's there now?"

"Good chance."

Too many questions. So much he needed to do.

With Carmichael shot and probably dead, Grigg had to go see the detectives about the gunfight. He needed to get in that container, and he needed Freddy Popov to surface.

First, he needed to get some sleep—and sober up.

CHAPTER 20

Thursday, September 29, 2016

The rental car swung around the exit ramp, giving Grigg and Charlotte a panoramic view of Newark Airport, then the Port Elizabeth Container Terminal. Here was where all of transportation in Jersey came together—planes, trains, trucks, ships. It didn't look like anyone had planned it. More like a six-year-old armed with wood blocks, Legos, and Lincoln Logs had thrown together a home for all his favorite things.

The wipers, set at their fastest, couldn't keep up. More rain sheeted across the glass before the next wipe.

Charlotte drove the rented Hyundai. Grigg didn't have a license. Neither did Charlotte, for that matter. They'd grown up subway kids. She was able to get a fake and claimed to have practiced. Grigg grabbed the door handle and the dashboard as they rode up to the ass end of a container truck. Not for the first time, he wondered how much practicing Charlotte had actually done.

"Calm down, dude." Charlotte braked. They slid, then the tires caught, and the car slowed. "I got this."

"You're going to *get* the bumper of that truck, which, is, oh, at about the height of our heads."

"Ye of little faith."

The ramp led them onto a road running between the Jersey turnpike and various fenced-off sections of the port. Docked ships were stacked so high with containers that Grigg wondered how they stayed upright at sea. Giant cranes crouched over the vessels, looking only several whizz-whir spins and clacks from turning into Transformers. He'd played with dozens of the robot toys as a kid, in part because his father loved them as much as he did. Toys, games, anything to do with play fascinated Dad. He said it was because he'd grown up in a place where work was the only religion.

Grigg blew out a heavy breath. The sadness was still there, a constant internal rainstorm, like today, unceasing. Not even the mixture of thrill and fear of this covert mission cut through the gray, which was what the black gunk had mutated into. He wondered if that meant he was starting to deal with his father's loss in some small way. Which made him feel like shit. He didn't want to deal—to let go.

After almost three weeks and no word from Freddy Popov—and no results from Charlotte's searches for him on the web and the darknet—Grigg had decided to get a look in the container before it disappeared. He'd gotten nowhere with all his other leads, hampered by his fear of getting caught out in the neighborhood by Joe the Borscht. The morning after Carmichael's shooting, Grigg had learned the ex-cop had died at Coney Island

Hospital. The three-paragraph *Daily News* story said he was a former NYPD detective, though not why he'd been booted from the force. The Precinct 60 detectives on the case hadn't been pleasant when he reported in later that morning to tell them he'd been at the gunfight. One break: Ho and Wilson weren't assigned to the murder, though they spent a fair amount of time telling the other detectives Grigg was full of shit. Problem for the cops: His story matched what they found at the scene and what witnesses told them.

Carmichael's rule on investigations: *Witnesses, witnesses, witnesses.*

They continued behind the container truck, and another followed them. No cars for as far as Grigg could see. How were they going to convince anyone to let them in the terminal in a rented Hyundai?

The car was another reason they'd waited so long. He'd needed to save up to pay for the rental. His two credit cards were maxed from the memorial and the lunch, and he still owed the funeral home. Once he'd collected a couple of paychecks, Charlotte rented a car for a day to scope out the place. She'd reported a sixteen-foot fence topped by concertina wire around the terminal filled with stacked containers. Private security guards in blue- and yellow-checked Priuses circled the area every twenty-five minutes. The only way in was by ship or a long swim from Bayonne. Or by using the paperwork Charlotte had spent a good deal of the past week forging, telling an impatient Grigg repeatedly it was "a whole lot more complex than a fucking driver's license." Port of Elizabeth IDs and corporate IDs for the fake company Matryoshka Trading Inc., bills of lading, and other shipping paperwork that Grigg didn't worry about understanding. The whole time, Grigg made Charlotte check for the target container every twelve hours, fearing the image would show it had disappeared forever. Every time, it was there. But Grigg knew the images were themselves twelve hours old.

Tick-tick-tick-tick.

The container had been there in last night's picture, now twenty-seven hours ago, according to his father's watch.

They could get to the spot and find the blacktop empty—or a new container that had nothing to do with the case. *Assuming the one I'm obsessing on does?*

Charlotte insisted on renting the car for three days this time, just in case. Grigg didn't even ask. He imagined the two of them fleeing south on the Turnpike, chased by God-knows-who.

That brought his thoughts back to Joe the Borscht, who had obvious reasons to want Grigg's ass on a plate. The upside: Joe the Borscht was lying low. Two of his men were on the run. One was dead.

Grigg hadn't told Charlotte, not even Katia, but he was now seriously thinking of disappearing somewhere into furthest Queens after this caper. He could go back and forth to his day job with the city without running into Joe or his men. Work his investigation from outside the neighborhood. He'd lose the cash from his arcade work, but he'd find something else. The idea of moving even farther away had occurred, a vague beyond-the-city place he couldn't imagine. He didn't *want* to leave the neighborhood, but he'd do it to stay alive. He was still standing. Unlike Carmichael ... Grigg couldn't let go of that. The man had chosen to help and died trying to rescue him. Grigg was learning there could be many different kinds of guilt. This one burned, acid and gravel grinding in his gut.

They approached the entry gate to the terminal, which had twenty-one lanes for tractor trailers. They plodded along behind six or seven trucks, each pulling a container: Maersk, SCS, China Shipping, Hanjin, even Hyundai.

Their Hyundai was the only car in any of the twenty-one lines.

We're fucked if Charlotte's paperwork isn't convincing.

Ten minutes later, a security guard reviewed the papers from the driver of the truck in front of them.

Tick-tick-tick-tick.

His father's watch read 5:55 p.m.

The timing had been Grigg's idea. Before dinner, a hungry guard might not be as focused. Charlotte had laughed and agreed.

Cleared, the truck ahead of them pulled into the terminal. Charlotte eased the rental forward. The car looked as out of place at the security gate as a pigeon at an elephant convention.

"Afternoon, officer." Charlotte had never sounded that demure before.

"Identification, please."

Grigg passed over his laminated fakes; Charlotte added hers and offered all four. "Here's the bill of lading and delivery instructions."

The female guard, chubby with curly yellow hair that was brown at the roots, took everything and looked at Charlotte, then Grigg. She held on Grigg, glanced down at the ID, and then stared at his brown face for the long count. A frown. His face warmed. She stepped over to her counter inside the booth. The car's radio blared the Arctic Monkeys. Grigg turned it down. Charlotte side-eyed him.

The guard returned. "You're visiting the offices?"

"No, we've got to check the container listed."

"That doesn't happen here."

"We were told someone tried to break in," said Charlotte. "We need to make sure everything's okay."

Why the fuck did she say that?

"I didn't hear anything about a break-in."

"Oh." Charlotte sounded befuddled.

Fuck. I am *going to have to swim from Bayonne.*

"Let me see." Charlotte flipped through her clear plastic portfolio. "Here's the incident report from your security office. As our IDs indicate, we're from the company's loss investigations division."

The woman took the additional sheet inside the booth.

Grigg stared at Charlotte for several seconds, then faced forward.

The woman shuffled the papers around.

"Odd, but okay, you're good."

"Thank you, officer."

Charlotte went along an access road toward long rows of containers stacked two and three high and spaced far enough apart for the Hyundai to drive between. Farther even, for whatever forklift equipment they used in here.

"You didn't tell me about the break-in story."

"Had the paperwork ready. Didn't want you to freak any more than you already were. Truth is the best lie. Or a thing closest to the truth. Someone's gonna break in. Us."

Charlotte abruptly turned down a lane between containers, following the routing on her phone to their target, which was near the water on the far side of the highest stacks.

The sun disappeared. The narrow canyon of steel reminded Grigg of a scene from a movie. That Harry Potter film where they're chased among endless towering shelves holding glass globes. He and his father had loved those movies.

"Fake magic, real magic. It doesn't matter, Grigoriy, as long as it's magic."

Transformers. Movie memories. What's wrong with me?

They emerged in sunlight, turned left, then right into another lane, rolling across cracked blacktop to a yellow container sitting at the end of a lonely row of four. Beyond was the edge of the pier and brown-black water with oily rainbows and clumps of foam skidding across the surface.

Grigg climbed out of the car, took the bolt cutter, and limped quickly through the rain to the container. He didn't know how much time Charlotte's paperwork would buy them. Stickers on the door held safety warnings. He was about to break the law, cross yet another line. He couldn't have cared less. The four locks were like nothing he'd ever seen: straight bolts through holes on the door handles with red combination devices capping the ends.

He didn't wait. He opened the cutter, closed it on a bolt, and snapped it off. *Thank god.* If the tool hadn't worked, this would've been a perilous *and* stupid mission. Charlotte carried two padlocks for when they were done. She'd insisted on it, not to fool people but to keep others out after they left.

"It's the same in hacking," she'd said. "You lock it back up even if you leave signs of your exploit. Make everyone else work for it."

Grigg didn't care about her hacker ideals, but he knew if Popov did resurface, he'd probably want what was in here to still be here. And if Popov knew everything or anything about Grigg's dad, Grigg wanted him happy—or as happy as this fucked-up situation allowed.

He made short work of the other locks. Charlotte tossed all the pieces in the water. Grigg glanced around. Charlotte had said the video cameras were all on the fences. Management wasn't worried about someone using fake paperwork to break in. He lifted the handle on one side, turned the pole it was attached to, and opened the door. His heart dropped into his stomach, which dropped into his groin.

Empty.

Charlotte clicked on a small flashlight.

No, the back quarter of the container held eight milky-white plastic tubs—more depending on how many rows were behind—along with what looked like a couple of metal boxes. He approached, half-soaked from the downpour, his footsteps echoing loud inside the box.

Someone used a shipping container to move this? *Guess it depends on what* this *is.*

Again, he didn't wait. He snapped open the plastic handles securing the lid of the tub at the top of the stack on the left, pulled out crumpled newspapers covered in Cyrillic type, and reached in for a square object, a plastic-wrapped brick of hundred-dollar bills—at least based on the two he could see, top and bottom. Similar packs filled the box.

He tried another box. Same result.

"Jesus fucking Christ. What is Freddy Popov up to?"

"Bad things. If it's his cash, he's a bad guy."

Grigg shook his head. "Why would Freddy steal from himself?"

"Maybe he got it to the U.S. but couldn't get to the container. Your dad was meeting with Popov. Maybe it was his money?"

Grigg's laugh was grim. "No way. *Maybe* I'm wrong about my father being a criminal. But he was most definitely poor."

"This is a criminal enterprise." Charlotte made quick work of the lock on a metal box and swung it open. "Legit businesses move money electronically. Not by container ship. This is a big fucking pile of illegal— Holy shit." She grunted as she brought out a gold bar from the box.

"You think it's real?"

"Do you think all those bills are real?" She hefted it. "Heavy enough." She shined the light back in the box. "There're four more." She fiddled with her phone. "Worth half a mil apiece."

Grigg knew *what* he was looking at. His confusion made the facts dance. How could all this and his father possibly go together? A Harry Potter movie would've made more sense.

Charlotte leaned against the wall, shining her light at the back of the container. "Four rows of mainly tubs and a few more metal containers. One square cardboard box here in the front row. Okay. We've been here a long time already. I'll keep watch while you check as much of this as you can. Come out in ten minutes."

He took out his own flashlight. "I'll inventory what I can."

No answer. She was already gone, somewhere outside on the other side of the open door.

Okay, get organized. Learn everything you can. In case Freddy gets back in touch. Figure out how this connects to Dad's murder.

He pulled out his phone and noted the number of gold bars and bricks of hundreds he'd seen, though he had no idea how many bills the latter held. Took pictures, then closed the tubs.

The fourth plastic container was different. Binders, stacks of papers, most in Russian, some in English. He took a picture of the stack but didn't have time to take shots of individual pages or start reading the English docs, for that matter.

Next, he used his knife to slit the brown tape sealing the cardboard box.

Inside, standing four by four … what looked like sixteen nose cones. He lifted one gently out and realized it was a one-foot-tall *matryoshka* doll. The biggest he'd ever seen. Grigg could only laugh.

We named our fake company right.

He turned at a noise, thinking Charlotte had spoken.

The noise became a man's voice moving closer. "You there!"

Grigg hustled for daylight, which disappeared as the door slammed shut. He skidded to a stop. Something clicked on the other side once. Twice.

Charlotte's locks.

"What're you doing?" he whispered. "Let me out."

Charlotte hissed back. "Shut up you idiot. Wait."

"What is going on here?" said the man, now quite near the container. "Who are you?"

"Charlotte Webb. We were cleared at the gate."

"No container is supposed to be opened in the terminal."

"We were checking on a report of an attempted break-in."

"Or maybe you were trying to pull one off. You're coming with me."

"I haven't finished—"

"You sure as hell have. Let's go."

Steps, the sound of an engine.

Grigg slid down to sit against the locked door. Was this another part of Charlotte's plan she'd kept from him so he wouldn't freak? Lock him in if they were discovered? He pointed the beam at the pirate treasure his father's killing had led him to. People *would* kill for all that— motive by the quarter-container load—but it still didn't begin to answer his questions.

He wanted a definitive link to the murder. Like another bone record. *Well, I've got time to look.* That didn't make him feel any better. He snapped off the flashlight.

CHAPTER 21

Thursday, September 29, 2016

Grigg opened the first nested doll. He hadn't gone right to work. He'd sat for an hour in the dark, cursing Charlotte instead. His back on the cooling metal wall, he felt rather than saw the sun set on the other side of Jersey. Finally, as the container got chilly, he decided he'd better move around.

He began checking out the *matryoshka* dolls first because in the game one-of-these-things-is-not-like-the-others, the dolls were the one thing that definitely were *not*. Really. Why was a box of toys in here with all this illegitimate … illegal … fucking dirty money? Anyway, there wasn't much else productive for him to work on. Counting the hundred-dollar bills wouldn't tell him much he didn't already know—it was a shit-ton of money—and breaking open the packages was a step he didn't want to take.

He gripped the slightly smaller doll from inside the big one, unscrewed it, and then the next and the next. He touched something strange inside the bottom of the innermost one. It was not what *should* be there: a small, solid doll that did not open. No. It was cold. Metal. The electricity of the find tamped down what had been the slowly building panic at being locked in the can. He put the smallest doll's cup-shaped base between his crossed legs and held the beam like a spotlight from on high, revealing a flash drive.

What now? Cash, gold ... and data? Dad, what's going on here?

He picked it up. It was the longer type made before the drives shrank to the size of the end of your thumb. One side said *Visit Moscow* with a silhouette of the onion-turreted towers of St. Basil's Cathedral in Red Square. Nothing on the other side. A key chain ring. Probably bigger because it's supposed to be a souvenir. *Yeah, supposed to be.*

He pulled out the next *matryoshka*, finding another drive at its core. He put both dolls back together so as to leave the shipment looking undisturbed—sort of—if you ignored the fact the carboard box had been cut open. And that he'd taken the two flash drives. So, not really. He was following Charlotte's weird rule of semi-covering up a break-in—even if she had left him stuck in here. The methodical unscrewing, checking, unscrewing, checking to get the now inevitable device, then reassembling each doll calmed him some.

If they detained Charlotte, or called the real cops to arrest her, how long would it be? She'd have to tell security or the police about him. Wouldn't she? Charlotte was difficult, but she wouldn't leave him here. Once she confessed, this lead in the investigation would be lost to him forever. He'd probably be thrown in jail, and the bad guys would know what had happened and … disappear? Seek revenge? The break-in would have been worth it if he'd seen anything that pointed to Dad. Nada, so far. He'd have to get the flash drives out of here to find out if they meant anything, which would not happen if the cops came.

Why ship a box of souvenirs with piles of cash and bricks of bullion?

Fuck that. The details are blinding you.

The container was the obvious clue. The cash and gold were the motive for murder. What he couldn't fathom was why Dad would get involved with it or Freddy Popov—even to pay off his debts. That wasn't the Dad he knew. But if the unbelievable were true and his father had been working with Popov and they'd had some kind of falling out … The container put Popov at the top of Grigg's list of suspects.

He made the mistake of leaving the doll project to use the flashlight and search the can's walls for chinks or gaps. Nothing. Fingers crept up his throat. The metal box had to be watertight to go on ships. Did that mean airtight? Was he running out of oxygen? His breathing quickened. He should have researched these damned containers ahead of time. He pulled out his phone. One bar and only twenty percent battery. Not enough to waste on web searches. There had to be gaps for air. Right? He checked the door twice: an overlapping seal. He could call Charlotte, but if she was still with the rent-a-cops, she wouldn't pick up.

His tongue was dry as paper from his quickened respiration. He felt like he was going to hyperventilate. *Gotta break the cycle.* Grigg forced a slower rhythm with deep breathing. Kept at it. He pressed 9-1-1 on the phone almost automatically. Held his thumb above the green call button. No. Courage or crazy, he wasn't blowing this lead until he had no other choice.

Dad's murder was explained by the contents of this container. Had to be.

He clicked the light off. The darkness felt like it didn't end, though he knew how close the walls were. That didn't help. Brought him back to thinking about his air supply.

Continuing his breathing exercise, he picked up another *matryoshka*, twisted the head, and caught the odor of pine. He pulled it apart faster than the others, lining each smaller doll next to the previous one until he got to the flash drive. He dissected another even faster, the process stilling his anxiety.

With the doll project finished, he gave himself a half hour of flashlight time to go through the paperwork. He skipped the documents in Russian, cursing himself again for giving up on the lessons his father had urged. Back then, his reasoning had made sense. The language wouldn't help him fit in any better in their neighborhood. Now, it could have helped him investigate the murder.

The sheets in English were all numbers, financial ledgers of some kind. Maybe. Page after page meant nothing. He checked his father's watch. Time was up. He switched off the light having learned not a thing. Charlotte could figure out if there was anything on the drives. He jammed them in his windbreaker pockets.

Tick-tick-tick-tick.

The sound seemed to come from his pockets rather than inside his head. The total darkness was messing with his mind. It pressed up against his eyes, like the world ended right there. He thought it had a taste: dust, copper, and salt.

He lost track of time. After three hours, he dialed Charlotte's phone. It rolled over to voicemail with Verizon's pre-programmed greeting. Only old folks recorded their own messages.

"Charlotte, where the hell are you? It's getting cold in this box." *And I'm thirsty and hungry. And maybe running out of air.*

Grigg leaned against the wall. Too cold. The plastic boxes were better; he started to doze. Shook himself awake. *Is the CO_2 getting to me? It will if I keep hyperventilating.*

An hour later, he tried Charlotte again. This time it sounded like she answered and hung up. What the fuck was that supposed to mean? He turned the phone off to save battery for what would be his final call—to the cops.

He shivered as the can got colder, rain pattering against the top. His eyelids dropped, popped open, closed again, opened. Fear for himself was countered by a heavy sadness over what he was about to do. Expose the contents of this find. Tracks would get covered. The bad guys would escape. He'd lose the drives.

His father screamed when the killer broke into the house. And again, as they raced across the roof. When he fell. And after he was dead, Dad kept screaming. The voice that narrated his dreams, his voice only different, like a play-by-play announcer: *Your father never screamed, not then or ever.* Dad's mouth, inches from the ground after his neck had twisted around the wrong way, continued making the horror-show noises of a zombie.

Grigg woke to the sound of his own screams bouncing off the steel walls.

He grabbed at his phone: black and silent. He flicked on the light, half convinced something was in here with him. He heard a noise and checked around the interior for the source. It had come from the left wall.

No, the front. A metal-on-metal groaning screech. The door opened. Charlotte stood in the opening. The landscape behind her was the same and different. Artificial lighting rather than the sun illuminated the container stacks. Between two, a small rectangle of black sky.

He rushed into air warmer than inside the can. He shook, nonetheless, as the sweats from his nightmare chilled him. His eyes adjusted. The clouds had cleared off.

Charlotte closed the doors and relocked the container. "Let's go. We've got zero time."

She ran for the fence. Grigg followed as best he could.

She slipped through a hole cut in the chain link and picked up the bolt cutter on the other side. Grigg started to pass through as a patrolling Prius put on its revolving blue light and sped toward him. He was halfway through when a jagged piece of fence snagged his jeans.

The car skidded to a stop. "You. Hold it!"

The guard flew from the car and came for him.

Fuck, a rent-a-cop with a rent-a-gun.

He pulled his leg.

The fabric tore but he was still caught.

The guard moved closer.

Not after all this.

Closer.

A giant yank and a loud ripping. His pants flapping, he broke back into his awkward run toward their rented car.

I'm going to get shot in the back by a fake cop, unarmed. That even qualify as tragic?

Charlotte hit the accelerator hard as he was shutting the Hyundai's door, sending the car over bumps and barriers you weren't supposed to hit at speed, definitely not with a rental that had no collision coverage. They made the access road moving fast and the highway faster.

"Where the fuck were you?"

"Getting grilled. Trying to explain why you weren't there when the guard first grabbed me. As in, definitely *not* in the container. Figuring out an escape plan for you once they took my paperwork to review. I talked them in circles."

"You'd said going through the fence was a stupid idea when we were planning this."

"Stupid if we wanted any time in the container. Once they took the papers, my only way to get you was the smash-and-grab."

"Got it," Grigg said, suddenly exhausted almost beyond care. "Uh … the owner's gonna get a call."

"Maybe. They didn't know you were in there, and they won't cut those locks. Not without the owner's permission. Containers are the Swiss banking of shipping. That said, what you learned is probably going to have to be enough."

"There's these." He held up three of the flash drives.

"Data?"

"Yeah, in a box of nesting dolls."

"Fucking Russians."

"Can't argue that."

Charlotte turned thoughtful. "Could be information they didn't want to move on the net. Instead, they shipped it with lots of money and other goodies meant to stay off the books." She glanced at him. "Don't get your hopes up, though."

Tick-tick-tick-tick.

His father's watch said 11:35 p.m.

Charlotte unlocked the apartment door. Grigg stepped in behind her, put all the flash drives on her bed, turned around, and swung the door shut. It stopped prematurely.

A uniformed cop stood with his foot against the wood, his gun pointed at them.

"All right, shitbirds." The cop waved his Sig Sauer at Grigg. "Took me long enough tailing this one to find where he lives. This isn't for out on the street. We're going to have a nice talk in here."

CHAPTER 22

Friday, September 30, 2016

Fire sparked in Charlotte's eyes as she turned on Grigg, not seeming to care a weapon was pointed at them. "Everything I've done. You lead a fucking cop here?"

"I don't know how. I've been careful the whole time."

"Which just ended."

"He's telling the truth." The cop laughed. "He gave me the slip four times. Took two more stakeouts to find this comfy crib. Now sit the fuck down."

They did, on the inflated mattress. Charlotte sat straight, stiff. Her cheeks flushed to a deep red.

They needed to play this chill. They didn't know what the cop was here about, and she would be stupid to give him something he didn't have because she was pissed off at Grigg.

The cop was short, maybe five eight, white, with curly salt and pepper hair—more salt than pepper—bushy white eyebrows, and a big lumpy nose that had either been broken or was plain bad luck. His nameplate said FURILLO. A uniformed cop here on his own seemed odd. Detectives should be the ones coming after Grigg about his father—or about Carmichael or the container or any of the rest of the shitshow he referred to as the investigation.

"You watched the arcade?" Grigg said.

"Asked around the neighborhood. Your first name—not Russian, but not *not* Russian—is easily remembered." He backed up to close the door, holstered the pistol, and took a position in front of the balcony, out of their reach.

"Why not grab me on the street?"

"Wanted to see who else you might be working with."

Charlotte turned to Grigg, glaring harder, if that was possible.

"What's your name, miss?"

"Marcy Molotov."

Charlotte could afford to screw around. Not the Brown Outsider. Grigg sat as still as possible in front of this white cop and his gun, and a single witness who right now was furious with him. No fast moves. Running for the door was out of the question. Getting a gun pointed at his back twice in one day by a white man in uniform was tempting all the fates.

That was when Grigg noticed the shoulder patch on the cop's uniform. It had the shape and colors of the NYPD's, but where *City of New York* should have run along the two sides, instead was stitched:

SEA GATE
NEW YORK

With 1899 at the bottom.

"You're a Sea Gate cop? What the hell are you doing harassing us outside your fence? You've got no authority here."

Charlotte turned toward Furillo. "We're being held by a security guard from that gated community?"

"We're a legitimate public safety agency, with full police powers." Furillo sounded insulted.

"*Inside* Sea Gate. That's why you couldn't grab me on the street."

Grigg knew it. Everyone knew it. The Sea Gate Police Department was a private/public entity. They could do what most cops could, but within the enclosed neighborhood at the western end of Coney Island.

"I'm a detective investigating a case."

"In *uniform*?" Grigg said. "How far are you going to stretch this scam?"

"We're a small force. Someone was sick today. I had to man the Neptune gate. Just got off."

"Fucking security guard. Go ahead and shoot me. Though, hot tip: you probably want to plug him instead." Charlotte pointed at Grigg. "It's men of color sprinting the other way you guys are hot for these days."

Though she now sounded madder at Furillo than at him, Grigg didn't need her making any suggestions. Fear tingled from his throat down to his nuts.

Furillo turned remarkably calm, given the onslaught of insults.

"Jamie Carmichael used to be my partner in the Six-Seven. Thirteen years together in Bed-Stuy. I had a pop with him the night before he died. I'm after his killers."

Probably more than one pop, if he was with Carmichael. "Then we're on the same side. He was my boss."

"Right. He told me he was helping this guy who worked for him. Looking at the murder of his old man. Jamie sounded like he was into it—whatever he was doing for you on the side. He hadn't been into anything in a long while. He got screwed by the NYPD, and I'm gonna make sure that doesn't happen again with his murder. Owe it to him. He was a good cop. A good partner. The guys working his case here knew him too. And aren't fans. Wouldn't tell me shit. I also checked into your dad's case, since that's my one lead. My source in the Six-Oh said Ho and Wilson are sitting on their asses. They're not doing a damn thing about that murder. Someone's got strings in the Six-Oh, and they're pullin' real hard." He paused. "Now, I want you to tell me everything you know about the shootout that got Jamie killed."

Grigg calculated fast. If he gave Furillo the right lead—like Joe the Borscht—it might get the detective off his back and keep that damn mobster occupied. On the other side of the equation, Grigg's side: a new lead. Was someone really stalling the investigation of his father's homicide? If so, Grigg needed to know who that was and why. He went with it, a desperate move. The only one he had.

"Carmichael offered to help me check out Joe the Borscht."

Furillo's brow furrowed into one gray, bushy clump.

"The shooting happened outside his club. How did you get onto him?"

Grigg described his encounter with Joe the Borscht at the arcade, then tailing the gangster with Carmichael to the warehouse. Charlotte shifted on the bed. Grigg skipped her work on the case and what was going on inside the warehouse—talk about complicated—and jumped to the day of the memorial and the gunfight.

"Carmichael saved my life."

"Fucking stupid of you to go there alone. Joe the Borscht pulls serious weight in this neighborhood."

"You think he's bribing the detectives at the Six-Oh to do nothing?"

"Never heard me say the word bribe."

"You know what I mean."

A half nod from the old cop. "He's a good bet. How've you avoided him since?"

"I assume he's lying low because of the shooting. They can get him on conspiracy, at least, if they can catch and flip one of his guys." It was Grigg's turn to shrug. "Me? I'm being careful. So, what happened to Carmichael that put him off the force?"

"He was set up. Forced to resign. I'm not going into the details because that just spreads the lies. I caught some of the blowback. Made retirement a good option." Furillo fell silent and looked out the window at the Atlantic.

That much fit. The Sea Gate force was made up of double-dipping NYPD retirees with a sprinkling of former state troopers and cops from other jurisdictions. Grigg wasn't going to say anything else. No bone record. No shipping container. No Facebook Factory. Let Furillo stay focused on Joe the Borscht and his gang. The risks were high. He'd pointed this guy at danger and not told him everything. He'd crossed another line, probably into the most dangerous territory.

Furillo turned from the window. "I'll make a deal with you two."

Perspiration sprung up on Grigg's neck.

Fuck, not a deal from a cop. Those are never good.

"You let me know when you hear anything that might bear on Carmichael's homicide. You make yourself available when I want to talk." He whirled his index finger in the air to indicate the squat. "As for me, I don't know nothing about this place."

Charlotte and Grigg both stared at him.

"Like you said, it's outside our gate."

"Right," Charlotte said. "Don't forget that."

"Deal," said Grigg.

Furillo nodded and left, pulling the door closed; it looked much less secure and secret than when Grigg believed he was hidden in an apartment deleted from the bank's records.

The cop's departure meant Grigg needed to pack up for another sleepover at the arcade.

As he turned, Charlotte swung a bottle toward him. He flinched, then realized she was handing him a beer, not attacking him with it.

"No poison in it?"

Charlotte chuckled at his joke. Her moods came and went, like the storms off the ocean that could leave anything from wet pavement to fallen trees to wrecked houses. This time, he'd expected the roof to fly off.

He popped the top of a Belgian beer stronger than the IPAs he drank. You were supposed to sip this dark stuff that was twelve-percent alcohol. Grigg didn't feel like sipping. He took two big gulps instead, and the buzz moved into his head like his neurons couldn't get out of the way fast enough.

"I can stay? Why?"

"That's how the script had to run."

"I have no idea what—"

"A script. A computer program. Your dad was murdered. If Carmichael talked to somebody about helping you, which he did, and that person—Furillo—wanted to get Carmichael's murderers … well … coming after you becomes the obvious solution. That script runs one way. You didn't know that cop was on your ass. He said he lost you four times. You were doing your best. Can't boot you for that." She air-toasted him and drank. "Something out of my control was bound to happen if I started mixing it up with other people."

"You're taking a chance."

"Probabilities. Numbers. It always comes down to numbers." Now she was drinking almost as fast as Grigg. "Damn, it's late."

Despite the statement, she opened two more beers. Grigg would fall asleep easy tonight, though probably to enjoy a looped nightmare inside a container.

"I'm working second shift at Joe's warehouse tomorrow," Charlotte said. "I've almost got a backdoor built into their network. Two weeks it's taken me. There's some high-grade security running in that place. Nothing I've seen commercially. They watch us all the time. I think they're tracking everyone's keystrokes. Or believe they are." A sly smile over the bottle top. "I'm close."

"Then what're you gonna do?"

"I dunno. Get what they're doing into the wild somehow, so people know what those Oxford fucking Russians are up to."

"WikiLeaks?"

"Nah. Can't tell who Assange is fucking with anymore. Or fucking. There're other sites. Maybe my own special site to show off what Coney Island hackers can pull off."

He coughed on his beer. "You can't put your name on it."

"Duh."

Grigg picked up one of the flash drives and handed it over so she could have her first real look.

She turned it in her hands. "From a souvenir stand?"

"Looks like."

"What if I find a shitload of tourist pictures?"

Grigg shook his head in dismay. He hoped like hell the drives would point where to look next, because nothing else in the container had.

"You going to check the drive out now?"

"No."

"Why not?"

"I'm not sticking one of those in anything but an air-gapped computer. I don't have one here." Grigg didn't know what she was talking about; it showed on his face. "A laptop with no Wi-Fi, no Bluetooth, no connection to the net. None at all. If there's something nasty on here," she held up the flash drive, "it's staying on the computer. The way things are going with your investigation it will either be tourist pictures or *very* nasty. There's no middle ground with you."

"Hey, I'm not doing it."

He'd been lying on the mattress for about twenty minutes when his phone rang. Katia.

"Did you get in?"

"Oh yeah."

He told her about what they'd discovered. The whole long day, plus Furillo's surprise visit.

"Good God. How much is all that cash and gold worth?"

"Too much."

She repeated his conclusion like she needed to hear how it sounded. "You think Popov's the killer because he and your dad were going to steal it and they fell out?"

"That's my theory. Popov is crooked."

"But your dad wasn't." She became insistent.

"Maybe I didn't know him as well as I thought."

"No! He wasn't that kind of man. You have to believe that."

"Then why was he meeting with Popov?"

"That's what you need to find out."

"Charlotte's trying to trace Popov, or at least give me a lead."

"Things okay over there?" Katia asked some form of that question every call.

"Yeah, no problems. Surprisingly. Even after Furillo found us. She got over it. Can't say I understand her logic. She was a real hero getting us into the container. And me out. She's obsessed with the Facebook Factory. Almost done hacking a backdoor in. Going to put all those crazy-ass political posts on the Internet somewhere."

"That's our Charlotte."

"How's things at work?"

"Hard to concentrate with you two breaking into the container terminal. Didn't like my job in the first place. Now you're getting all the excitement."

"There's such a thing as *too* much excitement." He closed his eyes. He jumped back in time to when he'd last been able to relax. "Had fun at McSorley's. Just talking about normal stuff. Can't believe it's been more than two weeks." And to something that still bothered him. "Two weeks since Dad's service … two weeks since Mr. P told me about Victor Voronin. Dad's friend. Your father's too. They were all into bone records in Leningrad. I'm still drawing a blank on the name. Don't remember Dad ever mentioning him."

"Same." He imagined her shaking her head, black hair loose, swinging across her face. "Nothing from my father's stories about growing up. He told enough of them." A beat, then a second one. She spoke in a quieter voice. "I had fun too."

"How about tomorrow? I know it's a pain to go into Manhattan but—"

"I'd love to."

"Oh … Great. The White Horse Tavern at seven? Let's keep it to the classic old bars of Manhattan."

"Nice. Smart, too. Russians like to go to all the shiny new places."

She told him to be careful, as she ended every call. He made no promises. He couldn't. He planned to test Furillo's information about the detectives at the Six-Oh tomorrow.

CHAPTER 23

Friday, September 30, 2016

Grigg crunched on his cinnamon raisin toast, sans butter, the regular breakfast at the squat. Charlotte's choice, and he'd decided to go in with her on groceries.

A deep electronic tone—like the ones radio stations use when they test the emergency alert system—sounded from Charlotte's phone. Time for the news. She'd written a program, more like a homebrew app, that trolled for stories and had Siri read them off when enough arrived. She hadn't been a news junkie before she started working at the Facebook Factory. The job had changed that as she worked to put up hundreds of posts that were someone's idea of propaganda. She needed to compare what was being reported with what she was seeing at the warehouse.

Siri started: *"Story one: In the latest Reuters/Ipsos poll, Hillary Clinton held her lead over Donald Trump, forty-three percent to thirty-eight percent. These are the earliest figures since the candidates debated for the first time Monday.*

"Story two: Hillary Clinton attacked then-primary rival

Senator Bernie Sanders's supporters as ill-informed, naive 'children of the Great Recession' who are 'living in their parents' basement.' The just-released hacked recording comes from a talk she gave to donors in February. Clinton went on to say, 'There's just a deep desire to believe that we can have free college, free healthcare, that what we've done hasn't gone far enough, and that we just need to, you know, go as far as, you know, Scandinavia, whatever that means, and half the people don't know what that means, but it's something that they deeply feel—'"

"What is her problem?" Grigg said. "Does she not have a filter?"

"Shh." Charlotte touched the iPhone's screen to rewind the feed a few seconds.

"Story three: According to New York's attorney general, Donald Trump's charitable foundation never registered to collect money from donors. The Donald J. Trump Foundation was set up by the presidential candidate in 1987 to make grants from the royalties of his book, The Art of the Deal. *However, it has been primarily funded by outside contributions in recent years. If the attorney general rules the foundation broke the law, he could order it to cease soliciting donations."*

The stories trailed off into this batshit crazy year's version of the mundane. Charlotte went back to her keyboard. Grigg got ready for work. He shoved the spiral notebook with all his case information into his messenger bag.

"Holy shit," Charlotte said.

"What is it?"

He came back into the living room/her bedroom.

"Holy shitty shit shit. A bone record found on a dead body." She stared at her screen. "Bullet hole in the forehead."

"Where?"

"Moscow."

"How are you getting this?"

"Deaddit. The Reddit for criminals and other scumbags. I posted a general, 'anything happening with bone records' query. Victim was Nikolai Popov, managing director of some natural-gas company in Siberia."

"Popov, as in Freddy Popov?"

She looked up. "Pretty common Russian name, isn't it? The family reported Popov received a bone record in the mail three days before the shooting. The killer also left one on the body. The Deaddit post isn't clear on whether it was the same record that came in the mail, or if the murderer brought his own. Did your dad get one in the mail?"

"Maybe. I remembered him opening an envelope the night before he left. A black object fell out. I'm not sure it was a record."

"Must have been. One to scare. One to take credit for the kill."

"How do you know any of this is legit?"

"Links in the post to two newspaper articles about the Popov murder with pictures of the bone record. It's also an X-ray of a skull."

"When was he killed?"

"Ten months ago. My new friend CharlesHardin59

says 'Rave On' by Buddy Holly was recorded on the disc." Her hand went up to shush Grigg. "Scrolling … Oh, this is creepy. Maybe he's not my new friend. He also writes about your father's murder." She looked up. "This guy put the two killings together. Maybe he knows the killer. Maybe he *is* the killer."

"Shit," said Grigg. "Can he trace you?"

"Not on Deaddit, thank fuck. That's the point."

"So CharlesHardin59 can't know you or that you know me."

"No way. He only posted because I asked about any crimes involving bone records."

"Evidence and a mystery at the same time." He waited for the information to organize itself into a clear picture. It declined. "Keep looking for Freddy Popov."

"I told you. He's a ghost."

"We need to find him. Nikolai Popov killed in Moscow. Freddy Popov meets with my dad before his murder. I have to know what's really going on with him."

After work, Grigg walked toward the 60th Precinct, a dangerous place for him, but he couldn't avoid it. Furillo had leveled serious charges against Ho and Wilson. Grigg planned to take a big chance to find out if they were true. His heart thumped inside his chest wall like a fat moth hitting a window. His stomach tightened; the pain made him grunt out loud. He was going to accuse the detectives of stalling—and worse. He had a plan, something more than a fishing expedition, but the two could easily drag him into that windowless little room and thump him. Or worse. "Resisting arrest" was a good reason for a cop to pull his gun.

He blew out air. His guts were in an uproar, but he was clear about the questions he needed to get answered at the precinct. He also understood how many other questions there were. For those, he had no plan as of yet. Freddy Popov and Joe the Borscht topped his list of suspects, but did either of them kill Nikolai Popov in Moscow? And Grigg knew nothing about the Russian gunmen who'd attacked Freddy's apartment. Or how all evidence of their bloody gunfight in the park had vanished. Could Russian nationals do that on American soil? How was he supposed to track down ghosts?

Detective Wilson met him at the front desk, holding an Egg McWhateverTheFuck wrapped in stained yellow paper. A drop of grease fell to the floor, then another. Wilson contemplated the problem, reached out with the toe of a scuffed brown shoe, and smeared the grease across the yellow tile.

"What do you want?"

"An update on the investigation."

"We're pursuing leads."

"Is that where Ho is now?"

"It's police business. None of yours."

"You have a nice touch, you know, when dealing with the son of a murder victim."

"You're more than that."

"Right. I forgot. I'm a suspect. Because of a witness."

Here was where things would start to get interesting. "A witness who must be the shooter."

Wilson didn't flinch. "No one told you that."

"No one had to."

Wilson took a bite of his sandwich and chewed with a smacking sound.

"Have you talked to Joe the Borscht yet?"

"We're interviewing anyone relevant."

"Pretty relevant, that guy. He's come after me. His guys killed Jamie Carmichael when he tried to save me. Now Joe's in the wind. How can a guy that big be so hard to find?"

"Like I said—"

"Maybe he's not in the picture because he's painting the picture."

"Be careful. We've got plenty to keep you here longer than you want."

"Yet you aren't. A police source told me Joe the Borscht is pulling strings in this precinct."

Wilson set down the sandwich on what looked like important cop paperwork. He wiped his greasy hands with a greasy napkin and stepped around the desk to Grigg. He was a full head taller. "One, it's not true. Two, it's not an accusation a smart *boy* makes when he tops our very short list of suspects."

"Don't call me boy." The thumping in his chest was so loud Grigg thought Wilson might hear it.

"You're not smart, either. We got a gym downstairs. Do a little boxing, little martial arts. Just messing around, of course. You want the tour?"

This was cat-and-mouse in the tiger's cage. No going back. His big move: "You know what? I'm gonna get with my source. Nail down what's *really* going on. Find out who's stymied the investigation."

A total amateur move. He was gambling Wilson had Grigg down as a total amateur.

The detective offered an unimpressed grunt. He picked up the remains of his breakfast and walked back to the squad room.

Grigg left the precinct, rounded the corner, and crossed the street, gaining a view of the front of the building from a tight angle. A minute later, Wilson came out. As soon as he did, Grigg turned and walked away, keeping the pace easy. He had no intention of letting the detective lose him.

He pulled out his cell phone.

"Didn't expect to hear from you so soon," said Furillo. "Actually, didn't expect to hear from you clown-boxes at all."

Grigg told him what he'd done and what he needed.

"Are you fucking nuts?"

"I'm checking out your info—and the detectives. Two for the price of one."

"You're checking me out?"

"Don't show, and I'll know you were bullshitting us."

"Where?" A grudging growl.

"Nathan's."

"Wait ten minutes before you go in. I'll be there."

Grigg walked once through the grounds of the New York Aquarium, letting Wilson keep him in sight. When he headed back along Surf Avenue, Wilson was gone, replaced by a tall, muscular guy in the telltale uniform of black T-shirt and jeans. Wilson had handed off the tail to this goon, who Grigg would've bet a containerful of dirty money worked for Joe the Borscht.

Grigg pulled the thug along Surf Avenue toward Nathan's Famous, Coney Island's center of gravity. Eleven minutes after the call, he went inside, ordered one hot dog plain, pumped on mustard and ketchup, and sat.

His shadow leaned against the doorframe at the far corner, doing a rotten job of looking inattentive.

Grigg's phone went off: Furillo's name on the screen. "I'm here."

"I've got a tail. Switched off with Wilson."

"There's two of them I can see. I'll move when they do."

A rippling charge rose from Grigg's roiling stomach to his throat. "I hope you're fast."

"I am. And I'm close."

Grigg started to turn his head.

"Don't look around."

He stared down at the hot dog with its too-yellow mustard and ketchup that looked like blood.

CHAPTER 24

Friday, September 30, 2016

A Mercedes pulled to the curb in front of Nathan's. Joe the Borscht grabbed the top of the open car door to pull his bulk up and out. The Bookkeeper came from the other side of the car, his small steps making it look like he was scuttling to keep up with the bigger man. The goon who'd followed Grigg broke whatever he thought was cover and opened the door to Nathan's for his boss. Duty over craft.

Joe took the chair across from Grigg, the Bookkeeper sitting to his right.

"You're hard to find, Grigoriy."

"You've been scarce yourself. Told you my name is Grigg."

"After everything, you pick that to argue about?"

"I can argue about other things. Let's start with why you're bribing detectives. Specifically, to do nothing about my dad's murder. Wilson's not only your stooge but a stupid one."

"You didn't come here to meet your precinct 'source,' then?"

"Fuck no. I said *Wilson* was stupid, not me."

"Maybe you are as intelligent as some say you are," said the Bookkeeper. He smiled. "Maybe we should listen." He looked over at Joe the Borscht, then back to Grigg.

The more Grigg heard the Bookkeeper, the more he thought of a museum guide. What did he really do for Joe?

"And you are?" Grigg said.

"Anthony."

Joe leaned forward. "Never mind fucking introductions. You broke into my container."

A brief look of surprise crossed Grigg's face, and not brief enough.

"I protect my property," Joe the Borscht said. "Video surveillance. You were in the container for more than four hours after the woman was picked up. I want to know what you did. What you took."

Ask something without admitting anything. "You familiar with a guy named Freddy Popov? Either of you."

There were beads of sweat on Joe's forehead, though Nathan's wasn't warm. One droplet ran past his eye and stopped at the top of his fat cheek. Maybe he was hot from carrying all that weight.

"Freddy fucked up. There will be a reckoning. There will be a reckoning with you, too."

"You know him, then. Thanks. Helps. Why can't you check your own container? If it *is* yours."

Joe the Borscht erupted. "I'll fucking kill you!"

"Let's not get nasty," said Furillo, suddenly sitting next to Grigg.

"You are?" Joe the Borscht's large brown eyes leveled on Furillo. "People who involve themselves in my business don't stay involved in anything long."

"Furillo, detective with Sea Gate PD. You're responsible for two killings. Where are the men who shot Jamie Carmichael?"

"You don't understand the mistake you're making."

"I've got a pretty .22 under the table pointed at your nut sack. After the round splatters your testicles, it will bounce around tearing up your guts. The joy of a low-caliber weapon."

Grigg had thought Furillo would be good backup. Now he feared he'd brought a cowboy along. This was supposed to be an interview, not a wild west standoff. He caught movement. Two gangsters were coming toward them from across the restaurant.

"Tell your boys to back up," Furillo said.

Joe the Borscht signaled with two fingers. The men moved to separate exits.

Furillo's voice got louder. "Why don't you want Andrei Orlov's murder solved? One of your guys the shooter in that one too?"

"This meeting is no longer productive," said Anthony, sounding like he wanted to move to another gallery in the museum. He tapped Joe the Borscht, who rose slowly, like he was sitting at a table in the middle of a minefield.

"You got nothing?" Furillo stood up, a small black revolver in his left hand. "Carmichael was my partner. I will settle accounts."

Joe the Borscht and Anthony walked toward the door. After three steps, Anthony turned to them, and the smiling, benign face was gone, like another personality had crawled up from inside him.

"You've made a terrible mistake disrespecting our Joe. A bigger mistake stealing from him. The settling of your accounts will be at a time and place of our choosing."

He spun. They exited and got in the Merc.

Grigg sat on one of the stools for the two-player Star Wars game at the back of the Conquistador Arcade. He bounced his good right leg. The case had hung a hard left down a dark tunnel. Furillo had turned into a movie tough guy. Joe the Borscht knew Grigg and Charlotte broke into the container—which he claimed was his. Grigg's throat tightened. He swallowed. The appetite he'd lost at Nathan's was still missing in action. Had Furillo heard the conversation about the container? Would he have to explain it to him? Should he?

Furillo, who had been checking to see if they'd been followed, joined Grigg in the back. "Who was blondie?"

"Said his name was Anthony. Not muscle. Maybe brains?"

"Joe could use fucking more of those. At least we got something out of it. You told Wilson you were going to check with your source. Next thing, Joe and company show up. He's the one interfering with the Six-Oh. Not enough to get *infernal* affairs involved. Too circumstantial. But it's something." He walked to the aisle. "I've got to get back to work."

After Furillo left, Grigg put his head down on the game's console and went through the list of what he'd achieved. Figure out if Furillo was on the level. *Check.* Discover who on the outside was stalling the investigation. *Check.* Find out who owned the container. *Check.* Learn that his visit to said container was known to Joe the Borscht. No check there. Because that was the fucking opposite of what he needed, now or ever.

Freddy Popov had given Grigg the location of the box, and Joe said he knew Popov. In fact, wanted to punish him. If Joe the Borscht's men murdered Dad, was it because Dad was involved with Popov? In that case, wouldn't Joe have known Popov was planning to hit the container? Or maybe there was bad blood between Joe and Freddy over something else—something Grigg hadn't figured out. Either way, he'd connected his two main suspects. The other connection in the case he didn't have an answer for: the Moscow bone record killing. Freddy had the same last name as the victim, and despite his lies, he hadn't been in the U.S. that long. So, he could have killed someone related. Grigg didn't yet have a way to link Joe the Borscht to that crime.

Grigg sighed. Still too many unknowns.

He needed IDs on—or an idea how to find—the men who'd attacked him and Popov at the apartment. Russians, but not Joe's men. That was all he knew, and it wasn't much.

Katia was meeting him at the White Horse in about an hour. She'd listen, give him her thoughts.

CHAPTER 25

Saturday, October 1, 2016

Grigg sat on Charlotte's mattress. She slid next to him after giving him a serious warning about messing around. He wasn't sure why she was worried. He'd showed no interest—and he didn't want his credit history wrecked.

"This is the airgap." She pointed to a Toshiba that wasn't her regular laptop. The computer had a rugged steel and rubber exterior, nicked and scratched, like it was more weapon than computer.

Weren't they all weapons now?

"To keep any viruses on the flash drive trapped, right?"

"That's right. Could be code that starts hacking into the seven firewalls in front of the CIA's network. Or maybe it'll spew out Facebook shit about the election. These drives did belong to Joe the Borscht."

She slotted one of them into the computer. They watched a green screen with a prompt and a blinking rectangular cursor—a real old-school interface. No windows, icons, pictures of her dog—if Charlotte ever had a dog. She typed. The cursor slid to the right on its own, spitting out lines and lines of words that weren't words—gibberish, with more semicolons than Grigg had ever used in his lifetime.

He had squeaked through one computer course at Kingsborough Community College with a C minus. He took it because he thought it would be cool to hack systems like Charlotte did. Except in the end, it was all math. Nothing cool about that.

"What's going on?"

"There's a program on the thumb drive. I loaded it onto the laptop. Looks like it will take a while."

Tick-tick-tick-tick.

His father's watch read 2:39 a.m.

After a half hour, he put on a sweatshirt and sat on the balcony, watching the water and waiting. He so wanted his bed … correction, his air mattress.

"This is why I air-gapped," she called out.

Grigg went back inside to stare at what he didn't understand.

"It's looking for a way off the computer. It pinged for every sort of port to get on the net. I had programs looking for anything like that."

"Where does it want to go?"

"Don't know the where, what, or why. I'll have to plow through the code to figure out what it is while it worms around, trying to get away." She typed. Shook her head. "A lot of programming here. Thousands and thousands of lines, and I'm just getting into it. Which is weird. Viruses are usually tight little things. This could take weeks if each drive has a different program that's this complex. Unless we farm the work out."

"No! No farming. No one else."

"Then weeks."

"I'm gonna hope you can figure out something from this one."

"Don't be stupid. This one may be the easiest. Or you might need all sixteen to understand what's really here. What it does."

Grigg's chest tightened, and the pressure moved around to his back and shoulders, squeezing like a hug he didn't want. He knew he needed to give her time, but his nightmare that the drives were not a lead at all felt like it was starting to come true. He'd be left with the knowledge of Joe the Borscht's secret stash—*and* the knowledge Joe had learned they'd broken in. Then they would have bought nothing but trouble and wouldn't be a step closer to knowing what was going on.

"What would happen if you let it out and, I don't know, followed it?"

She gave him that look. "It can't be traced once it's loose in the wild. We don't know what it'll do. I'm *not* letting it out."

Grigg locked the front door of the arcade after closing for his last night on the job. He had his final paycheck in hand. Quitting was going to cost him, but he couldn't keep working a job so many people in the neighborhood knew about. Especially one person: Joe the Borscht.

He walked down the middle of The Bowery.

A hand grabbed his wrist.

He twisted away, at the same time reaching for the stun gun.

Steel fingers squeezed his arm and another hand stripped him of the weapon.

"Don't move."

Contrary to instruction, he struggled.

The man, who wore a dark business suit, half turned him and put him in a hammer lock.

A second man appeared in front of Grigg. "FBI. We'd like to talk."

"That's a new one in this shit show," Grigg said, wincing at the pressure on his arm. "Prove it."

An ID card appeared three inches from his eyes. The red letters F-B-I were so close they blurred. Grigg quit twisting as they took his sap and messenger bag. The two men escorted him to a black Ford SUV on West 15th Street that must have been chosen to let the entire neighborhood know the feds were in the hood.

His stomach dropped into a deep frier. He shook his head and groaned.

"What's the problem?" said the second man.

"You can't just kidnap me."

"We want to talk."

Famous last words, as in the ones too many people heard last. The pain spread through his gut.

They drove onto the Belt Parkway, exiting at the edge of downtown Brooklyn. The stocky agent who'd grabbed

Grigg parked the vehicle, yanked him out, and escorted him to an ugly glass-fronted stub of a three-story office building. They rode to the third floor and stepped into an open room with five occupied desks.

Late hours for whatever they're chasing. Must be urgent.

No one looked up.

Probably FBI policy.

Grigg was plopped in a chair in one of three offices off the main room. His escort stayed with him, standing by the door reading his phone. The agent was only a little taller than Grigg, barrel chested with a lumpy face so scarred by acne it looked like a moonscape.

After about forty minutes, the other agent from the kidnapping opened the door.

"My name's Carlyle. We're hoping you can help us."

Help, huh? Grigg remained silent. Whatever this was, he had to play it stronger than he felt.

Carlyle crossed the room on long legs and took the chair behind the desk. He had a thin, pointed nose under a low forehead and black hair parted at the side. FBI haircuts were a kind of time travel.

Carlyle opened a laptop, then folded out a second screen. He placed a digital recorder on the desk.

"You are Grigoriy Orlov, and your father was the late Anton."

"I go by Grigg."

"Your father immigrated from the Soviet Union in 1987 …"

He trailed off, giving Grigg's face that searching look,

like the Russian part of him was hiding. "You were born here."

"My mother was Jamaican. You should have that too."

"It's your father we're interested in. He was meeting with a person of interest named Freddy Popov. Do you know why?"

"I talked to my dad for less than five minutes before he was killed. I don't know what he was doing for the six months before that."

"Why did he leave?"

"Don't know."

"Do you know Freddy Popov?"

"Yeah. Met him twice."

"He didn't tell you why he was meeting with your father?"

"He didn't tell me they met at all. I learned that from a third party."

"How did you and Popov come in contact?"

"I thought maybe Dad went somewhere outside the neighborhood, somewhere he'd blend in. I'd worked my way to this building full of Russians in Midwood, and I showed Dad's picture to the people there. Popov claimed he'd seen a picture of the same man when it was displayed by a federal agent. Was that guy one of you?"

Grigg expected to hear *I'll ask the questions.* Carlyle surprised him.

"No. Your father first came to our attention after he was killed."

"I only learned later about Popov's meetings. He lied,

really."

"Lying is one thing he does quite well."

"What else is he into?"

"I'll ask the questions." *Ah, there we go.* "You said you met twice."

"The second time he claimed he was going to sell me this federal agent's phone number."

"Did you get it?"

Good time to test this strange part of the case.

"No. While I was at his apartment, two Russians broke in, started shooting. By Russians, I mean they sounded like they were off the plane from Russia, not living in the hood. Popov had a rope ladder at the window. He clearly expected unfriendly company. We both got out of there. They grabbed me in a park across the street. One of them told me Dad and Freddy had been meeting. They were pretty obsessed with finding Freddy. Problem was, I didn't know anything more about him, so they were going to drag me off somewhere. That's when the night really went off the rails. That park's gang territory. North Brooklyn Skins. NBS slingers and the Russians started firing at each other. At least one banger was killed—maybe more—by a third Russian who arrived after the shooting started. I watched him put a bullet in the face of a gangbanger who was already down. I got away, and the next day there was no record of that gunfight. Of what must have been murder. Not with the cops. Not on the news. No video of it from the cameras around the park. Zero blood on the grass, even. Again, an educated guess, but I thought people like you made it all go away. Maybe you did?"

Carlyle pushed a button on the desk phone. "Parker, in here."

Parker came in, closed the door, and stood in front of it. A brown-haired woman, she looked too small to deal with bad guys, which probably meant she knew extra-special ways of hurting people. Kind of like Katia.

"Repeat your story."

Grigg did. Parker asked the date, then left without another question.

"Who is Popov? What is he up to?" Grigg asked.

"As I said, a person of interest."

I've got to get something out of this. "Is he related to a murder victim named Nikolai Popov?"

"Where did you get that name?"

"He was shot in Moscow. There was a bone record left on his body, just like my father had in his pocket." He waited for Carlyle to ask what a bone record was. He didn't. Grigg figured Carlyle had read the police file on Dad's murder.

"You don't know what you've gotten into."

"You bet your sweet ass I don't. That's why it'd be nice to get some help. Have you guys thought about doing that?"

"It's not our job to help, but …"

Lunar Face, who was leaning against the wall, shook his head wearily, as in *bad idea*.

"So, you're half Russian?" Carlyle continued.

"I was born here. I'm American."

"I just didn't want you to think I was being insulting. That's all. Russia is a mafia state, run by a small, powerful group of people organized like a mob family. Nikolai Popov was a junior member of that family. Over there, mobsters and businessmen are interchangeable. They're called the *avtoritet*, which literally means the authority. They run straight and dirty businesses side by side. Don't even differentiate. The government certainly doesn't. Nikolai was an *avtoritet*. Freddy is his son."

"Fuck."

"Which brings up a pretty interesting question. Why was your dad murdered in the same way as Freddy's father?"

"Interesting? How about obvious? Problem is: if he were one of these *avtoritet*, I would have noticed. I've lived with my dad my whole life. My mother died when I was eighteen months old. He was a seventh-grade social studies teacher. Wrote history books no one wanted to publish. Wanted to write a book on Coney Island from the perspective of a Soviet immigrant. Never got to it. He was the authority on things no one cared about." Grigg's mind jumped to another question. "Are you working on Russian interference in the elections?"

Carlyle leaned back in his chair for the first time. "Why do you ask?"

Careful. Grigg was curious about the Facebook Factory but not so much that he wanted the FBI raiding the place while Charlotte was working there.

"I keep hearing about it on the news. Like I said, I'm

an American. Elections are what make the whole thing work, right?"

"Very patriotic. You really don't know anything specific about the elections?"

Suddenly, Grigg felt Carlyle was more focused on the Russian inside him than the brown he saw.

"No. Nothing." He went for blasé, but he'd probably caused the FBI to double whatever surveillance they might try to put on him.

"You can go. We'll be in touch."

Grigg stood up.

Carlyle turned the chair and eased forward. "Watch yourself. Freddy's not the most dangerous person in this game."

CHAPTER 26

Sunday, October 2, 2016

Urgent knocking on the apartment door.

Tick-tick-tick-tick.

His father's watch read 1:45 a.m.

Charlotte stirred. "What the …"

Grigg wasn't taking any chances. He took the revolver out of the gun safe, unlocked the door, and found Katia standing there.

He dropped the pistol to his side.

Her face was white, glistening with sweat, but so grim he was sure he'd done something awful—besides pulling a gun on her.

She reached into the gray duffel she was carrying. Her hand was shaking when she brought out a black disc.

Grigg already knew, but he checked it, taking the thing, turning it toward the light, and as he did, bones surfaced from the film. Two skeletal hands. Handwriting on the disc: "Heartbeat."

"I checked. Buddy Holly."

"Where did you get this?"

"Arrived in the mail today—yesterday. Plain manila envelope. Addressed to me."

"*Yesterday?*" Charlotte said.

"I had a long Saturday night at the office, catching up on work. Dinner on the way home. I didn't look at my mail until after midnight."

She came toward Grigg. He wrapped his arms around her, hugged her tight, trying to squeeze away the fear he'd mistaken for anger.

"Why didn't you come sooner? Call?"

"You'd texted me about the FBI. I decided to wait. Walked circles in my apartment. I didn't know what to do. Finally, I just got the hell out of there. I was scared to use my phone. To text. I'm scared shitless now. Who *are* these people? I'm next. Right? That's what it means."

Her question said prove me wrong. "I don't—"

"That's why your father told you to come to me. He knew. Our dads were friends from childhood. Mine's been dead for years, so … the sins of the fathers and all that. They're going to kill me instead."

Grigg wanted to say he didn't know enough yet but in a manner that wouldn't belittle her fears. Two bone records had already tagged two people for murder. He still didn't know how CharlesHardin59 knew about crimes committed eight months apart on different continents. He still didn't know the *why* of these killings. He couldn't think of any grudge Joe the Borscht had against Mr. Sokolov, so he should have no reason to go after Katia.

"First, we keep you safe. Then figure out what's going on."

Charlotte nodded slightly, standing with her arms folded, quiet for once, watching her friend.

"What's to figure? We have a bone record. A third bone record! How can I be safe?"

Katia was tumbling into panic. Grigg had never seen her like this. She was always the cool customer in tough situations. She'd been on the receiving end of all kinds of hate when she'd dated the brown boy. *The fake Russian.* Her response: no response. They never got a rise out of her. Even when her dad died five years after her mom, she'd kept it together, bearing the weight of all the condolences and comforting everyone else. Later that evening, he'd found her in a side room of the funeral parlor crying quietly. They were both eighteen.

"We're ahead in this game. Remember that. We know more than anyone. We know the pattern. We'll figure out the connection. I'll find the killer. Stop him."

It sounded too positive. And he knew it.

"How can you be so calm?"

"I'm not." He chanced a reach for her hand. "Focused and worried and working the case."

She took his hand. "Working it—or me?"

"The case." Grigg offered a little smile, hoping it would give her confidence.

She sat on the bed and deflated into herself. "We know my dad and yours were friends from childhood. They collected bone records when they were teens. I guess … maybe there is something there."

He knew she wouldn't let him change the subject so

settled on talking about all the other facts. "Mr. P says our fathers hung out with two boys, Viktor Voronin and his younger brother. Mr. P hasn't come up with his name yet. The older one, Viktor, died in a work camp in his early twenties. Tonight, the FBI gave me two decent pieces of information. One, Nikolai Popov, murdered in Russia, was Freddy's father. He was a mid-level gangster, and the FBI's actively looking for Freddy. Two, the agent said there are people in this case more dangerous than Freddy. He may have meant the killer, which means maybe Freddy's not our man. The FBI and Charlotte haven't been able to track down Popov—"

"But I'm still looking," Charlotte cut in. "If someone's threatening Katia, I'll be putting all my time into it. All. My. Time."

"What about CharlesHardin59? He knew about Nikolai Popov and my dad."

"He's stayed quiet. I'll post something. A teaser about a new record being released."

"Do we actually dangle the container? See if that gets a reaction."

"Dangle it where?" said Katia.

"Deaddit. Whatever works." He looked at Charlotte.

She nodded but said, "You might attract more of Joe the Borscht's attention."

"Not sure how much more I can attract. Let's see what our other moves turn up first before doing that."

Katia exhaled loudly and fell back on Charlotte's mattress with arms spread.

Charlotte reached for her hand, and they linked fingers. "You want to stay?"

"How did you guess?"

"That duffel bag—and I'm a shit-hot detective now."

"I know it's more than you bargained for."

"Screw it. We may as well have all the hunted watching out for each other."

Katia hoisted the big duffel and walked to the bedroom. Grigg followed.

She started unpacking. A tiny brown roll sprung open to form a mattress that looked too thin to be comfortable. Camping gear rather than something for the beach. A sleeping bag emerged from a tiny stuff sack. Katia's face shifted to focused intensity as she organized her things like every move was important, like she was setting up at some remote outpost and had to get it all correct before night fell and the wild animals approached the fire circle. They'd been apart so long, yet he remembered so much about the way she thought and acted.

Grigg sipped a 90 Years Double IPA, the sting of nine-percent alcohol piercing the round flavor of malt and hops—and settling his nerves but a little.

Katia sat down on her made-up bed. She was so low to the ground, her knees were up around her face, making her look like a little girl.

"Is that really comfortable?" Grigg swallowed more strong ale.

"Not bad—after a ten-mile hike."

"We don't do those here at Camp Charlotte." He took

one more swallow and set the can down. "You want one? I find it helps with the floor under a thin mattress."

She nodded. He went and got a bottle of Mermaid Pilsner, passing Charlotte, who kept her eyes on the screen, mumbling and typing faster than he'd seen before.

Grigg handed over the beer. "We'll get through this."

There was more he wanted to say, but he didn't have enough nine percent in him to give him the courage. The *we'll* was pretty big by itself.

Grigg suggested that if she was okay with it, they go over everything that had happened since Grigg's father was killed to see if they'd missed anything about her in light of the new bone record.

"Yeah, I can do it," she said, already sounding calmer. "I had my wipeout. I've got you guys."

So, they went through it all: The red-haired assassin. Dad's bone record. Detectives Wilson and Ho. Carmichael. Joe the Borscht's interest in Grigg. Joe the Borscht's interest in—and visit to—the Facebook Factory. The Facebook Factory itself. The Moscow killing. Freddy Popov and his lies. The attack on Freddy and Grigg by the Russians. The vanishing gunfight in the park. Furillo. The shipping container full of gold, cash, and hinky thumb drives. The friendly meet-up at Nathan's. The FBI.

Grigg tipped back his bottle to get the last of it and almost fell over. He was exhausted and riding a good buzz.

"Some list, but nothing pops." Katia said. "The only thing that's clear is the bone record is the key."

"Deaddit's given us one good lead on the records."

Grigg looked back in the direction of Charlotte.

Getting all the facts out—and the beer in—calmed Katia more. Her eyelids were heavy. They were talked out. He disposed of the bottles, then fell into the deep sleep guaranteed by the nine percent.

A hand touched his shoulder. He jerked around.

"Easy." Katia had her sleeping bag over shoulders. She wore nothing else.

He threw aside his blanket. Katia lay naked on top of him, the sleeping bag providing cover for both. Her hand reached down inside his boxer briefs. "You never were slow to react."

He didn't answer. Through the buzz and arousal, he wondered if she was using sex to keep the fear at bay. Were they coming together, only to separate again tomorrow? He let the worry flutter away as she stroked him slowly. He groaned. She lowered herself onto him, warm and wet inside. She kissed him once, twice, three times, then sat up and rode him the way she'd always liked it best, slow first, then moving faster. She was quieter than usual, what with Charlotte next door. He sat up and kissed a nipple, licked it, kissed it again as his fingers lightly touched the other, both low on her small breasts.

She worked for both of them until he came in a shudder, sending her into a final spasm of low moans. She leaned down to kiss him and lay there, the two of them sweating, wet, him still inside her, his throbbing a slowing pulse.

"Do you think she heard?" Grigg whispered.

"I'm hoping she's not still working."

"She'll just blame it on those *fucking* Russians."

She buried her face in his chest to giggle. A few moments later, she sat back up, her face serious. "Promise me."

"That's a scary word after sex."

"That you're not just trying to calm me down. That you *know* we can beat this."

The sex hadn't chased away all the fear.

"Believe it."

CHAPTER 27

Wednesday, October 5, 2016

Boyd dropped a stack of files on Grigg's desk. "Input every one of these field reports." The bureaucrats upstairs hadn't named an adjuster to replace Carmichael, which meant Grigg was doing everyone's shit work, plus some shit work that had never been done before. He shifted the stack over to his left, like he planned to get on it immediately.

Tick-tick-tick-tick.

His father's watch read 12:30 p.m.

Charlotte had spent four days trying to figure out the code from the flash drive. A big nothing. This morning, she'd repeated her plea that they farm the other ones out. Grigg scotched that again. They were already too exposed. Katia agreed.

So far, Katia had called in sick every day this week. Her dick of a boss was being, surprise, a complete dick. He said she had three more sick days, and then he'd start looking for someone to replace her Monday. After the first night's emotional explosion, the death threat—what else could you call it?—had become a weight she carried around. It pressed down on her. She didn't want to leave the apartment for any reason. "How can they know so much about us?" she'd asked him.

The only person left in Grigg's work area stood and left for lunch. Grigg picked up the phone and called the rental office at Gardenia Place, Freddy Popov's building in Midwood. For the first time in more than three weeks, a person rather than a recording answered. A woman's voice, deep and gruff.

"Don't you ever return calls?"

"We're fully rented. Why should I bother?"

"I'm calling about a tenant, Freddy Popov."

"That asshole doesn't live here anymore. He left his apartment trashed with two month's rent in arrears. Can't help you."

"I just want the place of employment he listed on his rental application."

"Why would I give you that?"

"He's a deadbeat, for one. You're going to protect his privacy? He owes others money too. Give me the information, and I'll share what I find."

"Hell. What the fuck? Hold on." The phone rattled on a desk or some other hard surface. After two minutes, she picked it up. "Morrison's Imported Furniture, 137-19 Cross Bay Boulevard in Queens. There's a copy of his paystub in the file. Same address as on the rental app. That's good confirmation to have because I wouldn't believe anything Popov said or wrote. The stub's handwritten. How often do you see those anymore? Everything's ADP."

Maybe a lie. Or maybe Popov did everything he could to stay off the grid.

"How long had he been renting?"

"He was four months into the lease."

"I'll let you know what I get."

Grigg hung the phone up and slapped his desk hard. Popov had left no digital trail for Charlotte to find, but his apartment application had left him a thin lead.

From the office, getting to that Queens address would take an hour, at least. He had to get there before five; he didn't plan on calling ahead to the furniture business. Grigg put a note on top of the stack he was supposed input. *Will finish when I return.* He left off *tomorrow*.

On Cross Bay Boulevard, he passed a bodega, a liquor store, a children's shoe shop, and, midblock, came to the address he wanted. The sign overhead read MORRISON'S IMPORTED FURNITURE. But a gray steel shutter was down and locked in place.

He banged, creating a rattling din. Nothing. He kicked at it. Same again.

He walked to the liquor store. A chain of bells tinkled against the inside of the door.

"Do you know anything about Morrison's Imported Furniture?" he asked the clerk on duty. "They ever open?"

"Why do you want to know?"

"I'm trying to find a Russian man named Freddy Popov."

The counterman's eyes widened at *Russian*.

"I don't know any Popovs. Any Russians."

An old woman came from the back of the shop carrying a bottle of Yellow Tail. "Oh, Veejay, why don't you ever speak up?" She put the bottle of chardonnay on the counter. "This is a nice shopping street. Or was. Whoever took over Morrison's left the sign up and pulled the shutter down and left it that way. It's an eyesore right in the middle of our block. You get one shop looking like that, then you get more. The street dies. That's what you should worry about, Veejay."

The man shrugged.

"Does anyone ever come and go?"

"Not out the front. From the back. My house is on the street behind."

God bless neighborhood busybodies.

"Thank you." Grigg left and walked along the side of the bodega to the small parking lot behind the single-story strip of shops. They all had back doors, dumpsters, and bundles of cardboard for recycling. Except Morrison's. A silver Lexus was parked across from the rear entrance.

Grigg pulled on the back door, and to his surprise, it swung open, fast. That was because someone was pushing on it. That someone was Freddy Popov.

"Hey, Freddy," Grigg said. "Before you head off in that sweet ride, let's have a chat."

Popov, tall and thin in another cheap suit, moved back enough so they weren't face to face. "Don't have time right now."

Grigg continued to block the doorway. "Someone else chasing you?"

"You have no idea what's going on."

"That's been the problem all along. I don't have a fucking clue. I know you do." Grigg reached back and brought out the .32. "And I need to get a fucking clue in the worst way."

"Are you crazy?"

"How about you go inside so we don't have to put that to the test."

Popov walked backwards the whole way, eyeing the barrel of the gun. Down the rear hallway, they passed a bathroom and a storage area and came out into the showroom for the furniture store. It was overcrowded with leather couches, dining room tables and chairs, and bedroom sets.

"There's a reason they call a cover a cover. Not making much of an effort at the whole retailing thing here, are you? Merchandise is piling up while you keep the shutter down all day. I guess all your importing is done by container. That's one serious fucking import job out there in Jersey."

"Don't tell me you went out—"

"That your desk?" One ornate piece, like something that would appear in grandma's house in a TV movie, had a laptop, a phone, and a mess of paperwork on it. "Sit."

Grigg came around the desk and settled on a couch behind him so he could make sure Popov didn't go for anything in the drawers.

"Your father was killed by the same person as mine," he told Popov.

"Yes, that may be so."

"Was it you?"

"No, of course not."

"Don't give me *of course not*. Some people don't like their dads. Hate them so bad, they kill them. Then my dad gets murdered after meeting you. Bone records left on both bodies. What's the connection? Did you and he fight over the container?"

"I was trying to help your father."

"Bullshit."

"I contacted your father before he got the bone record. Your father, mine, and late Alexander Sokolov were all friends from time they were kids. Until emigration split them up. A close group of friends in Leningrad."

"I know all that. Except no Popov was among them."

"You've not figured it out, maybe? Nikolai Voronin was one of original four friends."

"Nikolai Popov was Nikolai Voronin. He changed his name?"

"His older brother, Viktor, was arrested for anti-state activities. He was sent to work camp and fell deep into dark places in Gulag. He died. Or was murdered. My parents changed family name to Popov to escape shame."

"Who killed these two boyhood friends, then? My dad and yours. And why? Yours was a mobster. Or should I say, one of the 'authority.' That would make him a likely target for lots of reasons. Crime does that. Mine was over here doing nothing to nobody. So why the fuck? Who's behind the murders?"

"Why do you say *behind*?"

"It's organized. Two continents. The bone records. It can't be one person." Grigg waved the gun at Popov, who flinched. "How are you involved? You knew that my dad would be a target. You came all the way over here to help him? Yet you're pulling the container job, too. Make it make sense for me."

"I'm afraid I can't reveal everything. I have sources. I did try to help your father. To do what I could for family connection. The container was … is separate issue."

I bet Agent Carlyle can get a straight answer out of you. Maybe I take you to him myself.

"What the fuck does that mean?"

"I didn't get all my father had after he was killed. Most of his holdings were clawed away from my family and handed out to others. Putin and his people have turned Russia into land of animals. Container is my competitor's. I learned about it after my father's murder."

"From your 'sources'?"

He nodded.

"Joe the Borscht and your father were competitors?"

"Maybe."

"I'm getting tired of this. I've got the gun."

"You won't shoot me. You're your father's son."

"Who were the Russians that attacked us at your apartment?"

"I believe they were SVR. Russian secret service."

"Why were they after *you*?" Grigg's tone went to incredulous as Popov skipped from mob story to spy story.

"I can only guess. Perhaps there is something in container they want. You weren't supposed to enter until I took care of the owner's video surveillance. You *did* break in?"

"Oh, yeah. Found cash. Gold. Paperwork. You never fucking called me. I got tired of waiting."

"You needed to be more patient."

"Nah, I don't think you were ever going to call. Your plan was screwed. *Is* screwed. Let's talk about the SVR."

"I can only guess—"

"Tired of your guessing. And your lying."

"Okay, so maybe I lie on some things. I do know who killer is."

"Everything okay, boss?" Another tall, thin man in a black suit, white shirt, and no tie stood at the entrance to the back hallway, pointing a long-barreled semi-automatic pistol at Grigg. Brooklyn accent. Popov hired local. Quiet one, too. Grigg squeezed the grip of his weapon. The confidence it had given him with Popov melted. If he tried to take on this guy, Popov could go for a gun.

"I'm fine, Rez." Popov stood. "I was trying to convince Grigg that I'm not his enemy. We're done," he told Grigg. Then to Rez, "Shoot him if he does anything but leave the store."

Rez stepped closer, easy, panther-like steps, the big weapon steady.

Grigg rose, carefully slotting his gun in its holster, then moved around the desk with his hands out, past the gunman. He opened the steel back door and let it slam shut behind him.

Back on the sidewalk, he called Agent Carlyle and told him everything Popov had said, along with the address of Morrison's and the tag number on the Lexus.

CHAPTER 28

Wednesday, October 5, 2016

"Do you believe him?"

Katia sat on Charlotte's mattress, her legs folded underneath her, one hand squeezing the first two fingers of the other. Grigg had finished recounting his interview with Popov. He knew her. She didn't want to hear he believed Popov, but that he'd gleaned a clue from what he'd heard, even if Popov didn't answer the most important question.

"He's a flat-out liar. He knows enough to be the murderer. He also knows enough to know *who* the murderer is. Claims he does know. I know it's not everything," he squeezed her forearm, "but it's more than I've accomplished in a while. Did Charlotte say where she was going?"

"No."

"Coming back?"

"No."

"Damn. I'd love to know what's up with the thumb drives."

Katia frowned. "I'm getting back involved. Three will

make more progress than two, and I'm done with hiding."

Charlotte came through the door, gave Grigg the evil eye for sitting on the bed without permission—he stood—and plopped on the other side of the mattress.

"What's up?" Katia said.

"It's what's down." She flipped open the laptop. "I had someone take a look at the code."

"You what?" Grigg moved to her side of the bed. "We agreed. We're already too exposed."

"We didn't agree. You fucking ordered. I don't take orders from anyone, including guests in my home. I asked an extremely discreet, extremely talented friend to consult on this. The woman who taught me a lot of what I know."

The invisible hand grabbed Grigg's guts and squeezed until it hurt. "You should have at least talked with me."

"You would have said no."

"That's because it was a fucking stupid thing to do."

"Hey, c'mon, guys," Katia said, standing. "Let's work this out."

Why is she calm while I'm freaking?

Charlotte wasn't having it. "You know what's fucking stupid? Trying to check the code on sixteen of them." She scooped up the pile of drives on her mattress and let them fall through her fingers like pirate treasure. "What's even stupider is that it was pointless. My work. Your precautions."

"What are you talking about?"

She pulled one of the souvenir storage devices out of the pocket of her black denim jacket. "This contains MyOffice."

"What the fuck is that?"

"The Microsoft Office of fucking Russia. You know, word processing, email, spreadsheets. Office productivity. It's sold by a Russian company that pirated Microsoft." She waved him off. "Don't insult me. I took precautions. I met my friend in person. When hackers meet face-to-face, you know they're taking things seriously."

Grigg's mouth went dry. He looked at the mini fridge that held his beer supply. Held off. He needed his leads to lead somewhere, *not* turn into … what was it turning into?

"And?" he asked.

"Nothing. Once my friend figured out what it was, she ran an application that compared the commercial version of the program with what's on the drive, line of code for line of code, character for character. No variation between the two of them. None whatsoever."

"Then why the hell was it trying so hard to reach the Internet from your air-gapped laptop?"

"It's programmed for automatic updates like all commercial software."

"Fuck." Grigg stretched his back to get rid of the tension. No go. "There're fifteen others. We don't know they don't have something that's suspect."

"She can check a couple more. I'm not asking her to do all of them. I'll get the app and do the same. That sample should tell us whether to waste any more time."

"Anything to be sure. Or as sure as we can be."

Grigg pushed four of the drives toward Charlotte. He picked up the rest and put them in his messenger bag.

"What? You don't trust me now?"

"No, it's not that." Guilt replaced anger. Charlotte had been good to them. "I'm sorry. I need a breakthrough—*we* need a breakthrough. Instead, our best leads turn into more questions. I believe you. But these had to be in the container for *some* purpose. There's a reason the SVR wants them."

"SVR's a guess based on what Popov told him," Katia clarified for Charlotte. "Even assuming Popov's right—or not lying—we don't know what they want. Could be something Grigg didn't find."

"Or the cash and gold we did," said Charlotte. "What exactly did Popov say?" She looked from Katia to Grigg.

He recounted again, with less detail, the meeting.

Katia reached to touch Charlotte's forearm. "We both owe you big time. I've been selfish. You guys need help. I'm going to stop hiding out. Work on the investigation. Figure a plan to get to work. I can't lose that miserable job."

"Fucking Russians." Charlotte shook her head and chuckled. "You can stay as long as you like. Him? He's a real pain in my ass."

CHAPTER 29

Friday, October 7, 2016 - Sunday, October 9, 2016

Grigg crossed the street two blocks from Charlotte's squat in the Neptune's Manor condo tower. He was anxious to get home. Boyd had made him work late on the stacks of paperwork he'd been diligently ignoring.

He dragged his left leg faster. He wanted to see Katia. He was worried about her. She'd gone back to work today after a false start Thursday. He'd sent her a text and they'd had a quick exchange six hours ago:

How are you doing?

Too busy. That's good. Talk when we're home.

Okay, thinking of you.

A woman walked away from the building in the opposite direction. She wore her brown hair in a ponytail. Charlotte? She had on a black denim jacket with a splotch of color on the back that Grigg just made out as the Coney Island Funny Face, the clown that was the neighborhood's unofficial logo. That confirmed it. As did her orange bell-bottoms.

Must be a grocery run. Too early for the Facebook Factory.

He let out a long breath. It would be nice to have some private time to talk with Katia … Despite his apology to Charlotte, things had been tense in the apartment after the argument over the flash drives. Because of what he'd said. Because Katia was still rattled even if she was dealing with things better. Her decision to go outside had come from her head; her heart wasn't in it at first. Several times, he caught her staring at the door like she was getting ready to storm a castle. Or run from a monster. They'd talked about it. He'd said she didn't have to go. She said she did. Which had only driven him to try harder to find leads on the killer. Drive wasn't enough, though. Not two days' worth. How long would he need?

An Escalade flew past him and skidded to a stop in front of Charlotte's building. Two men jumped from the SUV, leaving the doors open. The first sported a blond crewcut and wore a gray turtleneck and pants a darker shade of gray. The second, in a suit, was a redhead with a close-trimmed beard and that flattened nose.

Katia!

Grigg threw himself down the block. If he could only have a working knee one time, he wanted it to be now. He reached the glass outer door and put in his key. Inside the lobby, Red Hair disappeared into the elevator. Grigg drew the .32 and yanked the inner door so hard it smashed into the vestibule wall. He lunged toward the elevator to stop the men. Disarm. Shoot. Whatever it took.

The elevator door slid shut.

Shit!

The other car was on the tenth floor. Grigg holstered the gun. He texted:

Killer in elevator. Get out now. Take stairs.

He went for the stairs himself, shoving the phone in his pocket. He took two at a time with his good right leg, pulling himself with both hands on the banister. He passed the door to the second floor. No sign of Katia. *Fuck. What was she doing?* The apartment. He had to get to the apartment.

A loud banging from above. Door-banging, not shooting.

Grigg redoubled his effort, moving as fast as he could with his three good limbs.

On the fourth-floor landing, he pushed open the door, hoping surprise would be on his side.

A crash down the hall.

Red Hair, leading with the big, nickel-plated revolver that he'd shot Dad with, stepped into the open door of Charlotte's apartment.

The crack of a gun.

Two more shots.

Grigg crossed the hall, flattened himself next to the apartment doorway, and, crouching low, started to move into the opening. He'd shoot at anything that wasn't Katia. Red Hair surprised Grigg, sprinting out of the apartment and almost knocking him over. The killer ducked around the corner toward the elevators. Grigg put two bullets in the wall where the hallway turned.

Goddammit, Grigg, faster!

Pursuit was not an option.

He entered the apartment swinging the gun wildly, too wildly. The man in gray was sprawled half off the bed, face up, mouth open, a ragged red hole in his cheek. Blood soaked Charlotte's blankets.

Katia lay facedown on the other side of the door to their bedroom, her head out of sight.

"No. No!"

His vision blurred. He wiped his eyes with his sleeve.

Not now.

He had to hop to her because his left knee had given up completely. Katia's hand gripped a large semi-automatic that looked like a .45. Had *she* put the hole in Gray Guy's face? Where'd she get the pistol?

Blood leaked from a wound in her other hand. He came around to see brown hair in a ponytail ... *What?* He became dizzy as the scene stopped making sense. Charlotte on the street—*and* in the apartment?

He collapsed next to her and gently turned the body over. It was Charlotte. The instant of relief when he realized it wasn't Katia turned into guilt that speared his heart.

He put his hand above her mouth.

Shallow breathing.

Charlotte had a second wound on the right side of her chest, clearly the threat to her life. He pressed his hand to it. She groaned.

He tried to take the gun away, but Charlotte's hand was locked on it.

He used his phone to call for an ambulance. He took his shirt off to apply more pressure on the wound. Katia had responded to his last text during the shooting:

What are you talking about?

What's going on?

Grigg?

As he pressed to stop the flow of blood, he one-hand texted her the news, an agonizingly slow process, particularly as he had to explain his own earlier messages.

Oh God no! How bad?

Bad. GET SOMEWHERE SAFE.

I know a place.

Keep disguise on.

Kk. Let me know what's going on.

Sirens coming. We'll meet when they're done with me. Take care of yourself.

Grigg put his gun down in front of him and kicked it toward the door, so it was in clear view. There was still the problem of Charlotte's .45-caliber security blanket.

"Did you get the other one?" Charlotte's voice came low and thick.

"No."

"Gotta get that fuh …" She faded.

He pressed harder on the wound. Too hard? He had no idea. He had to keep the life from ebbing out of her.

Two cops—blue uniform, white skin—came in fast and saw Charlotte's head in Grigg's lap, his hand pressing on her chest. And her gun.

"Get rid of the weapon."

"She won't let go of it."

"I'm serious. Right. Now."

They were both in a shooting stance.

"Okay." Talking slowly. "I'm going to try to take it away."

If he was not careful, this was where it all ended, trying to disarm his wounded friend after bringing the killers to her door.

The cops stiffened, both training their service revolvers on Grigg.

"Charlotte, let me have the gun." Grigg grabbed the barrel, keeping it pointed back into the bedroom and away from the patrolman. She didn't have the same strength as before. She tugged once, then her whole body went limp. He dropped the pistol on the rug, and the lead cop kicked it away.

"The other one's mine."

"Who'd you shoot?"

"Only the wall in the hallway. Trying to get the second assailant."

"Are there any more weapons?"

"Check the guy on the bed."

The cop at the rear found a Glock in the blankets. He waved in the EMTs. The lead officer frisked and cuffed Grigg. Charlotte was prepped for transport and wheeled out of the apartment.

The night and the entire next day were a blur of conversations, interviews, demands, and swearing harangues—good cop, bad cop, and Grigg-didn't-know-what-the-fuck cop. When he started, he was committed to telling them everything. No more secrets. He described the red-haired, red-bearded assailant who got away, who looked like the man who shot his father, who carried the same gun: the nickel-plated magnum. He told them about the bone record Katia had received—exactly like the one he'd found on his father's body—so they'd understand she could've been the intended target.

In between, he begged to hear about Charlotte's condition. Late Saturday morning, a cop said Charlotte was hanging on but wouldn't offer anything else, except that the bullets they pulled out of Charlotte didn't come from Grigg's .32. Grigg asked if the slugs were from a magnum. A detective sergeant yelled at him, "Don't do the fucking police work!"

Grigg told them about the murder of Freddy Popov's father in Moscow, complete with bone record—it was here they started to look at him funny—and the shipping container. They conferenced right in front of him, talked about state jurisdiction, needing a warrant, U.S. Customs—and whether this guy was spinning fairy tales.

At that point, Grigg put the brakes on full disclosure, leaving out the Russian secret service, the Facebook Factory, and the thumb drives, because, at this point, he wanted them to believe him—and find the man who was his dad's murderer and Charlotte's assailant. Wilson and Ho might be bent, but not all the detectives in the Six-Oh could be. Not with something this big. Senior officers were involved. At about midnight, more than twenty-four hours after the shooting, a female lieutenant delivered coffee and word that the bullet that tore up the gunman's face was from a .45, maybe the one Charlotte was holding.

Tell me something I don't know.

When Grigg wasn't trying to answer the same question in the same way again and again and again—following his rule that cops like stories that don't change—and when he wasn't picturing Charlotte tubed and wired up in the hospital, he worried whether Katia was safe. The cops wanted to know where she was, since he'd said she was supposed to be the next victim. Several of them asked. Yelled. Since he didn't know, he didn't have to lie about it.

Early Sunday morning, having told the full story twenty or more times, he waited to get charged with something or several somethings. Instead, they let him out of the interview room, and he sat on a bench outside the detective squad with his phone returned. There were a dozen worried texts from Katia. He tapped a message to her, and she answered, despite the hour.

You all right?

The longest day. How are you doing? I'm really worried.

So far, so safe.

Good. Sorry I was out of touch. Cops took my phone. They may do it again. I'm still in the station.

How long?

No idea. Please stay safe.

Oh I'm resourceful. I'll be fine until we can meet.

He deleted the text thread—didn't need the cops again screaming for her location—and flipped to the news as a distraction. The top story was about a joint statement from the Department of Homeland Security and the Office of the Director of National Intelligence:

> "The U.S. Intelligence Community is confident that the Russian Government directed the recent compromises of emails from U.S. persons and institutions, including from U.S. political organizations. The recent disclosures of alleged hacked e-mails on sites like DCLeaks.com and WikiLeaks and by the Guccifer 2.0 online persona are consistent with the methods and motivations of Russian-directed efforts. These thefts and disclosures are intended to interfere with the U.S. election process. Such activity is not new to Moscow—the Russians have used similar tactics and techniques across Europe and Eurasia, for example, to influence public opinion there. Experts believe, based on the scope and sensitivity of these efforts, that only Russia's senior-most officials could have authorized these activities."

No shit, spy guys.

Grigg reconsidered reporting the Facebook Factory. No, it was too James Bond for the 60th Precinct. He needed them focused on the shooter. Maybe he'd take it to Carlyle at the FBI when he wasn't dodging killers. Given the U.S. spymasters' analysis, Carlyle would have to believe Grigg. Might even be what he was working on.

The lieutenant escorted him to the front door.

"We'll want you back, one way or another," she said.

"And everything I told you?"

"It's a lot. We're working on it." She glanced to the side, looking like she had a sour taste in her mouth. "Right now, we have a dead man with no ID, a badly wounded woman in the hospital, and a messy crime scene. That's before we get to your ... er, complicated story."

"Carlyle at the FBI? I told the detectives about him. He can back my story."

"We've been calling him. He's not found the time to get back to us."

"I don't understand."

"You've never worked with the FBI, then. They get points off for playing well with others."

Maybe he *wouldn't* take the Facebook Factory to Carlyle.

Tick-tick-tick-tick.

His father's watch read 5:45 a.m.

Outside, a chill was in the air and a deeper one settled in Grigg's chest. Was someone again manipulating the 60th Precinct? He'd been on the scene of three shootings, two of them murders. He didn't look kosher no matter what. His gut said someone wanted him out, and he was now easier to get at, naked without the .32. He chose a direction at random and slipped into the shadows of a side street, thinking, if the detectives of the 60th weren't gonna help, Grigg would have to bring down the killer himself. His gut told him one more thing: the red-headed gunman was somewhere nearby.

CHAPTER 30

Sunday, October 9, 2016

The sun brought a smudged fire to the east end of Coney Island, though likely not a whole lot of warmth, and would soon begin to shine on the beach for the entire day. Grigg hunched against the ocean-facing side of the West 16th Street lifeguard station. If someone wanted him out on the street, he was going to be damn hard to find. Joe the Borscht. Freddy Popov. The SVR. The red-headed hitman. Or thugs working for one or any of them.

He'd made one quick stop at a locker in a privately-run shop on Mermaid that beachgoers used to stow their stuff. He was there to get the thumb drives, which he'd stowed for safekeeping after Charlotte returned the four she and her friend tested, finding nothing suspect. At that point on Thursday, Furillo knew about the apartment, and Charlotte's friend knew about the drives. Two people too many for Grigg. He didn't want the drives in the squat. He still held hope they meant something. It was a good call in one way: the cops had taken from the flat the bone record Katia had received, and other less important items. On the run now and not knowing where he'd end up, he had no choice but to keep the drives in his bag.

Katia was on her way from her alma mater, Hofstra University, to meet Grigg. Ever resourceful, she'd contrived to get herself locked in the library for two nights running.

He ached to know how Charlotte was doing. That would mean visiting Coney Island Hospital to even have a chance, as they'd never tell him anything over the phone. He fiddled with the zipper on the messenger bag.

One of the drives glinted in his hand. He'd pulled it out without thinking.

There's got to be something.

While waiting for the ambulance back in the squat, he'd told Charlotte she'd be okay. Her eyes were open, fearful. She didn't say anything. The only noise she'd made was a shallow, labored wheezing. She was hurt and alone in that hospital. On the phone, Katia sounded upset but together. She'd wanted to know about Charlotte although she herself was in mortal danger. Anger filled his head, a deep red, swirling cloud pressing on his skull. He had to stop the killer. He'd been inches from the fucking bastard. Reactions too slow. The mistake that might spell the end for all of them.

Fuck it.

Before he could check himself, he hurled the thumb drive against the concrete footing of the lifeguard station and screamed long and loud.

His rage expressed, he sheepishly looked down at the

broken drive. He picked it up and, checking the damage, saw that something white shone from within the cracked shell. A piece of paper? Grigg pulled it out:

Franklin Crosby.

Handwritten neatly in pen. Nothing else. Quickly, he took out another drive and pried it open with his pen knife, this time taking care not to damage the drive. The device swung open on tiny hinges like a clamshell.

Lawrence Miller.

Another.

Michael Cardoza.

When he was finished, he slid sixteen slips with sixteen names in his wallet, then put the drives back together. More of Charlotte's hacker protocol: he didn't want it to look like he'd discovered the names. He buried the busted one in the sand so at least, at first glance, it would appear as if the secret hadn't been discovered. Until someone counted the devices …

It was a cute trick, hiding physical information in the flash drives. Probably the last thing anyone would look for.

That much you got, genius. But who do the names belong to? What do they mean?

They could be real people, or codes for other names, or codes for anything.

At least they were *something*.

"Grigg." Katia slid next to him, whispering his name.

"I was so worried," he said. "The whole time. I missed you. I really missed you."

"Charlotte …" With the name, she fell onto him,

wrapped her arms tight around his neck, and sobbed.

"I know. I know."

"They were coming for me—not her. The disguise."

"Charlotte had a gun I didn't know about. She killed one of the fuckers. The other one shot her. Same guy who came after Dad. I had to choose between chasing him and helping Charlotte."

"We've got to find out how she's doing." She eased her grip and pulled away to crouch on the sand. She was tear streaked, her nose running. She pulled Charlotte's black jacket off to use her shirtsleeve to wipe her face.

"Last the cops told me, she was alive, but the hospital's one place I'd watch if I were looking for you or me. If either of us goes, it should be me."

"Why you?"

"No one's sent me a bone record."

"How did the shooters find the apartment?"

"Two ways I can think of. I located Freddy Popov. Maybe he returned the favor and fingered the squat. Or Charlotte's friend who checked the drives. Does she know where Charlotte lives?"

"Don't know. Maybe. There's a third person. Furillo was in the squat."

"But he's helped me. Took a big risk with the Russians."

"This is all so fucked up."

"You don't know the half of it." He told her the news about the slips in the thumb drives. "I'm thinking someone got me released from the precinct. No way I should be out already after that bloodbath Friday night. One of the bad guys wants me on the street."

"Red Hair wants me dead."

"Yeah. That is the worst of it. So close, and I let him get away. I don't want to sit in one place too long. I'd know by now if I'd been followed here from the Sixtieth. Let's head down the beach a bit."

Grigg and Katia strolled close to the water in the light of the risen sun. A steady breeze off the ocean cooled the air. Grigg put his arm around Katia and drew her close.

She shivered and slid a hand into his back pocket. "What are we going to do?"

"Figure out what we're going to do." He shook his head at the circles his thoughts were running in.

"You know Charlotte plays it tough, but she only wants to help people. That's why she took you in."

Katia started crying again, burying her head in the crook of Grigg's neck. This slowed their pace, a worry, but he didn't have the heart to hurry her up. He cried too. They stopped walking, and his tears misted over Deno's Wonder Wheel, the Parachute Jump, and the rest of the Coney Island skyline. Assholes were ruining this place for him. His place. Covering it in the blood of the dead.

Tick-tick-tick-tick.

His father's watch said they'd been standing still for ten minutes.

Grigg gently urged Katia along.

She sniffled until they reached the New York Aquarium. Construction gear and stacks of material sat on the beach all the way up to the aquarium's wall, surrounded by a plastic-web barrier fence. The repairs from the damage caused in 2012 by Superstorm Sandy were still ongoing.

"More than anything, I want a shower and somewhere to warm up a bit." Katia faced him. "What about my apartment? A quick stop. They won't expect it. They attacked the squat. Knew I'd left my flat. So, probably no one's watching it anymore."

Grigg considered the idea for a moment. He could see Katia needed it. He needed it. "Okay, but a close, close check before we go in. The slightest sign someone's on the place, and we're gone."

They slogged through the sand in the direction of Brighton Beach.

"Among many things, this has been bothering me," Grigg said. "Let's say the SVR is involved in this, like Freddy claims. How do we stop the Russian secret service?"

"Get the CIA involved?"

"It's the FBI that does counterintelligence inside the U.S."

"You sure?"

"Yeah. It's not like *Homeland*."

"We'd have to get them to believe us. You know Carlyle … maybe the names you found …?"

He nodded, unsure who he could trust at this point.

Once they neared her apartment, Grigg spent two hours driving Katia crazy by staking out her building and making her identify everyone who came in and out. He worried that his own desire for a shower, not to mention thought-hazing exhaustion, was clouding his judgment.

That made him extra careful, walking both sides of the block, checking cars for local or imported muscle.

He came up dry.

"All right, let's go."

"*Finally.*"

"Be ready to get out fast."

While Katia showered, Grigg called Furillo. The Sea Gate cop was pretty much the only person left he could call. Maybe Carlyle, though he needed to get his thoughts together before facing a brigade of FBI agents. Voicemail picked up. Did someone get to Furillo? Grigg wasn't going to walk all the way to Sea Gate only to find Furillo wasn't there—or end up in a trap. Nowhere in the open was safe. He hated using his phone. Someone could have done something to it at the 60th. He knew he should dump it, but they needed a way to connect with the world. Paranoia. Exhaustion. Mournful sadness. *Can't hide here. Got nowhere else to go.*

Then there was Dad. A jolt across his gut. He realized he'd thought little of him since Friday night, except when he told the cops, all of which had turned into a drone by the end. He should have felt guilt, but it was only tired astonishment. The case had expanded in so many ways and caused so much collateral damage.

He chanced the Sea Gate Police Department main number. They said Furillo was on the 4 p.m. shift.

Grigg showered under steamy water, dozing while leaning against the red tile for several minutes. He dried off, put on sweats and a T-shirt that Katia had left out for him. Her dad's, he guessed—too big, but clean and not awful looking. Since no one had kicked the door in, he extended their stay, lying down next to Katia, only to arrive in that netherworld of strange dreams that comes during naps you drop into with a shuddering suddenness. Nightmare monsters, the wrong people doing very wrong things, Grigg doing even worse. And nothing to do with his father, bone records, or anything else in the real world.

He startled awake. Hands were on his chest.

"Whoa." Katia, leaning over, squeezed his shoulders. "Lot of yelling there. Nightmare?"

"Nap-mare."

Tick-tick-tick-tick.

His father's watch read 1:35 p.m.

"Shit, we've been here a long time."

"We eat, then we go." She made it a command, not a request.

His stomach weighed in, convincing him. He cooked omelets while Katia took a second shower. "Saving up," she joked.

He shoveled in a forkful of egg as she joined him at the table. "Where can we hang out for a couple of hours before we stroll down the beach in the direction of Sea Gate? Assuming I can reach Furillo."

"We're using the beach a lot."

"Unlike on the streets, you can see the bad guys coming. Thugs are street people, anyway."

"We could wait down in the basement. Use the door out the back of the building. Gets us out of my apartment for the next two hours. No one will see us leave."

"Great idea." Grigg kissed her.

Two hours later, they were back on the beach, passing the amusement area, the ballfield, the Ford Amphitheater, apartment buildings. It was a reverse of this morning's panorama, except a notch warmer under the October afternoon sun.

Tick-tick-tick-tick.

His father's watch read 4:10 p.m.

He called the Sea Gate police station and was put through.

"Jesus motherfucking Christ. What are you doing?"

"Our friend was shot. She's badly injured."

"I know what's going on. What I need to know is why. Because whatever it is, it's gotten way out of hand."

"You're not wrong. Can we meet somewhere to talk?"

"Sea Gate Food. Come in at Surf Avenue. I'll leave word with the uniforms."

They were passing the Poseidon Playground, walking in the middle of the wide beach, when a man with a ponytail appeared on the boardwalk and matched their progress. He looked enough like one of the thugs from the park that night near Popov's place to put Grigg on high alert.

Someone finally started watching the beach.

They were four blocks from the Surf Avenue gate. Grigg turned to check, kept doing so. Katia noticed. A block later, the guy dropped straight off the boardwalk and jogged in their direction.

"Run!" he whispered.
Katia took off.

CHAPTER 31

Sunday, October 9, 2016

Grigg's right foot, then his left sunk into the sand as he tried to sprint away. He needed several steps to gain traction on the loose surface.

Katia, with two good legs, sped ahead of him, while their pursuer moved at a jog. Long, easy strides. He didn't look worried. Good news: He hadn't pulled a gun. Yet.

Two of the blocks covered, Katia, running thirty yards ahead of Grigg, visibly slowed. Their pursuer had cut the distance by about the same amount. Grigg didn't like the math. He winced at a cramp in his left side. He waved at her to go on.

Katia turned up West 37th and stopped before reaching the Surf Avenue gatehouse.

"Go in!" His breathless words were gasps that didn't carry.

The bad guy was ten yards away as Grigg made the turn for the gate. He strained to cover the last twenty feet as the thug got closer.

Grigg lurched like a drunk.

Closer.

He reached Katia and pulled her up to the booth's window.

Panting hard—never helpful when talking to cops—he told the officer in the box that Detective Furillo had left their names.

"Yeah, he's here. Something wrong?"

"No, just jogging on the beach."

The gate lifted.

The bad guy stayed on the sidewalk and watched.

Grigg and Katia passed the Sea Gate Police Department, a rambling building that looked like two houses stuck together. Probably because it was. The restaurant was conveniently located next door, a part of the Sea Gate Beach Club.

Their pursuer strolled away from the gate, crossed the street, and stopped. He lit a cigarette. He might have been waiting for a bus—if there were a bus stop. He was making no bones about watching them. Waiting for them. Inside the restaurant, Furillo sat at a corner table with a window view of the gate and the street and a mug of coffee in front of him. "Take a seat."

Grigg and Katia settled in chairs across from the detective. Grigg huffed to catch his breath.

"What the fuck is going on?" the detective said.

"Right this minute, the SVR—the Russian secret service—is on us. I'm pretty sure. He's right across the street."

"What makes you think he's SVR?"

"Something Freddy Popov told me. The guy who

chased us looks like one of the thugs who were at Freddy's apartment."

"Why you?"

"They may think I have something."

"Do you?"

"I might."

"What the fuck does that mean?"

"I'm not sure if I do."

Furillo finished his coffee and ordered a second. "You *broke* into the container?"

"Seemed like the only plan at the time."

"You're nuts, pal." Furillo frowned and blinked hard like he'd developed a tic. "All this spy shit. I'm not buying it. In my career taking killers off the street, I learned people don't get dead as a result of complicated plans. It's usually something simple. Love. Money. Fury. Fury over love or money. You're selling an international conspiracy based on guesses. I don't even know what to make of it. How does it fit in?"

"I don't know. It's one of the jokers."

"You got a deck full of jokers."

Grigg looked into the water he'd half finished.

Maybe Furillo isn't the one to help us. Maybe we're on our own.

"Let's see what your friend out there has to say about all this *intrigue*." Furillo picked up his hand-held radio from the table. "204 to Gate 1."

"Go ahead 204."

"See the guy standing across the street from you?"

"10-4."

"Ask him to come into Sea Gate Foods for a chat. *No* isn't an option."

"10-4."

Two officers crossed the street. Grigg expected the man to take off; he was wrong. He stood his ground. The cops forced him to assume the position, searched him, held up some kind of gun, checked his ID, and handed that back.

The three of them walked into the restaurant.

"Detective, we took a Glock 43 off him," said the shorter uniformed officer. "No permit."

"Surprise, surprise. How very up to date. Lock it in the station. I'll think about charges."

"We also—"

"I'll take it from here."

The uniforms retreated slowly. They clearly wanted to say more.

"Have a seat."

Aside from the ponytail, the man's distinguishing characteristic was the left side of his face: it had suffered a landslide, making his head appear to tilt in that direction. Grigg couldn't tell if it was a birth defect or the result of an injury. He knew which way he'd bet. He was now almost certain this was the goon who'd held him up against the ladder in the playground. The man slowly lowered himself into the chair at the end of table around the corner from Grigg. He wore a purple button-down shirt, black sport jacket, and black slacks.

"What are you doing at our little end of Coney Island?"

"I am tourist."

The Russian was spring-loaded. Ready to move in an instant.

"With a shiny new Glock 43?"

"Nervous tourist."

"Yeah, that's bullshit. Let me see your ID." Without hesitation, the man pulled out a burgundy passport. Furillo's bushy eyebrows slipped up his forehead. He glanced at Grigg, turned to the Russian. "Well, Vladimir I-can't-pronounce-your-fucking-last-name, you seem to be here on a Russian diplomatic passport."

"No seem. You understand then my cooperation is totally voluntary. I may depart at any time."

"We've got a lot of bad shit going on around here right now. *Seems* by Russians. By Russians from Russia. Maybe by you?"

"No. Not me."

"What's your job at the embassy?"

"Cultural attaché."

"Isn't that the job they give to spies?" Katia asked.

"There are many important cultural exchanges going on between our two countries."

Furillo laughed, loud and cheerful.

Katia pushed away her half-finished mug of coffee. "Why did you come after us?"

Vladimir turned toward Grigg instead. His eyes, the dark blue of the ocean during late afternoon, vibrated slightly.

"*If* I did follow you, I could have picked you up when you left 60th Precinct early Sunday morning. *If* I did, I might want to wait to see who you meet after. Which it seems is your woman and detective here. All ifs, of course. Possibilities."

"I'm not anyone's woman, Vladimir," Katia said. Then something in Russian.

Furillo banged the table. "Let's keep this in English."

"I only told him to go fuck himself." A breezy smile. "There's worse I could say to this secret policeman's errand boy."

The look Vladimir gave Katia was not breezy. More a glower.

"Everything you described is harassment," said Furillo, slamming the table again. "All of it."

"For which I'm covered under diplomatic immunity."

"Did you get me kicked loose by the cops?" Grigg said.

The man's twisted face creased into a smile. "Such an imagination."

Grigg was only getting one shot at this guy. He didn't expect to hear anything straight. But there might be something true in the lies. Collect as much disinformation as possible and sort the leads from the shit. *Witnesses, witnesses, witnesses.*

"Are you working with Joe the Borscht?"

"No."

"Is he working with someone else?"

"I'm afraid I can't say."

"How about bone records—bones," Katia said. "What do you know about them?"

"Bone records?" He tipped his head in what looked like actual ignorance.

"Pirated music recorded on old X-rays in the Soviet Union in the fifties and sixties." More Russian talk. Then, "The way people listened to black-market Western music back then."

A small smile. "I have heard old people talk of such things. Much simpler times. Simpler crimes."

"Simple, huh?" Grigg said. "Have you heard of those records being sent to people—before they were shot dead? And records being left at the murder scenes? One case in Moscow, one here. Both in the last eight months. They're a death sentence nowadays."

"I'm sorry. Whatever you may think I am, I have nothing to do with local policing like your detective here. That is for Moscow Police Department. Formally called Main Directorate of Internal Affairs."

"His father was killed," said Katia, voice firm, eyes locked. "Then I received one. We want to know what is going on and who's doing it."

"No one I know. That is truth."

"Because nothing else is?" Furillo tossed the passport back at him. "You're talkative enough. What are you here for? Must be something, since the usual procedure is to clam up with the police, claim immunity, and walk away sly and happy."

"Property of ours has gone missing. I need to get it

back. I will do whatever I have to, including sit down and have nice cup of coffee with you, which—you are right—is strange assignment for me."

"For a member of the SVR?" Grigg said.

"As I explained, I am cultural attaché."

"Yeah, you keep fucking saying that." Furillo waved for another refill. "Would this missing property be a shipping container?"

"A container with precious *cultural* items."

"Precious gold and precious stacks of U.S. currency," Grigg said. "Did Freddy Popov get it?"

"Popov wanted to steal it from its owner, but he missed his opportunity."

"Russia isn't the owner?"

"No, a third party who was in dispute with Russian state."

"You're trying to do *police work* on U.S. soil," said Furillo. "The immunity of Christ Jesus won't protect you if we come down on you for that."

"Perhaps you misunderstand. We already have container. We worked out our differences with owner. Business is done differently in our country."

Grigg's jaw tightened, muscles pulsing. The game was coming to its last hand, and he'd always had a terrible poker face. *Try to rattle him.* "More like the mafia does business?"

"I had not met so many criminals until I came to what you call Little Odessa."

"That's because you call them the *avtoritet*. Businessmen and crooks are one and the same."

"Enough with words." He waved his hand as if to swat Grigg's away. "To get to point, we have this container, but it is missing certain items. We have received intelligence that he knows where they are." Vladimir pointed at Grigg, who had to force himself not to move his hand onto his messenger bag. "We know that Grigg Orlov and Charlotte Carter were the only ones to enter container. We don't know if either gave items to other associates. That's why we're following you. The shooting of Carter on Friday night made things complicated, too complicated. My boss's patience is at an end."

"Is Grigg right?" There was an urgent look on Furillo's face. "The container is loaded with cash and gold?"

"There are items in container that are still owned by person who shipped. Is not my decision what happens to them. I'm responsible for what's missing."

Play the hand.

"Why are *these* so important?" Grigg pulled out one of the flash drives.

Vladimir's dark blues eyes locked on the silver rectangle. "You'd be smart to turn those over."

"They're what you're looking for, right?" Grigg knew not to say anything about the slips with the names inside the nested dolls. "Do you know why?"

"Is not my job to know. Is my job to get."

The Russian was fast, grabbing Grigg's arm as the coiled springs released. He yanked Grigg in front of him as a shield.

Katia gasped.

Furillo smiled like nothing was wrong. He pulled his semi from his shoulder holster. "I know you secret agents got tricks, but I've got a gun, we've got yours, and you're next to a fucking police station."

In the time Furillo spoke the sentence, Vladimir ducked low behind Grigg-as-shield and dragged him across the restaurant to the door opposite police HQ. With his hands on Grigg's neck and arm, he backed the door open. "Do anything but walk with me and I'll snap your neck." He squeezed—iron fingers digging into the muscle—to show he could.

As the door closed, Grigg heard Katia. "Do something! He's getting away!"

Grigg didn't panic. He expected to be surrounded by armed police in seconds. They ducked under the gate and walked up West 37th Street.

No one followed. No one did anything.

CHAPTER 32

Sunday, October 9, 2016

Vladimir forced Grigg to turn onto Mermaid Avenue, which was smart, because it kept them from passing the next gate at Neptune.

What the fuck is Furillo up to?

"No one comes. Are your friends your friends?"

"They're figuring the best way to nail you."

"What's wrong with your leg?"

"Bad knee."

Vladimir's phone rang. He spoke briefly to the caller, but the only word Grigg understood was *da*.

Row houses lined Mermaid Avenue for the first few blocks, followed by a strip of one-story shops.

Vladimir pushed him into an alley between the Avenue Deli and a line of newish-looking, two-level houses with bars on every window. He straight-armed Grigg against the dull green plastic siding of the last house and stood in front of him.

"Waiting for our ride?"

Vlad didn't answer.

Grigg watched for his captor to relax his guard, even a little. Grigg was an amateur, small in size and damaged—easy to underestimate. He counted on that. These weeks had changed him. Vlad no longer had a gun, but he had two good legs. From the corner of his eye, Grigg saw an open dumpster.

"Do you like Coney Island?"

"Cheap and tacky place. I don't understand popularity."

That made the Russian an enemy for life.

The spy pulled out a pack of Marlboros.

The cue for Grigg to move.

As Vlad flicked his Bic and brought up the flame, Grigg drove his heel into the toe of Vlad's dress shoe once, then stomped on it a second time. The Russian yelled. Grigg lunged for the dumpster, pulled out a short piece of lumber, and swung for Vlad's head. Connected. The agent bent over, grabbing at his scalp with a yelp.

Grigg ripped away his messenger bag, even though the slips with the names were in his wallet. Better no one knew he'd discovered the drives' real secret.

Out of the alley, he pushed open a door and plunged into the deli.

"Quick, call the police. There's someone after me."

"We don't want no trouble," said the Chinese American man behind the counter. "Take it somewhere else."

"You've got to help me. This guy's a killer. Russian. Just call."

"You need to go!"

Running out of time.

He hustled down the single aisle of household goods, grabbed two aerosol cans, and hunched down by the candy rack next to the front door.

It swung open.

Grigg counted off two beats, started rising—and dropped back again when a blue-haired old lady passed his position.

"What are you up to?" she asked. "Ben, what's going on in here?"

Vlad came right behind her, blood streaming down the collapsed side of his face, wobbling to one side like a drunk, but a drunk with a knife.

How'd the cops miss that?

"I've called the police on both of you."

Really? Now?

Vladimir scanned the store in front of him, missing Grigg at first, then spotting him. He lunged forward. At the same time, Grigg extended his arm and pressed the button on the first aerosol. It was carpet cleaner. White foam covered Vladimir's eyes. He screeched, using his weaponless hand to wipe the foam away and waving the knife in dangerous patterns. The serrated blade passed inches from Grigg's shoulder, then his face.

Grigg bobbed back, darted in, and hit the button on the Lysol can. Vladimir screamed louder.

Grigg exited the Avenue Deli.

He went as fast he could—still too slow, always too slow—toward the next cross street, West 32nd. If he rounded the corner, he could get lost in the little winding streets that wrapped around a public housing project before Vlad reached him. Grigg wheel-stepped down the sidewalk, swinging his right leg out as far as he could, every other footfall igniting the agony in his bad knee.

He made the corner.

A hand grabbed him from behind, spun him, and Vladimir punched him in the face. Before Grigg could get up, the Russian lifted him to his feet and started choking him. One of Vladimir's eyes was swollen shut. Grigg clutched at the strong hands on his throat, getting nowhere. It was like trying to bend iron.

The need in his lungs rose to pressure, rose to pain.

He became woozy … spinning … dropping out for good.

A car skidded to the curb, capturing Grigg's last bit of attention. Furillo opened the door, got out, and aimed his Glock over the roof.

"Let him go, asshole, or I air you out. Do it now!"

Grigg dropped to the sidewalk, coughing and massaging his neck. Vladimir kicked him.

"Shit, Mr. Super Spy, you let him do *that* to you?"

Grigg's vision cleared as he inhaled in gulping gasps. The skin of his neck stung like an eight-hours-with-no-SPF sunburn.

"Get over here!" Furillo kept his gun on Vladimir. Katia was in the back seat of the unmarked Ford SUV. "C'mon, now!"

Why's he yelling at me?

Grigg was halfway to the car when a Mercedes G Wagon heading toward them pulled across the lane and stopped, facing Furillo's vehicle bumper to bumper. Two men sprang out of the Merc, both with pistols pointed at Furillo. A third stayed behind the wheel.

"You don't wanna go shooting cops," Furillo called out. "That's an entirely un-secret crime, Secret Agent Men. Bad for business. Your passports won't cover it."

"We heard our friend was in trouble," said the Russian on the passenger side, tall and bald. "We came to help."

Again, the night in the playground flashed from memory. This guy could be the leader who did the killing.

"Oh, he's in trouble? Seems we have something you want. Some flash drives?"

Grigg stopped next to the SUV. He whispered loudly: "Furillo, what are you doing? We already know they want them. Get us out of here!"

"Shut the fuck up!" Furillo yelled at Grigg but kept his eyes on the Russians.

"You should take your own advice," said Baldy. "The more you talk, the less likely you will stay healthy."

Furillo clicked his radio and spoke: "Unit 204, 11-99 at Mermaid and West 32nd Street. Also advise NYPD." He clicked off. "We've got a minute or so to cut a deal or we're all going to be talking to the Sea Gate police and officers from the Six-Oh. You want this secret stuff? I want what you recovered from the container. The cash, the gold, all of it."

"I would need to consult—"

"You don't have time to consult. Grigg, get in the back *now*." This time Furillo briefly pointed the gun at Grigg, who did as he was told.

Sirens came from the direction of Sea Gate.

"The spy shit for the dough. Make up your fucking mind."

"Orlov?"

"I'll trade him too. With the woman. In fact, I insist."

Katia turned to Grigg. He shook his head. Mouthed, "No clue."

"Follow us," said Baldy.

Furillo slid behind the wheel as the Mercedes did a three-point. He keyed the mike. "Unit 204 is now 10-26 at this location."

"10-4. You okay, detective?"

"False report. All under control."

Grigg looked at Katia. They needed an escape plan. She flicked her eyes outside. She understood.

Furillo followed the G Wagon out of the neighborhood, through Sheepshead Bay, and merged onto the Belt Parkway heading east. Traffic flowed easily, the rush hour over, and a string of well-spaced taillights moved ahead of them along the edge of Brooklyn toward Queens. Grigg tried a couple more questions. He got profanity-laced non-answers and finally the gun pushed into his face.

Tick-tick-tick-tick.

His father's watch read 6:15 p.m.

They exited the highway at Flatbush Avenue and drove about a mile along the edge of Floyd Bennett Field. Grigg knew the old airport well. A big X formed the out-of-use runways; the concrete was cracked, broken, and weed-infested like out of a dystopian movie. The field was now part of a nearby national recreation area.

"Oh God." Katia stared at her phone. Her hand started shaking. Grigg steadied it to read the story from the *Brooklyn Eagle's* website:

> Charlotte Carter, the squatter who was involved in a three-way gunfight in a Neptune Avenue apartment, died Saturday night, according to Coney Island Hospital.

Furillo reached back and ripped the phone out of their cupped hands. "Give me yours too."

"The fucking Russian took it, asshole."

"Maybe he'll give it back when he sees you."

Furillo entered Floyd Bennett's main gate and followed the Russians around the sports center. They drove past the cricket field used by people from the Caribbean, Pakistan, and India and onto one of the runways. Furillo's SUV bumped and rattled over cracks. They kept going to the far side of the huge airfield, as far as you could get from the buildings, heading toward an area of dark woods. Furillo had to weave around concrete construction barriers placed without pattern, though there was no evidence of work being done.

The G Wagon veered off the runway.

"All right, fuckers." Furillo held up the gun with his right hand and steered with the left.

He followed, driving on a dirt track at least one hundred feet into the woods, where a familiar shipping container stood in a clearing like it had dropped from the sky.

CHAPTER 33

Sunday, October 9, 2016

Furillo threw the SUV into reverse, spun it around, and drove back toward the airfield, not stopping until he was parked on the other side of the runway that ran nearest the woods. He killed the lights and left the engine running.

"Get out," he told Grigg.

"Why?"

"You're going to go in there and get the cash, as much as you can carry." He took the messenger bag off the car seat. "Tell them I'm watching from a nice, safe distance." He climbed out, opened the back, and pulled out an AR-15 with a scope. "With this and their flash drives. They'll get some drives when I get the money." He held out the messenger bag.

Grigg stared at the bag. He couldn't help himself. "What about Carmichael?"

"Carmichael?" He snickered mean and small. "He tried to do some good and look where it got him. He told me about the container when he started helping you. Russian mobsters. Shipping container. Odds on, that thing wasn't going to be stuffed with Hanes V-necks from China. And I was fucking right. I just had to bide my time until the container was off the docks and you led me to it. Finally, you're right where I need you."

"You didn't give a shit about Carmichael." Grigg was talking to himself, but Furillo answered anyway, hatred in his voice.

"You're a fucking genius. I'm the one who set up the goddamn boy scout. Internal affairs was getting too close to me back in Bed-Stuy. Needed to throw them off, so Carmichael got busted with some drugs I was moving. Weeks ago, he told me about the container. If it hadn't turned up, you and I would never have met. Walk straight there and back. You're in the crossfire."

"What else is new?"

With the barrel of the AR-15, Furillo pushed Grigg in the direction of the trees.

The worst part of the walk was Grigg's slow realization that he had no way to escape a double-crosser—the guy he'd trusted—and four Russian agents. Furillo had Katia in the car, while the Russians all had their guns trained on Grigg when he approached the Mercedes and the container. He was furious with his own stupidity. Conned by a dirty cop who was going to turn them over to these assholes. He was the amateur. The idiot. He strained to use the anger to focus on what he saw, on what he heard to find a way out of the trap he'd walked into. Because, yeah, he was the amateur, but he'd changed in so many ways since that August night.

"He wants the cash," Grigg told the Russians. "He's watching from a safe distance with a semi-automatic rifle."

"What do we get?" said Baldy.

"Some of the drives when he gets the money."

Baldy frowned and spoke in Russian. Grigg's wallet with the slips weighed heavy in his pocket. If he was correct about the names, everything they wanted was in his billfold. The drives weren't going to do it for them—assuming these Russians knew what they contained.

One of them handed a package of bills to Grigg.

"Tell the cop this is his taste. You come back with our items, or we come out with guns. Weapons are no problem for us."

With Katia and me in the middle.

Grigg returned with half of the drives—the wrapped hundreds had excited Furillo—which satisfied Baldy enough to give him three more bundles of bills. The third trip found him struggling to lug two gold bars that weighed more than fifty pounds together. Even if the SVR agents didn't know about the slips and their names, Grigg worried about his fourth trip. That was when they'd realize that one of the drives, the one he'd broken, was missing. That they had fifteen instead of sixteen. He was dragging his left foot by the time he got to Furillo, whose eyes lit with fire when the moon reflected on the bullion.

"Clock's ticking." Furillo jingled the remaining drives in his hand, then seemed to weigh his options aloud. "They must have called in more people by now. Don't like being out in the open this long. Nothing worse than getting greedy when you're ahead."

He opened Katia's door. "Get out. Both of you walk slowly to the woods."

"With what?" Grigg said.

"Big smiles."

"They're not going to like that."

"They already don't like you, so I don't think that will change things." He turned toward the SUV. "This last set's my insurance. Tell them that for me, won't you?"

Grigg glared at the lying shit with his AR-15; Furillo's smile was tight. Grigg took Katia's hand and turned toward the gap in the woods he knew well. After three steps, flash-crack, flash-crack—the light faster than the booming sounds that followed.

"Down!" Katia pulled him to the tarmac. A spiderweb of cracks appeared in the window she had been sitting behind. Furillo dashed to the other side of the SUV and started firing from the rear corner.

The Russians were shooting from two places in the trees to the right. *They must have run out of patience. Or they were always going to take Furillo out and take everything. Well, they can have the shithead.*

Katia squeezed his hand hard. He had to do something before they died in this blazing crossfire.

Katia figured it out before him. "The construction barriers. We need to crawl about twenty feet left first. Stay as low as possible."

She started over the rough pavement, and Grigg followed. He got it. They needed to get out of sight while Furillo and the Russians focused on each other. Hand, knee, hand, knee. The crackle of weapons.

Finally, they were lined up with one of the concrete barriers out on the runway parallel to the woods. The break in the trees was now on their right and the Russians who were shooting even farther away in that direction.

"You go first," he said. "Just crouch low and run for that barrier. Don't look up. Don't stop. Don't wait for me."

Katia followed his instructions and was hunched against the cement, breathing normally, when Grigg finally got there panting.

"You doing all right?" Grigg said.

"So far. What now?"

"We go into the woods."

"The Russians are in the woods."

"Yeah, and they're going to come out to get Furillo. They have him outnumbered. The moon is out, the night's clear, and there's more light coming from the buildings behind. We need the darkness under the trees. We get caught, and the Russians will shoot us for knowing too much. We'll work our way through the woods to Flatbush Avenue and get away. See the barrier sitting at an angle on the other side of the runway?"

"Yeah."

"Go for that. Then we make for the trees."

Katia looked at him, hesitating, then threw one leg and then the other over the barrier and ran. The gunfire increased. More Russians in the fight? As long as they shot at Furillo.

He crossed the no man's land as quickly as he could, then peered at the trees from this final concrete protection. Still no shooting from this side of the woods. The last distance was shorter than all the others, but somehow stretched out before him because they were closer to the line of fire to their right. When would the Russians make their charge?

Think too much, and you'll end up dead against this barrier.

"Ready?"

Katia didn't answer, instead took off and disappeared into the dark of the trees in front of him. Halfway across the grass, Grigg's foot caught on something unseen, sending him crashing to the ground. He scrambled to his feet—damaged knee burning—and couldn't decide which gap Katia had shot through. He limped toward his best guess, putting his back to a big tree once inside the woods.

He peered into the deep darkness that he'd wanted for cover but now cursed. He was going to lose Katia. He took slow steps. Strained to see something other than the darker shapes of trees. *Getting separated cannot happen.* A snap to his left. He moved toward the sound, saw a shadow moving past a bush, and hurried for it.

A hand fell on his shoulder from behind the nearest trunk as two fingers crossed his lips. Before he could cry out, Katia pulled him behind the tree. Her lips so close to his ear that he could feel them moving, in a bare whisper, she said, "It's one of them."

The Russian was going for Furillo's left flank. That

made three of the four SVR agents in the fight—that he could be sure of. Problem was, the Russians were on both sides of them now. They couldn't head left for the avenue yet. Grigg pointed straight into the forest and whispered one word: "Careful."

They slipped from tree to tree. Grigg had no sense of where he was. As a result, it was no surprise that they ended up at the edge of the clearing looking in at the G Wagon and the container. The gunfire ceased. That could only mean one thing. Furillo was dead. Three of the four Russians were behind them now, at least for the moment. One camping lantern glowed yellow in front of the SUV, while the moonlight made everything in the clearing visible and the shadows blacker. No sign of the fourth man. Maybe he'd joined in the fight. Grigg knew he had to take that chance. There was no time. They had to get far the fuck away from there, fast. The Russians were going to come back. They'd want the two witnesses dead. Limping through the woods wouldn't cut it.

"I'm going for the SUV. Wait here. I'll signal."

Katia nodded firmly, clearly agreeing that it would be better to drive than run from the gunmen.

He moved through high, dead grass to where the plants had been pounded down by human activity, checking from side to side as he approached the Mercedes. There was a gap of about ten feet between the vehicle and the container behind it. Someone could be crouched in that space. He checked. No one. He opened the door, slid in, and reached for the keys. A button? *Right, you idiot. Keyless ignition.*

He'd hadn't been in many new cars. He caught sight of the fob in one of the cupholders and pushed the start button. Nothing. He pressed the brake and hit the button again. The engine hummed. He waved to Katia, who ran to the passenger side. As her door closed, his opened, and he was yanked from the G Wagon and thrown to the ground, landing on his bad knee. Sizzling pain shot from the joint to his skull. He gasped.

Vladimir stood over him. "Boss would not be happy if I killed you. Yet. I will pound you to death when he gets back."

On his hands and knees, Grigg found his voice: "Katia, go! Get out of here."

Vladimir lunged in through the driver's side and pulled Katia across both seats as she yelled obscenities and kicked. He slapped her hard—"That's for rudeness earlier"—and she dropped on the ground next to Grigg.

"Get up."

Vladimir aimed a semi-automatic rifle with a banana clip.

"I said, get up."

When Grigg and Katia were on their feet, he waved them around the back of the SUV toward the container.

"Shit, not again," Grigg said. "I've already been locked in that thing once."

Needed Charlotte to get me out. She's gone. Forever gone. I keep getting it wrong.

"Shut your fucking mouth."

"Been hearing that a lot today."

The container's doors were unlocked and open. Of course, to feed Furillo's greed, the greed that got him killed.

"Get in."

Katia looked back once and stepped into pitch black. Vladimir was courteous enough to shove Grigg hard so he landed on cold metal. His bad knee raised further serious objections to the abuse, while his hands burned from sliding across the steel. The doors slammed shut with metallic finality.

"Would not get comfortable," Vladimir called from the other side. "We'll be moving out soon. Well … you won't."

Laughter as he walked away from the door.

Katia's hands felt for him. "Move over here by the wall."

"No, down to the end. It's not so cold leaning against the tubs, if they're still here. I learned that the first time."

They were there.

A chill colder than the metal floor settled in his stomach. Fear raced through his veins like ice, threatening to freeze him where he was. The anger evaporated. He hadn't found an escape—he'd put them in a worse trap instead.

Don't go there. Check on Katia.

"How's your face?" he said. "He hit you hard."

"Stings. I'm fine, just pissed off. Fucking Russian men."

"Close your eyes. It'll be bright." She did. He clicked on the mini flash on his keychain. He examined a nasty red welt on her cheek. "No broken skin. A bad bruise for a few days." He kissed the other cheek.

Talk like there's a future. Maybe you'll believe it too.

So cold.

"What do we do?" Their situation was sinking in.

"Baldy will want to talk to me, especially if he knows about the names. With all the gunfire, they're gonna have to leave the container behind and get out of here fast. We'll look for any opening."

"You got the jump on Vladimir before. He underestimated you. And they don't know I'm trained. He caught me off guard in the truck. I'll take the first shot. You improvise."

An indistinct noise from outside the box.

Grigg pressed his ear to the steel wall, wincing at the prickling sting of the cold. He strained to make out what was being said. The sound moved closer. Voices, but they wouldn't resolve into words.

He returned to Katia. "Sounds like they're back."

As the right door started to swing open, gunfire erupted.

CHAPTER 34

Sunday, October 9 – Monday, October 10, 2016

Grigg threw up his hands defensively, like they'd stop bullets. He brought them down when he realized the shooting wasn't coming from the doorway. The silhouette that had partly opened the door disappeared, leaving it ajar. A one-foot stripe of trees in the moonlight. The Russians outside yelled in Russian.

"What the hell?" said Katia.

"I don't know," said Grigg. "Can't be Furillo. They must have killed him."

A ping sounded near the front of the container.

"Lie flat. Whoever's shooting, they must be aiming at the Russians—and the container's behind them."

Katia lay with her hands over her head. Grigg shifted tubs from the back to create a second wall along the inside of the metal skin that faced the clearing. Two more dings echoed. He threw the last ones in place.

He flattened next to Katia. The weapons fire was louder now, the bullets hitting rapidly.

"We need to move," Katia said.

"Need to know what we're stepping into. The Russians will shoot us. Whoever's attacking could do the same."

A circle of light appeared near the top of the wall in the middle of the container as a round passed through.

"They're shooting high at least." The effort at sounding brave didn't. He wanted to do what Katia suggested and fly out of this steel hell. He imagined an aerial view of the clearing, the container, the SUV, the dirt track in from the airfield. He convinced himself he saw an escape route that wasn't pure panic. "If we work our way to the open door on our stomachs, we can slide around to the back side of the container and take off deeper into the woods without being seen."

"Works for me. Gotta get out of this."

"As long as no one's near the door."

"We'll deal with it." She sounded convinced.

They scooched along, then froze halfway when the container took three quick hits. As they started crawling even faster, a scream echoed, and the sound of gunfire decreased. One combatant down? Who were they up against? The gunfire rose, then dropped again. No scream this time. Reloading?

He could hear Katia's breathing, quick and pressured. With a third of the way to go, he repeated to himself they were safe on the floor. The litany kept him moving.

As they got to the doorway, the guns went silent.

"Let's go," he whispered.

Grigg rose to slide around to the back. A light blinded him.

He used one hand to shield his eyes.

"Put your hands up." American accent.

Grigg and Katia did as they were instructed.

"I told you there were people more dangerous than Freddy Popov."

"Agent Carlyle?"

The light dropped, and Carlyle was revealed in his FBI windbreaker. Red and blue flashing lights washed over him and the grass and trees around.

"C'mon, get out of that thing."

Outside, two big black SUVs with strobing lights stood at the entrance to the clearing, while an ambulance was pulling in from Floyd Bennett Field. Vladimir lay spread across the hood of the Merc. Grigg wasn't sure if the ambulance would be of much help. Based on the blood pooling on the black steel, it didn't seem so. Another man lay flat on his stomach, and two, including Baldy, were being shoved into one of the SUVs by men in the same FBI windbreakers. A sedan sat at the opening into the trees. Carlyle led them to that vehicle, had them get in, and drove off with lights flashing. He used the two runways to get off the airfield by the quickest route, veered onto a road out of the complex, and navigated to the Belt Parkway.

"Did someone call in the gunfight?" Katia asked.

"We're not the NYPD. We've been watching the container for a long time. We'll go over what *you* were doing there at the office."

Grigg sat in the same office-cum-interrogation room

as before, waiting for an hour and a half while a special agent sat outside the door. Through an interior window, he could see Katia sitting in a similar office across the hall.

Carlyle came in, sat, and went through the same setup procedure. Folded out the extra screen on the laptop. Put down the digital recorder.

"Sorry to keep you waiting. That's some crime scene. What the hell were you doing out there?"

"Held captive."

"I figured that out using my finally honed investigative skills. How'd you get there?"

Grigg folded his arms. "I'm not telling you anything until I know what's going on around here."

"Now why would I tell you that? The last time you were here you didn't mention anything about the container. We know you broke into the thing."

Jesus, how many people were watching that damned box?

"I've already got charges I can put on you. Be good to cooperate."

Grigg let go an exhausted sigh. Too many players. Too many chess boards. And he so hated chess, ever not the good Russian. "We ended up at Floyd Bennett because we were kidnapped by a Sea Gate cop named Furillo."

"It's going to be hard for him to confirm that. He's dead."

"Did you find gold bars and bundles of cash in his car? He got it from the Russians."

"All the loot was in the G Wagon."

"The Russians took it back, then. Furillo sent us to them so he could get away. The gunfight started. We tried to escape but were caught. One of them—Vladimir—locked us in the container."

"Furillo went there for the loot?"

Grigg nodded. "Made me play go-between."

"What were the Russians getting?"

Here was Grigg's endgame. "C'mon. Tell *me* something for what you're getting. Who owns that goddamn container?"

Carlyle spread his hands. "We don't know."

"You're tracking it and you don't fucking know? Not Freddy Popov, right?"

"No. He was planning to hit the thing. He told us you knew that."

"You got him?"

"Thanks for the tip. He's talking. A lot. Hoping for a deal. He claims he was going to steal everything in the container as revenge for the murder of his father."

"So, the container *is* linked to the killer." Grigg paused as the chessboards multiplied and started spinning. "Whoever owned what's inside is the same person who killed my dad. If Freddy was after revenge, then he knows who did the bone record killings."

"We believe so. He refuses to give up that name. Says the owner has long arms. Wants us to provide protection."

"Long arms that reach all the way inside the FBI?"

"I doubt that, though Freddy seems to believe it."

"I still don't get why you need him to find the owner.

How could you be staking out a container and not know whose it is?"

"Five months ago, we received intel that an unnamed Russian with money and other resources was going to move funds into the U.S. to expand their criminal operations."

"The *avtoritet* sort of Russian?"

Carlyle gave a curt nod. "Or maybe farther up the food chain. An oligarch into organized crime."

"Aren't they all?"

"Pretty much. Like I said, no name. We were just given the number of the container. A worrying sort of tip. Could be bait for a trap. Disinformation. A distraction. The box is owned by a shell corporation inside of a shell corporation inside of a Grand Caymans partnership."

Grigg envisioned yet another Russian nesting doll: the shipping container hidden within a set of larger and larger boxes constructed of legal documents.

"We put surveillance on it when it got here. For reasons we don't yet understand, the SVR was after the same container. In fact, we only learned that angle recently when they stole it and moved it to Brooklyn. We were going to let it play out, see how many of them we could reel in. Then our stakeout reported tonight's fireworks, and we had to move. We're no closer to the owner, and we don't understand his relationship with the SVR cell that took the box from him. If indeed it was theft. But," he looked up from the screens, "you're the one sitting here. I don't get how you're tied up in this."

"All I've been trying to do is solve my father's murder. Furillo was willing to help. Or I thought he was. As for Freddy ... His father Nikolai changed his last name from Voronin. Freddy tell you that?" Carlyle nodded. "Good. Well, Nikolai Voronin and my father were boyhood friends. They were both murdered recently after receiving bone records. The other two members of their friend group from St. Petersburg are dead, one long dead. Voronin's older brother Viktor died in a Soviet work camp decades ago, and the other friend, Mikhail Sokolov, passed away in 2011. *But* ... Sokolov's daughter, my friend Katia in the other room," Grigg indicated her with his head, "was sent a bone record on Sunday. A death warrant. If the container's owned by the killer—we need to know who the fuck that is to save her."

"How about this idea? Tell it all to the cops, rather than upending a major FBI operation."

"Are you kidding? You saw how Furillo helped us. And the NYPD isn't trying to solve my dad's killing. Furillo claimed someone was bribing the detectives at the 60th Precinct."

"You believe him now?"

"I know this much. A mobster named Joe the Borscht showed up when I told one of those cops I was meeting my source about the bribery. Today, the cops cut me loose after a friend was murdered Friday night. They found me with her, a dead assailant, and three guns ... And I get sprung? Someone *wanted* me back on the street. I'm guessing it was the SVR, since they're the ones who came after me."

"Or Furillo. You were his lead to the container. That's for internal affairs, if they care about a dead dirty cop."

Frustration boiled up in Grigg. Carlyle was giving him the brush-off.

"Here's the deal: You're not gonna let the NYPD near anything having to do with that container. Which is linked to the killer. Which means the murder case is *yours*."

"No to the last. You're right about the rest. The container is a matter of national security."

"Yeah, I've heard that one before."

"From who?" Carlyle sounded worried.

"Movies, TV. They always say that."

"This isn't a joke."

"No, it's not. It's too fucked up for that."

"When did you first visit the container?"

"We only went once. End of last month. The twenty-ninth."

"How did you know where it was?"

"Freddy gave me the coordinates and told me to wait for his call."

"At least that matches what he told us."

"Then why the hell are you asking me?"

"Checking stories."

"Check this. The night Popov gave me the coordinates, that's the night the Russians—the SVR agents—nearly killed us in his apartment. I already told you about some of that—the gunfight in the park that no one found evidence of? When I didn't hear from Popov, Charlotte …" Grigg had to stop, take a breath. "Charlotte and I went to check the container out."

"The park shooting remains a mystery. Popov confirmed the men that night were SVR muscle. Not spies. More like weapons."

"Two were at the field. The one on the Merc, Vladimir, and the bald guy."

"Popov says he doesn't know why they're involved. He's afraid."

"Uh-huh. Of a lot. Tell me how the SVR got the container if it's owned by some secret mobster."

Carlyle shook his head. "I've told you way too much."

"Answer me and I'll tell you exactly what the SVR is after. I'll even give it to you."

"How could you do that?"

"Because I took it from the container, and the Russians came after me for it."

"You better not be shitting me."

"I am not."

"Seriously. I can keep you tied up a very long time."

Grigg shrugged indifferently, not really a bluff; Katia and he would be safe in custody, after all.

Carlyle turned from the screen, took his hands off the keyboard and looked straight at Grigg. "When the container was picked up from the terminal—for transit to its owner, we were pretty certain—the SVR hijacked it. They must have figured someone was watching—"

"Most watched container in history."

"They engineered a five-car pileup on the turnpike as a diversion. Fires. Smoke bombs and flares, the whole nine yards, while the tractor-trailer vanished up the highway. But not far enough. Another of my teams picked them up four exits north and followed them to Floyd Bennett."

Grigg nodded and began to recount the tale of the flash drives from the wooden nested dolls through his discovery of the names. He pulled out his wallet and handed the paper slips to Carlyle, who raised a hand to stop him while he donned latex gloves.

"Doubt that will help at this point."

"Never know. Paper's tough to get prints off anyway, but I'm taking no chances. How do you know these are important?"

"Like I said, they want the drives, and the slips were hidden inside them. My friend Charlotte, who was killed by the person who's hunting Katia, scanned the drives and found only a Russian rip-off of Microsoft Office."

"Interesting …" As Carlyle looked at the first, second, and third slip, his eyes went wide in an un-FBI-like way. True surprise, shock maybe. "I know these first few names. They all work in FBI counterintelligence here in New York. One's number two to my boss." He laid out the rest on the desk. "Four are out of Washington, including two senior people and two agents, and one in Chicago. The others look familiar, but I can't quite place them." He tapped on the keyboard of his laptop. "Hmm. Let me try another database …" Seconds, then minutes went by. "Nope."

"What's that mean?"

"The names I'm not sure of are classified."

"Even for an FBI agent?"

"Sure. Could be CIA, NSA, military. Hard to say without making inquiries."

"What could it be? A hit list?"

"Needs legwork. The FBI agents' identities are public enough. Could also be disinformation. Could be anything."

Grigg, who had twice checked to find Katia wasn't yet being interviewed, looked through the window again. Her smile was fake, her eyes concerned. Now sitting across from her was a man Grigg knew. Could never forget. Red hair, close-cut, same for the beard. The flat nose and wide-set eyes. Katia him knew too, from Grigg's description.

Grigg's body went to battle stations. His breathing came fast. His heart slammed inside his chest.

"Who's the agent with Katia?"

Carlyle didn't even look up. "That's Larry Miller."

Grigg ran his dry tongue against the roof of his dry mouth and spoke what he already knew. "His name's on a slip."

"Yes, it is."

Grigg made a quick and desperate calculation: Carlyle wasn't named. He'd played things straight with Grigg so far. The whole world couldn't be crooked, could it? What choice did he have?

"Miller murdered my father. He murdered Charlotte Carter."

CHAPTER 35

Monday, October 10, 2016

Carlyle arranged the slips of paper in rows on the desk. He played his own odd chess game, moving them around like he was looking for patterns. Upside down, they finished in what appeared to Grigg—based on their numbers—to be columns for the three FBI offices and the names Carlyle couldn't identify beyond the fact they were classified. His face looked like that of the victim in a mystery movie who's been told he swallowed poison right after setting down the glass.

Grigg glanced at Katia in the other room. She was listening to Miller and appeared outwardly calm, except for one jittering foot. Grigg could guess what was going on inside her head. She was the mouse trapped by the alley cat.

What was the fucker planning? Miller knew who they were. Did he want to protect his cover? He wasn't acting like he knew he'd been blown.

Grigg managed a skittish, photographic awareness—Katia, snap, Miller, snap, Carlyle, snap, slips, snap. Tingling washed across his skin. Every part of him was ready to act, move, do. The stakes were the highest; he had to win games in two offices or Katia was dead. So was he, for that matter. He knew he couldn't push Carlyle too hard, had to keep the agent on his side, give him enough time and reason to believe.

Tick-tick-tick-tick.

He had no idea how much time he had.

"None of this makes any sense." Carlyle waved his hand over the desk. "Three of these people hold top positions. Larry Miller … I've worked with him for ten years."

"I witnessed him kill my dad. I saw him go into Charlotte's apartment to kill her."

"You must be mistaken."

"Uh, that's definitely not possible. You don't mistake who shot your father."

Carlyle's dark eyes dropped, ran the columns quickly, then looked at Grigg. The skin on Carlyle's face was tight, his jaw muscles clenched. "There is one pattern here." He waved a hand over the paper slips. "Russia. Every one of the bureau people works on Russia. Have for a while."

"Working on what, exactly? Stray shipping containers? Interference in elections? Or something else?"

"I can't tell you assignments. That's—"

"A matter of national security. I know."

He took a glance at Katia. She appeared to be answering a question. She was talking, wearing her serious paralegal face. Just-the-facts, sir.

Keep it like that, Katia. Don't give away what you must have guessed.

"I'm serious, Special Agent Carlyle. You need to get Katia out of there."

"I have to check something," Carlyle said almost absently, focusing on the laptop. "I may have a way of identifying the non-FBI names."

He put his latex-covered index finger on one of the slips, slid it closer to the laptop and started typing. It was happening in slow motion. He'd just finished doing the same with the second when his phone rang.

"This is Carlyle … yes, of course I'll hold." He sat up straight. A long pause. "Yes, sir. I, uh, got the names as part of an investigation into Russian mob activity … No, I had no idea about his position. I was trying to—Yes, I'll explain from the beginning."

Carlyle started to recount in precise detail the story of the container, the flash drives, and the little pieces of paper. Slower slow-motion.

This is taking too long. No way I can get her out of there on my own. Miller draws down on my "escape attempt": game over.

When Carlyle was done, he listened to the person at the other end of the line.

Katia was still talking. Miller leaned in toward her, staring into her eyes, and she edged back. A sign of fear.

Carlyle, still on the phone, responded with short sentences to questions from the important person on the line. For the first time in two meetings, the agent looked confused.

Miller stood up and led Katia out of the office to the

elevators in the middle of the one hallway that ran the length of the building.

Fuck.

Grigg was out of his seat, Carlyle's "Wait!" trailing behind. As soon as he hit the hallway, he forced a big smile, spread his hands wide, exaggerated the limp—anything to be nonthreatening—and spoke. "Hey, Katia, where ya going?"

Miller was behind her next to the elevator buttons. Down, the only call button, was lit. His wide-set green eyes drilled into Grigg.

Yeah, he definitely knows who I am.

She closed her eyes slowly, held and opened them. "Special Agent Miller wants to take me down to the first floor to look at mug shots."

The sign in the lobby had said the first-floor tenants were a commercial real-estate company and a law office. Maybe they were covers. Grigg doubted it, and even if they were, Miller wasn't headed there. He was going to finish the job.

Grigg kept walking like he was the happiest boob on the planet. "Carlyle says I have to go look at the scene at the squat."

"Give me a hug goodbye, then."

She was totally overdoing it, but he came in for the squeeze anyway and she pulled him tight. Her voice was the lowest whisper. "Say hello. Shake his hand. Give me room—just keep his hands busy."

They broke the clinch, and Grigg stepped over to Miller, whose expression, now that Katia was facing him, had switched from wariness to impatience.

Grigg offered his hand. "Grigg Orlov."

Miller didn't take it. *Oh well. Gotta do something about those hands.* Grigg the Gimp drove his knee with all the force his right leg had into Miller's balls and fell when his left couldn't take his weight. Katia stepped up with a left roundhouse kick to Miller's head and a double-front punch to the side of his face. The agent crashed into the far wall as Grigg regained his feet.

"Stairs are the other way," Grigg said. "Go!"

Katia took off running away from the elevators.

Following behind her, Grigg slammed into Carlyle at his office door, bounced off the FBI man and ended on the ground *again*, this time behind Carlyle.

Carlyle addressed Miller: "Larry, we need to talk."

The gun Grigg and Katia had been trying to keep holstered went off. Carlyle staggered, slumped against the window next to his office door and left a long red smear as he slid into a sitting position.

Grigg pressed himself flat to the carpet, pulled out Carlyle's service weapon, and peered across the special agent's heaving chest. Miller had dropped to one knee, his head down—he must have been able to get off the shot before feeling the delayed cramping caused by a blow to the nuts. Didn't matter. He'd be up shooting soon enough. Grigg wasn't waiting. He heaved to his feet and sprinted for the stairs. Katia held open the door. He sidestepped through as Miller started firing.

"What are you doing up here?" Grigg said.

"Not leaving you."

Grigg didn't bother arguing. Following Katia, Grigg hopped down two stairs at a time using his right leg only, thanking god there were only three floors to descend. They'd hit the landing between the second and first floors when the third-floor door opened and slammed. It had taken Miller longer than Grigg expected to get to the door. Maybe Carlyle had bought them some time, or Katia's kicks had slowed him more than it seemed.

Once on the first floor, they burst into the darkness of a side street. Grigg immediately turned left toward an all-night diner he'd seen on his first visit to the FBI office. This was the time that night drinkers started showing up to eat. He was counting on it.

An Uber pulled up to the diner, and a couple started climbing out.

Grigg walked toward the driver's side of the blue Honda Accord.

"What are you doing?" Katia said.

"Trick I learned in the movies."

The driver rolled down his window. "We don't pick up street hails."

"This is more a grand-theft-auto hail." Grigg raised the Glock. "Get out."

"Shit, shit. All right." The door opened. "Don't shoot me."

Grigg signaled to Katia with his free hand. "You're a better driver then me."

"You mean because I can drive at all."

"Qualifies."

Miller flew around the far corner, following their path out and back up to speed.

"Let's go!"

Both doors slammed shut. A shot hit something at the back of the car. The Uber driver ran across the street screaming.

Another shot.

Katia gunned the engine, throwing them back in their seats. She took a hard right out of the line of fire.

"I hope that dude's okay. Tough enough working for Uber."

Katia turned again onto Atlantic Avenue. "How was that a trick from a movie?"

"You know. The guy without a car always waves a gun and throws some cabbie or housewife out of their vehicle."

"That's usually the bad guy."

He looked at her. "Improvising. We weren't going to get away from Miller on foot."

Grigg wrenched the Uber light from the dash and, as much as he wanted to chuck the thing out the window, shoved it under his seat.

"Where now?"

"Head over to Prospect Avenue. We'll go south between Prospect Park and the cemetery. After that, it's going to be all local streets, stop signs, and lights until we can make our way through the neighborhoods to Coney Island … While we figure out what to do."

"Shit, Grigg, that will take forever."

"The drive or figuring out what to do?" Lame, but he was trying to lighten the heavy atmosphere of threat and fear that descended every time they dodged killers. Neither of them smiled. "I'm hoping Miller won't find us this way. Staying off the radar—the expressways—is a good idea. By the time we're back in Coney Island, maybe things will have calmed down at the FBI offices. Maybe the agency will be onto him. Maybe I can call and get some help."

"Miller killed your dad—*and* he's an FBI agent."

Grigg nodded. "I know. And his name's on one of the slips." He filled her in.

"Jesus. This is a whole new universe of bad. What if Carlyle's dead? There'll be no one to back you up."

CHAPTER 36

Monday, October 10, 2016

They were somewhere between Flatbush and Kensington on the way to Borough Park. New York-born and raised, Grigg rarely thought of his city as a great sprawl. He jumped from place to place on the subway—neighborhoods slipping past by the dozen. Only now, driving side streets through areas he rarely visited, did he feel the true scale of the place.

Tick-tick-tick-tick.

His father's watch said three o'fucking blurry in the morning.

On 14th Avenue, in what was probably Borough Park, they passed an institutional building with a sign in Hebrew—a yeshiva or something—then Kaff's Grocery, the offices of State Sen. Simcha Felder, Schloimy's Bake Shoppe, Walgreens, The Mens Fashion, Mila's Custom Wigs. Storefronts in English and Hebrew and a mix of both went on and on. The bakery made Grigg smile: Jewish name with the olde English spelling of *shoppe*.

He'd been taking in the passing view so his mind could

wander. He hoped his subconscious would come up with some kind of answer to the only questions that mattered: Where they should go and how they could get any help?

Nothing was coming.

Katia made a turn that put them on track for Coney Island. "Where are you right now?"

"Who to trust? Where is safe? It sucks when you don't even like the questions."

"Break it down. Maybe that will help."

"We can't go to your apartment. You're on the FBI's radar, including that scumbag Miller's. Can't go to the squat. As for who to trust? That's where I really fucked up. Trusted Furillo. Wrong. Used us instead. Trusted the FBI. The biggest mistake of all. The killer is a goddamn FBI agent."

"That's not on you. How could you know Furillo was corrupt? He pushed all the right buttons with Carmichael. Some of what you've uncovered probably has nothing to do with your father. There's so much going on. You're just the one who brought it out in the open."

He wasn't comforted. "Freddy *can* connect the murders and who's behind them. But the FBI has him. No wonder he was worried. Long arms … Shit, what's longer than an FBI agent working the inside for you? What're the odds Freddy makes it through the night?" Grigg blew air through his lips. "Carlyle's the key. He's got to survive. If not, then Miller can spin any story he wants. Even say I grabbed his gun and shot Carlyle."

Grigg reached to turn on the radio, switched to all-news 1010 WINS.

"You want to hear election news now?"

"No, I don't." He sounded annoyed. *God, I'm tired. One person on my side, and I'm griping at her.* "Sorry, I just wanna see if they're reporting on the shooting. The FBI uses the media."

The newscaster tossed to a report from a correspondent in St. Louis, site of the second presidential debate last night.

"They're calling this the ugliest debate in recent American history. Some in Trump's own party were stunned at his strategy after the video leaked on Friday showing him bragging about forcing himself on women. Ninety minutes before the debate, Trump hosted a panel with four women who previously accused Bill Clinton of sexual misbehavior. Once the debate started, Trump went into what a senior GOP official called a tantrum, accusing Hilary Clinton of smearing women who accused her husband of sexual attacks, saying she has 'hate in her heart' and threatening to jail her because of how she used her email account while secretary of state. Clinton replied Trump had offended women, minorities and the disabled. Here's how she summed up her pitch to voters."

Clinton's voice came out of the radio: *"This is who Donald Trump is. The question for us, the question our country must answer, is that this is not who we are."*

Katia took a right.

The anchor moved on to NBC suspending Billy Bush for his role in the Trump sex-talk video, then Hurricane Matthew heading out to sea after killing seventeen people and leaving two million homes without power.

"*Here in the city,*" said the newscaster, "*the FBI is seeking assistance after a shooting at a bureau office in Brooklyn. No reports yet of casualties. New York agent in charge Jeremy Kilroy said a brown-skinned male named Grigg Orlov and a white female accomplice, Katia Sokolov, are being sought. They were last seen driving a blue Honda Accord stolen from an Uber driver.*"

"Shit! I did not want to be right about that. Miller must be in control."

"We won't be in control if we don't get gas."

"Okay, do it. Pull in as long as you don't see any cop cars or FBI-like SUVs."

She frowned at that instruction, backtracked to 18th Avenue, and entered an all-night Exxon station with a bodega next door. Katia pumped gas. Grigg crossed the street to the bodega. He walked the aisles and grabbed items that were the closest to having any nutritional value and put them all on the counter. He added a six-pack of waters and one of Coke Zero for caffeine.

The radio report meant they were already behind in finding a hideout. There was no way they could go back to the neighborhood. Feds and cops would be all over Coney Island—joining the bad guys if Miller had reached out. Grigg considered staying on the road as a way to stay off the radar. Head into Queens and Nassau County, avoid highways, keep to local streets. He rubbed his eyes. At some point they'd need sleep. They'd be vulnerable then. Maybe they should flat-out run, bolt south until they were six states away from gangsters, the bone record killer (and crooked FBI agent), and the manhunt. Would Katia see running as a viable plan or way too desperate?

He carried the two heavy bags of road-trip supplies—whatever road trip that might be—back to the gas station. Katia was already in the car. As Grigg stepped up on the sidewalk, a black SUV came around the corner one block away and hit the gas, grill lights, and siren. Grigg covered the remaining distance to the car and hurled the bags in the back.

"Go, go, go."

Katia backed up fast and took off down the side street next to the bodega as Grigg was pulling his door shut.

"How'd they find us?" he said.

"What about our phones?"

"I haven't called anybody. I sure as shit haven't called Miller."

They flew under one green light, then another.

"They're the FBI. If Miller's in charge, he could probably track our phones without us doing anything."

"Oh, god, I am an idiot. Hate to lose them, but …" He took out his keychain, bent a strand of the wire hoop and used it to pop open the SIM card tray of his phone.

"What are you doing?"

"Can't track us without the SIM. All you need to do is lose them."

He snapped the little wafer in half and tossed it out the window. He picked up Katia's phone from the cup holder. Pieces of her SIM card fluttered into the night as a red light loomed ahead.

"I gotta run it."

"Uh, you can't go through *that*."

An Entenmann's truck rumbled into the intersection and passed the front of the Honda as it skidded to a stop.

Grigg turned around. The SUV closed the distance.

Katia floored the gas, and the Honda sprinted across. The pursuing SUV almost didn't make it, squealing around the front of a van.

"Damn. A crash would've been a big help."

"What now? The Gowanus? Another highway?"

"Too easy to chase us down."

"But—shit!"

Katia had misjudged the gap at the next red.

A sedan's grill bore down on her door, growing larger fast.

Her foot slapped the pedal back to the floor.

Grigg watched their rear end barely clear the front of the other car. Its driver honked at them like a madman.

Next moment, Grigg's chest slammed into the locked shoulder belt as Katia stomped on the brake. Her sprint had taken the Honda up to the rear end of a moving van. She drove for a block behind the beast as the siren came nearer and nearer.

"Gotta make a move," she murmured.

At a point where four or five parallel parking spots were empty, Katia went for speed again, using the extra space—and half the sidewalk—to pass the truck on the right.

More honking fading behind them.

They were halfway to the next intersection when Grigg made out an unbroken procession of trucks moving through it. That cross street had no light or stop sign, while Grigg and Katia's did have a stop sign.

"We're fucked," Katia said.

"That's traffic heading for the Fort Hamilton Parkway on-ramp to the Gowanus. Trucks, early-morning deliveries. Squeeze in."

"I thought you said no highways."

"Miller or whoever that is can't catch up to us in traffic that's bumper to bumper. They'll have to inch in somewhere behind. There's nowhere for people to pull over no matter how loud the siren. Maybe we dump the car and vanish. Maybe we book into Green-Wood Cemetery and hide there. Maybe I come up with a plan that makes even better sense."

Now an ace on the horn, Katia edged them into the traffic moving slowly to the Fort Hamilton. Seven or eight more cars filled the line behind them before the SUV and its red-blue strobes joined the convoy.

They passed under one red light, leaving behind the rest of the cars in the parade. They were halfway through the next intersection when the inside of the car exploded.

Noise.

Glass.

For a few seconds, Grigg couldn't breathe. He pushed and flailed until he realized he'd been hit by the air bag. He shoved the material away. Katia moved her head in woozy circles. The windshield had turned into a transparent jigsaw puzzle. They'd been rammed in the front corner on her side by another SUV.

Miller got out.

CHAPTER 37

Monday, October 10, 2016

Grigg pulled the handle and leaned against his door. Stuck. He put more shoulder into it, thrust his right foot against the floor, and it creaked open. When he turned around to help Katia get out on his side, she was already halfway through her window. Miller tugged her stumbling form to the curb.

Grigg raised his pistol but didn't have a clear shot at the rogue agent.

Miller aimed and fired twice as Grigg spun away, putting his back against the rear door. People who had left their cars to assist with the accident changed their minds once shots were fired. They took off screaming and looked like they were going to keep running all the way to Canarsie. Two FBI-looking types approached, moving along the line of stopped vehicles to the rear of the crash. They were from the original SUV, the only one Grigg had thought was chasing them.

He rose to peer through the car's windows and saw Miller headed down the intersecting street, leaving his wrecked SUV in place. He wasn't going fast because Katia wasn't moving well.

He needs to get a car that isn't stuck in this traffic jam.

The other agents were four cars away, one on each side, both with weapons drawn.

They see my gun, they'll blow me away. Maybe they'll do it anyway. No way they'll listen to my story. Chasing Miller will put Katia and me in another fucking crossfire.

The agents moved a car closer.

Grigg slithered to the front of the Honda, hoping Miller wouldn't have an angle as he moved away down the street. Grigg rose to get another look.

The two other agents were now together on the sidewalk, moving in Miller's direction. They must have seen him.

Grigg scrabbled low across the asphalt and crouched on the street side of a blue Fiat parked at the curb near Miller.

"Stop pointing the gun, Miller." *A raspy voice.* "Where's Orlov?"

"You two back off, and we'll be fine." *Miller.* "I'll take care of this one."

Grigg peered through the bottom of the Fiat's windows.

The two agents were maybe six feet from Miller and Katia. Grigg could see her blinking hard, like she was trying to clear her vision—or her head.

The guy with the raspy voice said, "Seriously. This is no joke. You caused a fucking traffic accident to catch them. It's going to take explaining. We don't have Orlov yet. They want us back at the office, pronto."

Miller was too fast. He fired once at the first agent, and the man fell straight back, becoming a dark exclamation point on the sidewalk. Miller caught the second as he moved to get behind the car; the agent dropped to the street with a yell, protected by the vehicle. Miller backed down the street away from his newest crime scene with Katia still a shield. She stumbled, was yanked, and moved a little faster.

Grigg slipped to the side of the agent who had been hit second. He held his lower leg, moaning.

"Lift your hand."

The man grunted. It was a slow leak, not a bright-red arterial pulse. A muscle or maybe a vein.

"What's your name?"

"William Handy. Think I sprung my shoulder when I dove. How's Phil?"

"Bad. Not moving at all. You both need help." Grigg spied a radio next to the agent. "What's Phil's last name?"

"Wasnetsky."

Neither name was on the slips.

Grigg took off his jacket and tied it tight above the leg wound. He picked up the radio, thumbed open the channel. "My name is Grigg Orlov. One of your suspects … I guess. Though if Carlyle survived, maybe you know that's not true. Lawrence Miller is a rogue agent. I'm at West Seventy-Sixth Street east of Tenth Avenue on the approach to the Fort Hamilton Parkway. Miller rammed our car, causing an accident, then shot special agents William Handy and Phil Wasnetsky. Repeat, agents down. Handy and Wasnetsky need immediate assistance. Wasnetsky's critical."

"Ten-four. Stay with the agents."

"Sorry, man. Miller has Katia Sokolov, and he's gonna kill her. I gotta stop him."

Handy grabbed Grigg's arm. "You can't go."

Grigg twisted loose. "Miller showed you what his deal is. I'm it now. Sorry."

He considered asking for—or looking for—the agents' car keys, but he'd have to backtrack to their SUV, which remained stuck in traffic. Giving Miller any more time to get away would be it for this chase … for Katia. He had to move.

He reached back, stowed the gun in his belt, and limped down the sidewalk on the other side of the street Miller and Katia had taken.

Tick-tick-tick-tick.

His father's watch said 4:24 a.m.

The empty sidewalks contrasted with the local traffic jam heading the other way toward the Fort Hamilton. Drivers pounded on their horns. Delivery trucks, taxis, and a few cars threw headlight beams on Grigg. He might as well have been standing on a Broadway stage. If Miller looked across the street, he was fucked. Caution and speed didn't mix. He had to take the chance.

He crossed Tenth Avenue, looking down it both ways. Would Miller try to hotwire a car—or steal one at gunpoint? He guessed the latter and figured Miller would do it after he got far enough away from the backup. Grigg was running out of time. Electricity swirled in his gut and traveled down to his groin. His armpits were slick with sweat, despite the cool air.

At the intersection with the parkway, two light towers brought near-daylight to a parking lot in front of some kind of warehouse or depot. Grigg picked up the pace.

Out front of the building, Miller struggled with the driver of a red Dodge Ram pickup. The guy was giving Miller far more trouble than the Uber owner had Grigg. Katia stood pressed against the truck, right behind Miller.

Grigg started crossing the street, squeezing between a FedEx van and a Shop Rite truck, the driver looking down on him and shrugging. In the time that took, the scene had altered. The pickup's owner lay on the pavement surrounded by a puddle the white lights turned black. Miller climbed into the cab, Katia already shoved in ahead of him.

Grigg threw everything he had into getting there, limping, stumbling, half-skipping, half-hopping.

Once three more cars passed the entrance to the warehouse, Miller would have the gap he needed to get away.

Grigg considered a shot but couldn't see anything through the truck's rear window.

The second car went by.

As he closed, Grigg saw the truck was jacked up high. No need to duck as he approached.

The final car passed.

Grigg grabbed the top edge of the tailgate. The truck accelerated. His shoes skidded across the pavement and onto the street. He pulled one foot onto the wide chrome bumper, then the other before the friction could yank him off.

The truck picked up speed, crossed over the Gowanus, and kept to the local streets. Miller didn't like the highways, either. Grigg crouched on the back bumper to keep from being seen through the rear window. His fingers and arms started to ache, matching the complaint from his ruined knee at being forced to squat. He'd have to get into the bed without being seen or else he'd fall off. But the streetlights made it too bright to move safely. That yellow-white glow vanished when they went under an overpass. It was what he needed. He checked ahead, saw the next overpass, rehearsed the move in his head, and when the truck entered the shadowed darkness, he slipped over the tailgate and lay down on his back as gracefully as any gimp in NYC.

He drew the gun in case he'd been seen or heard, but the truck kept moving.

The stars shone in the clear autumn sky, at least the ones he could see with the city's light pollution. Laying on his back, Grigg was blind to where they were going. Signs went by on each side, most darkened, except for a few all-night diners and bodegas. Told him nothing.

No matter. Miller would play this one way. Grigg had his own plan.

The blocks continued to pass. He strained to hear anything from the cab and only made out music but couldn't tell what kind. What did that murderous fuck like? Sappy stuff with strings. He smiled a little at that. Making Miller ridiculous helped. He'd keep at it.

Warehouses and industrial buildings appeared on both sides and retreated behind.

The truck slowed and turned.

This might be it. He rolled onto his stomach and slid across the bed to the driver's side.

Grigg's breathing came fast. Stay cool. Nose-mouth-nose-mouth. Jump too soon and Miller would get the advantage.

The truck stopped. The engine died.

The driver's door opened.

Grigg stood, the pistol aimed in a two-handed grip. He stared down a tunnel. Nothing but the back of a head with red hair.

"Drop it, Miller."

He spun.

Grigg saw half of Miller's face as he pulled the trigger twice, aiming for the chest, center body mass like they taught in the academy. Miller crumpled. Grigg dropped off the truck and landed awkwardly but managed to snatch Miller's gun. He stepped back, still pointing the gun, saw the man wasn't moving, pocketed the gun, and patted Miller for other weapons, finding nothing, not even a phone. *Must've dumped it.* Grigg considered shooting the fucker in the face. He checked for a pulse. The guy wasn't going anywhere. Ever.

The tunnel vision fell away as he walked around the truck into Katia's arms.

He started shaking.

"Oh, shit. Grigg."

"Never shot anyone before."

"He killed your father and Charlotte. He was going to kill me."

The shakes eased. His own force of will and her touch.

"It isn't over."

"What do you mean?"

He realized Katia had never been here. He pointed across the street. "That's the Facebook Factory. The lights are on. It wasn't just Miller."

Of course, it never had been.

CHAPTER 38

Monday, October 10, 2016

Katia stared at the yellow plumbing supply sign.

"Joe the Borscht," Grigg said. "Carmichael and I followed him here that first time. Must be tied into the whole thing. It's all *fucking* Russians." He pointed to the Mercedes sedan and a Cadillac Escalade parked by the front entrance. "Somebody's here. Waiting for Miller."

Shadows—men—moved through the yellow light of the office at the front of the building.

"Shit. They may have heard the shots. Behind the truck."

They both rounded it and crouched down with Miller's body two feet away.

"What if they come over?" Katia said.

Grigg squeezed the Glock and put his finger to his lips. Miller couldn't have phoned ahead, so they didn't know the make of the vehicle he'd stolen. He and Katia both flattened to look under the truck. They saw two pairs of shoes moving along the sidewalk until they were opposite the pickup. Something dropped into the street. A match that burned briefly and went out. The murmur of indistinct conversation. Grigg would give anything to know if they were discussing the truck. He held the gun with both hands, ready to use it again if he had to.

The shoes started moving back the other way and were blocked by the front tire. Grigg had to know where they were going. He crawled to the back of the truck and inched out to get a look.

Both went back into the glass-walled office of the Facebook Factory.

He rejoined Katia and told her. "They're waiting for Miller to bring you." He studied her face, calculating at the same time. "It could take hours to get anyone to believe our story. I don't trust the 60th, and the FBI is in total chaos right now. They're going to want to take us in and ask lots of questions. No way they'll raid this place on *our* say-so. Whoever is in there will be gone by the time we convince anyone. I need to be able to tell the FBI who's inside."

She hugged herself, worried but listening.

"I'll sneak in for a fast look at who's there in the very early morning hours. Just that. To see if it's Joe the Borscht. The rest of his crew. Other FBI agents we've seen. Or both. If I don't know who it is, at least I'll be able give a description. Miller came here for a reason. Miller was the triggerman." The anger was different now. A clear red beam in his head pointing in one direction. He understood. "I want everyone responsible for murdering my dad and Charlotte brought down. I want them to stop hunting you. They get away unidentified, they could get away for good. This is the last thing I have to do." He squeezed both her arms. "Wait here behind the truck. Be ready to take off."

Grigg ghosted across the street to the back end of the warehouse. He knew it was too much to hope that the rear door be unlocked. He was right. As he checked out the back of the building, Grigg realized something he should have caught immediately. Charlotte had said the Facebook Factory worked three shifts. Not tonight. Why?

Because of a special event—a murder.

But why kill Katia *here*?

Grigg edged forward, hand skimming over painted cinderblock, his mind loaded with more questions than the FBI-issue Glock had bullets left. A chill. He'd be stupid not to be afraid now, but the fear was balanced against a deep, pulsing anger at whoever had targeted Dad, Charlotte, and Katia. The rage, along with his aching need for answers, kept his fear in check. He was focused and alert in a way he never could have been the night his father was killed.

A light rain started, fell heavier, coming at him in waves, the kind you only got down by the ocean. Grigg reached the edge of the plateglass window and peered into the fluorescent-lit front office. No one at the desk. No guard at the front door.

So … in by the front. Bad knee. One weapon. Alone. *This isn't an assault. Just keep to the plan. ID who's here and beat feet.*

Grigg entered the reception area and crossed it to a dark hallway, which he followed slowly, sliding along the wall toward the soft glow ahead, which came through a doorway into the main warehouse. All the computers were turned off, and a single light illuminated a small area in the center of the room, where three men stood and one sat.

Grigg crouched to avoid creating a silhouette in the doorway.

"Where the fuck is Miller?" The voice of the man in the chair. American accent.

"No word from him since he grabbed her," said the one standing on the right. Russian accent.

"Nothing else?"

"No, sir."

"Goddammit, I want her here, dead in front of me. Because after that, I have to put out the dumpster fire Grigg Orlov started. Miller better be able to get the cash and gold back from the FBI."

None of them replied.

Grigg needed to move closer. He couldn't make out any of them in the dim light. He slipped from the doorway to the first row of computers, staying low behind the chairs pushed underneath the long table. Halfway along, he crawled under the table to a row nearer.

Just a bit closer.

He inched another couple of feet and stopped.

He was grabbed by the neck and the wrist of his gun hand, shoved forward into the light, and forced facedown on the ground.

"Motion sensor went off." Deep accented voice and

hot breath in Grigg's ear.

The man quickly disarmed him.

"I told you," said the boss. "That's why I keep an open-door policy. You never know who'll show up."

Grigg struggled against the hold. Something smashed the side of his head. Lightning in his brain. His vision contracted to nothing.

Dreamless dark for seconds, maybe minutes. Out? How long? He was picked up and slammed hard into a chair. The right side of his head thumped like beating on a kettle drum. Fist? Club? Sap?

"The black boy. Why did you ever get involved in this? You needn't have. Your father paid his debt." Laughter. "Believe me, vengeance is mine, and I'm good at it."

The deep voice of the man in charge became familiar as the muddle of Grigg's thoughts worked to organize themselves. Who was it? Grigg couldn't force the blurred, double images to come together.

"Though I'll tell you," the man continued, "there are people back in the mother country who would have killed your father just for mixing good Russian blood with a mud woman. I'm more open-minded. Just don't ever mess with what's mine."

Grigg's words came out slow. "Leave my ... my mother out of it. You sound as Russian as I do."

"Hard work. Coaches. Degree from Harvard. Change was coming. I knew."

The two faces merged into one. Blonde hair and eyes a light blue. Grigg had last seen him in Nathan's. The Bookkeeper.

"Anthony?"

"Did you think I was working for that fat fuck Joe the Borscht? Good. That was the idea. It's business. I'm taking over Coney Island. Expanding, in fact. Bring in my fat friend."

In the dark to the left, a wail that dropped to unintelligible words. Grigg's vision continued to improve. Joe the Borscht was dragged in by his feet and left near Grigg's chair. Joe's face was swollen and splotched the color of a spoiled melon, and one eye was black.

"We haven't properly met, Grigoriy Andreiovich Orlov," the Bookkeeper said. "I'm Entoni Voronin."

"Voronin? The brothers?"

A tip of the head. "Son of Viktor."

"But he died young in a work camp."

"My mother was pregnant when he was sent into the Gulag," said Entoni.

"You're killing your father's childhood friends—and the daughter of one? Doesn't sound like business to me. Sounds nuts."

"Oh, the killings are personal. Very personal. Nothing to do with business. My father was murdered in one of the work camps. When I was old enough to understand, my mother swore he'd been denounced by someone close to him. A good Russian son settles his family debts. I was going to kill whoever did it. But I needed to know who. Time passed. I had no leads for years, though for the longest time I believed it may have been the people he worked with—"

"The local mob, you mean, after he got into the black market."

Entoni ignored him. "The Soviet Union disappeared in an instant. I was finally able to make progress. Those with certain privileges—like myself—were allowed to see the security files. My father's included dozens of letters written while at different camps. He said his two best friends and his brother had informed on him to the KGB. Named all three of them. Each letter was the same. Word for word. He kept writing them. Over and over. To get the truth out to my mother. Demanding his family settle the debt. That I settle his debt. None were ever sent, of course. The KGB wouldn't want to give up its informants. The case notes said all four boys dealt in bone music. There was even a record in the file. 'Not Fade Away' laid down on an X-ray of a skull."

"That's your evidence? The letters of a dead man?"

"'They all must have been in on it,' he wrote. 'The authorities knew everything I'd done, even dealing in the bones.' I sat in when my Uncle Nikolai was interrogated by my people. A pleasure to watch professionals work. He denied sending my father to his death. Claimed he didn't know who did. Was I to believe him or my father?" A shrug. "Next, your father had to die, and Sokolov too. But since Sokolov escaped me in death, your lovely Katia will stand in for him."

"You don't know if you've got the right people. Based on the accusations of a gangster."

"I'm going to watch my men work on you. I like to

watch. A man begging for his life. It's the true blood sport."

"That's why he was bringing Katia here."

"I pay. I get to watch. Unfortunately, your father ran, and I couldn't be on hand. The punishment was more important, of course."

"You are fucking nuts."

"*You* must like pain. You're here, so I guess we can assume Miller isn't coming." He turned toward one of the men. "Get the cars started. We'll be done very soon."

The thug who had grabbed Grigg left with one of the others.

Time for Plan B: keep him talking.

"I have something you need. From the container, which I know is yours, not Joe's."

"Where are they?"

"Why was Freddy going after the box? Instead of killing you?"

"I asked you a question." He moved closer to Grigg's chair, and so did the remaining goon, like a shadow.

"I have information you need. We're trading."

"Why would I trade with a dead man?"

"Because you want the information. That should have occurred to a Harvard grad."

"Cousin Freddy didn't have the balls or the men to take me out. Small-time, like his father. He thought to steal from me. That was going to be *his* revenge. That and helping your father. Like I said, weak. What do you expect from those who turn on family?"

"This place isn't Joe's either?"

"Hardly. My very first venture in America. Set up before I came over. A contract directly with the SVR. American fear is the new growth industry." His bass voiced turned into a growl. "I shipped a couple million in cash over here just for the bribes that will let me set up legitimate bank accounts so I can move over real money. Sometimes I do business with the SVR. Sometimes we disagree. It's all very Russian." He leaned in closer. "Now, I need those flash drives to clean up the mess you made."

"Oh … I don't have them."

"What?" Entoni backhanded him.

Grigg spit blood. "Easy, tough guy. We both know sixteen copies of MyOffice are worth shit. Nice move, though, having someone hide the names of American agents inside the cases. Larry Miller. Franklin Crosby. I could go on. All working for you."

"No. Not for me!" His tone went from a killer's confidence to agitated. "The Kremlin. The list is my Putin insurance. That man can turn on you. I didn't see the names before the box was loaded on the ship. I learned of only Miller before that and decided I needed his services more than the SVR."

"Good thing I have all of them, then. I've got a deal for you. I provide the rest of the names and you leave Katia and me alone. Some of those names will help you get your millions out of FBI lockup. That was the plan with Miller, right?"

Entoni stepped back. "Hurt him until he tells where the names are."

The silent one approached with a blade.

A thundering bang came from the front of the building.

The lights went out.

CHAPTER 39

Monday, October 10, 2016

Grigg hurled himself out of the chair to the right. Instant fire in his left leg followed him to the ground. He crawled several feet, stopped, and felt for the injury. The knife stuck out from his lower thigh; his dodge must have thrown the thug off. The right side of his head still pounded from the earlier blow. Overcome by the spins, he vomited and started crawling again. Too slow with a blade in his leg. He reached down, pulled it free, and bit his lip to keep from crying out.

At least he had a weapon now.

Joe the Borscht must have had the same idea as Grigg. The big mobster roared. A chair clattered over. A gun went off in the dark. Crashing.

The Russian goon groaned in pain: "Get him off me."

Somewhere in front of Grigg, Joe the Borscht's body pinned the gunman. Perhaps a loose gun lay nearby. Far more useful than the knife.

"Stop shooting in the dark, idiot," said Entoni. "We need to go out the back."

Grigg, his left leg bleeding and nearly useless, crawled on the cement in the direction of Joe the Borscht, sweeping back and forth with one hand, feeling for metal. He touched a hand, maybe that of the gunman. The fingers wrapped around Grigg's like an octopus. Definitely the gunman. Grigg pulled to get free, but the grip was tight. Lancing pain. Knuckles cracking. One big yank drew the hand toward him, and he stabbed it. An agonized cry and he had his hand back, but the Russian had the knife.

He patted the floor to either side, the gun critically important now.

C'mon, c'mon!

Struggling, grunting. The gunman was fighting to get out from under Joe the Borscht. Grigg wormed around the dark mountain rising from the floor. A crash by the back wall. Entoni making for the rear door?

"Damn chairs," Entoni said. "Sasha, quit fucking around. Let's go."

"I'm stuck under this whale."

"Move it if you want to get out of here."

"Can't … Help me!"

Light flashed from the hallway leading to the front office. Not the blue and red strobing of police cars. Yellow, a liquid, dancing yellow … like that of fire. The front of the building was burning.

Grigg's hand landed on a pistol's barrel. He turned it, gripped the butt, stood, and almost fell from the knife wound's burning pain. He squeezed his eyes closed, then open. He had no choice. He had to get past the agony. Or he was a dead man.

He limped slow to the side wall. Right angles. That was how he'd get free. Choking smoke, all the more frightening because he couldn't see it in the darkness. How thick already? He started coughing. A thunderous crash from the front of the building, and flames and smoke whooshed from the hallway.

Seven flavors of crook in this, and I'm going to die by smoke inhalation.

He made the wall, though each step forced him to bite down so hard his gums hurt and red flashed through his brain. His eyes watered. More fits of coughing from the acrid fumes. The taste of burning plastic at the back of his throat. Leaning heavily against the bricks, he arrived at the corner of the building. There, five feet away, still open and outlined by the sky and the nighttime glow thrown by the city, was the back door—the door that had first brought him into the Facebook Factory.

He hobbled for the fifty-gallon drum outside, half diving to get hold of its edge and prop himself up. He waved the gun wildly around him but there was no Entoni.

He grunt-stepped, grunt-stepped toward the burning front of the building. Stopped. Considered sinking to the ground and waiting for whoever showed up. Somehow, he propelled himself on again, giving a wide berth to the building as flames shot out from where the big windows had been. In front, he found the cause of the fire. Miller's stolen truck had been rammed through the front doors and was fully involved.

Katia!

He tried to get close to the driver's door but was pushed back by blistering heat. He edged back from the fire, his eyes adjusting so he could see better.

Entoni shoved Katia into the front seat of the Escalade and ran to the other side, yelling and signaling to the two remaining gunmen to take the sedan. The SUV roared off.

The sirens of fire trucks approached.

The SUV was gone before Grigg could react. He turned to the sedan. The thug who had grabbed him earlier was climbing in the passenger side. Grigg shot him. The door closed anyway, and the car pulled past. He put two shots through the back window. He limped to where the car stopped, sweat pouring down his face, pain running through the entire left leg, blood soaking his pants. He halted at the rear end of the Mercedes and could do nothing but duck down, breathing heavily. He peeked under the car as the driver's side door opened. One foot, then a second hit the ground. Unsteady steps.

He sighted down the barrel and squeezed. The goon screamed, grabbed his foot, and fell over. Grigg pulled himself up, inched around using the car as a handrail, shot the driver in the leg, and kicked his gun away. The one in the passenger seat was unconscious or dead. It almost did Grigg in, pushing the big man out of the car.

He hit the gas.

Something caught his eye in the rearview mirror. A car following, lights off.

Let's make a party of it.

He crossed Mermaid Avenue.

A single set of taillights ran ahead of him toward Surf Avenue. He hit the turn at Surf Avenue too hard, almost spinning into the fence surrounding the new Thunderbolt coaster before straightening out.

The Escalade began swerving back and forth across lanes ahead of him until it made a looping turn and jumped the curb at West 12th Street, thumping to a stop. The passenger door opened, and Katia sprinted down the side street.

Grigg could either stay and take Entoni on or make sure he and Katia did not get separated again. It was hardly a choice. He exited the sedan and followed Katia. On the way, he turned back and fired twice in the general direction of the Escalade. Covering fire, to buy time. His left leg had gone numb, probably a bad thing, but Grigg would take it in the short term as he gained back a bit of speed.

Katia reached The Bowery.

Grigg screamed. "Left. To Deno's."

He reached her at the gate, pulled out the park keys he'd kept all this time, and unlocked it. "C'mon." He led them among the rides, needing little light to navigate here. "What *was* the plan with the truck?"

"When I saw two of them come, I got worried they were leaving. Maybe you were trapped in there. Maybe they had you. Decided to make a distraction."

"Kill the power and start a fire?"

"Those were accidental bonuses."

"Not how I'd have drawn it up, but it helped. In the

end."

"The guy who took me said he was going to kill me for something my dad did. Sounded crazy."

"Or Russian."

"That's when he got an elbow in the face followed by a couple of combinations. He's coming after us ... pissed off."

"So am I."

They were on Grigg's home ground now. They could get away. But then so would Entoni Voronin.

"Let's get the Wonder Wheel going." He threw over the handle on the ride as they passed, though it would still need power.

He dragged himself to the hut with the main switches and mike for the public-address system.

"What are you going to do?"

"Put on a show. This *is* Coney Island." He clicked one switch. The wheel revolved, an eerie, dark spinning circle. He turned on its lights. He keyed the public-address mike and spoke into it: "Hey, En-tone-eee." Grigg's voice echoed over the park, the beach, and out to the street in the early morning quiet. "We've put those paper slips of yours on Deno's Wonder Wheel. C'mon over. Though getting the wheel to stop ... now *that'll* be a trick."

Cars, few though they were, stopped on the avenue because of the turning Wonder Wheel.

A shadow jogged around the Thunder Bolt and the Bumper Cars and stood looking up at the wheel.

"Give them to me!" Entoni pointed his pistol like the

ride knew what he meant.

"Probably can't do that," Grigg said through the PA system.

Entoni shot at the cars as they rotated past him.

"We can't have you attacking the historic Wonder Wheel. It's got landmark status."

Two at a time, Grigg threw the switches. For the first time in its history, the park and everything in it was lit up at 4:55 a.m. The Carousel, Jump Around Dune Buggy, Dizzy Dragons, the Fire Engine, the Thunderbolt, the Pirate Ship, and half a dozen others, along with overhead, perimeter, and decorative lights. Flashing and blinking and running courses in wild and crazy summertime patterns. Entoni stood alone as the colors washed over him. The ocean remained black, and Astroland on either side was almost as dark.

Sirens. More cars stopped. A handful of people came out of the all-night businesses on Surf Avenue to see something that had never been witnessed in almost-everything-had-already-been-seen-before Coney Island.

Deno's Wonder Wheel had to be visible miles out at sea.

"I'll kill you both."

"Old threat. Getting boring." Grigg drew the gun and whispered to Katia. "Cops should be here soon. I'll hold him until they arrive."

As he moved to go around the carousel, three men ran in from the boardwalk, where there was a fence and a locked gate, or was supposed to be. One threw a black bag over Entoni's head. All three were garbed in black and balaclavas—the wrong choice for a fully lit amusement park. They looked like a performance art company from the East Village.

"What is this?" Entoni yelled at his captors. "You don't understand what I have."

One of the men threw a canvas tarp on the ground.

"A list of Americans working for Russia. FBI. CIA. It goes to the Yanks if I'm taken."

It already has, Grigg thought.

Entoni switched to Russian. One of the men knocked him on the head with a club and he dropped to the tarp. Terse Russian orders from one of the commandos. Quickly, the other two rolled him up. With a series of grunts, they carried him in the direction of the boardwalk.

Joining the people at the gates to watch the great oddity—a brightly lit, empty amusement park in the early hours—were three NYPD patrol cars, plus two unmarked vehicles. Flashlights bobbed down the boardwalk, too.

Katia appeared next to him. "SVR?"

"I'd say so. A car with lights out followed me from the Facebook Factory. Bet they were watching Entoni."

"Why now?"

"My guess? Once things went south at the FBI office, one of those other double agents at the FBI reported in on what Entoni and Miller were up to. SVR damage control. Entoni told me he had turned Miller to work for him rather than the Russian government."

"Probably blackmailed Miller. Said he'd expose him as

a Russian agent."

"Or offered him more money."

They waited under the lights for a police interview that would go way beyond trespassing at Deno's Wonder Wheel. Grigg hoped the cops would listen while Entoni vanished to receive whatever punishment the Russians could dream up.

Grigg put his gun on the ground and stepped back. The pain sat him down. He shivered, blood itchy and cold on his leg.

Five officers approached.

"What's going on here?" said a sergeant.

"It's a long story, but the murderer of my father was just abducted by the Russian secret service. They left on the boardwalk."

"Are you crazy or shitfaced?"

I was right. Goodbye, Entoni.

"How did this place get started up?"

"Coney Island magic, sergeant. For the rest, I'd suggest you call the FBI."

The ninety-six-year-old Wonder Wheel turned, lights shifting and winking. The empty, eccentric cars rattled back and forth on their tracks.

CHAPTER 40

Monday, November 7, 2016

"Donald Trump and Hilary Clinton are making their last appeals to voters after a final campaign weekend filled with more shocking news.

"On Sunday, FBI Director James Comey told Congress new emails linked to Clinton's server hadn't changed the agency's conclusion that there were no grounds for charges over how Clinton handled sensitive material. Comey had notified Congress eleven days before the election that emails that might be related to the server had been found. The director's announcement so close to voting was unprecedented in election history.

"Trump said the FBI's actions showed the criminal justice system is 'rigged' in Clinton's favor and told voters 'to deliver justice at the ballot box.'

"One day earlier, The Wall Street Journal *reported that the* National Enquirer *paid $150,000 to buy a story on an affair Trump had with a Playboy Playmate and then suppressed the news. The Trump campaign and the* National Enquirer *both denied the story. The* Enquirer *endorsed Trump.*

"*Meanwhile, the Clinton Foundation admitted it took a one-million-dollar donation from the government of Qatar while Clinton was secretary of state, possibly violating her ethics pledge.*

"*Final polls show Clinton with a slight lead. Sunday's Washington Post/ABC survey gave Clinton a five-percentage-point edge over Trump, while the Politico/Morning Call poll reported Clinton holding a three-point advantage.*

"*A 5.0-magnitude earthquake hit central Oklahoma—*"

Grigg killed the Bluetooth speaker. He'd started listening to NPR on Katia's recommendation. They had longer stories than 1010 WINS and tended not to get distracted by a shooting in Yonkers.

Katia leaned against him on the blanket. "No interest in those poor folks in Oklahoma?"

"Nope, just want to hear the political sludge." He put his arm around her.

"You're lucky. It keeps getting sludgier."

It had. He expected it now. Problem was, he wasn't hearing the sludge he knew about: The Facebook Factory, the list of Americans working for the Russians, or anything about Entoni Voronin. He hadn't expected to, but it still pissed him off. The FBI was investigating everyone on the list. That's all Carlyle would tell Grigg when he visited the agent in the hospital, and Carlyle was the only one who would give him any information. Grigg had no idea if U.S. agents had managed to take Entoni from the SVR operatives. It seemed doubtful.

The waves rolled one over the other. The wind blew

quick off the water. They were bundled up. Grigg liked the ocean most in the off-season. A blue-sky day and a wide, empty beach. Water the color of battleship steel.

Witnesses, witnesses, witnesses. There were no living witnesses to the incident that had started it all: the betrayal of Viktor Voronin to the KGB. Grigg had spent the past weeks wondering about the father he knew—and the one he hadn't. Had Dad really turned in his friend? Sent him to his death? His conversation with Katia on the subject had been short. She'd said she didn't believe her father or Grigg's would do that. Her legal mind then went to work. Even if they had, she said, they were kids back then—minors, under a totalitarian government. Voronin was a crook. Her legal logic left Grigg empty, and certainly no closer to knowing if there were things he didn't understand about his father. Whoever turned in Voronin had set off a killing spree that destroyed families. To whom did that tally get assigned? He'd thought his father a good man, if not perfect. Understood why he'd left Grigg without a word. A hit had been put out on him. The bone record. Because of one secret in his dad's past ... Were there others? Grigg hadn't only lost Dad, he'd also lost his grasp on who his dad was. Memory shouldn't be a question.

"It's been two and a half weeks since the FBI stopped grilling us," Katia said.

They'd both been interviewed over ten days following Entoni Voronin's abduction.

The interviewing came to an end after the 27th repetition of the Tale of the Bone Records. A day passed in "protective custody." A woman came in. She said she was the agent in charge of a special task force. On what? She couldn't say. A matter of national security. *Her people* had taken her through all the interviews.

"They must have them fucking memorized by now," he'd said.

The woman had let him know they were free to go, but, as always, to remain available. That's when he'd realized he wouldn't be learning more. He already knew the kinds of secrets the government shoved down a deep, dark hole. Grigg had shot three men, killing one. During those interviews, no one said a thing about charges. Grigg figured it was because the dead man was intricately involved in a spy case that would embarrass the U.S. when—if—it came out. There were fifteen other names that could still come out. Or not. Grigg knew them all. He'd gotten the full lecture on national security before he left the FBI offices.

"Grigg? You there?"

The light brown eyes of the agent in charge turned into the running-water blue of Katia's.

"Oh, yeah. I'm here."

"Which part of the clusterfuck are you replaying?"

"The whole damned thing."

"Gotta move on," she said, rubbing his shoulder.

"Yeah." He didn't see that happening soon.

"The new job may help."

The bureaucrats at the city claims adjustment office had promoted him to Carmichael's position as adjuster. As best he could tell, it had zero to do with the recent events in Coney Island. No one in the office seemed to know anything about what had gone down. They never mentioned Carmichael, probably because he'd had no friends there.

His father's watch said five minutes until a Mermaid Pilsner. The ticking had left his head. Tonight, he planned to put the watch away in a safe place and start using the clock on his phone, like a good millennial.

He got up, groaning.

"What still hurts?"

"All of it, just in different ways at different times. Still, better than a week ago. Be good to get the stiches out of my leg. You want to go over to Ruby's?"

A vigorous nod from Katia. "Let's go to the polling place tomorrow. Vote together."

A seagull raced above a breaking wave.

"Um ... I'm not registered."

"*Fucking* Russian."

Acknowledgements

Several people played important roles in the journey these words made from my keyboard to your hands. Editor Ed Stackler of the Stackler Editorial Agency and copy editor Amy Cecil Holm of Allegory Editing found so many ways to make the story and the writing better. Any errors that remain are my fault alone—and likely the result of my not listening.

My friends Baron R. Birtcher and Elena Hartwell Taylor—both great authors; get their books!—read the manuscript and provided the insights you can only get from pros who know their craft. I very much appreciate the time they gave to this project.

Thank you to cover artist and book designer Rafael Andres, who took my vague ideas and produced work I loved.

I am indebted to *X-Ray Audio*, edited by Stephen Coates and published by Strange Attractor Press (2015). It's the only book I found on the history of the bone records.

Our house in Pelham, New York, became a little office building when Covid-19 hit a couple miles north in New Rochelle, with three of us doing our thing in here. And it all worked. To Patrick, who seemingly tells everyone his dad's a novelist, I miss you now that you're out in the world. I love you very much. To Sheri—my first sounding board in her Zoom-central office downstairs—for her patience and understanding as the book finished taking shape during the pandemic. You have my thanks and love.

Rich Zahradnik is the author of four critically acclaimed novels, including *Lights Out Summer,* winner of the Shamus Award. He was a journalist for twenty-seven years and now lives in Pelham, New York, where he is the mentor to the staff of the *Pelham Examiner,* an award-winning community newspaper run, edited, reported, and written by people under the age of eighteen.

Find him at:
www.richzahradnik.com

richzahradnik

rzahradnik

rzahradnik

Made in the USA
Middletown, DE
07 October 2023